CRITIC'S CHOICE

Kathleen Yapp

METEOR PUBLISHING CORPORATION
Bensalem, Pennsylvania

First Printing February 1992.

ISBN: 1-878702-80-7

Printed in the United States of America

To Jason, Janice, Jayme, Ciara, and Brent.
I love you.

KATHLEEN YAPP

Kathleen Yapp was executive secretary to the president of a major corporation for many years, writing in her spare time, getting up as early as three o'clock in the morning to do so. Now she writes full time (and gets up at four a.m.) and lives in the breathtaking mountains of Southern California with her much loved husband, Ken. With grown children and young grandchildren nearby, she enjoys family life, singing and speaking for various groups, and traveling.

ONE

Whoever runs this bed-and-breakfast inn is going to get a piece of my mind, the tall, exasperated man promised himself after standing in the empty foyer for ten minutes, waiting for someone to come and check him in.

He was hot and tired and wanted a thick rare steak, a brisk shower, and a soft bed—in that order. His car had broken down, the garage mechanic had taken three hours to do a forty-minute repair, and his foot hurt because he'd picked up a stone in one of his boots. His temper was beyond frayed. His jaw was stone.

He snatched a well-used cowboy hat from his head, ran a hand through a thick crop of sweaty, dark hair, and with the same hand impatiently whacked a silver bell that sat on the corner of the registration desk. A card on the desk said, "Please ring bell for service."

Tossing the hat next to the bell, he planted his legs firmly on the floor as though preparing to face a charging bull, folded his arms determinedly across his chest, and waited.

It was days like this that made Marlis Kent wonder why she ever wanted to run a bed-and-breakfast inn.

It had started that morning, when Amy, her housekeeper, had called to say she'd broken her wrist. Winifred, the backup housekeeper, was caring for her sick mother in Oregon. Mabel, the cook, had strep throat and doctor's orders to stay home. Kathleen, the backup cook, was visiting her parents in Ireland.

Such a catastrophe had never before befallen the Sunrise Inn, a twelve-room Victorian bed-and-breakfast inn in Sutter Creek, California, that Marlis had owned and operated with loving efficiency for five years. The quirk of fate that had eliminated the availability of all her domestic help at one time meant she had to do the work herself. Cleaning and cooking were two things Marlis hated to do, and did not do well, which is why she had hired Amy and Winifred and Mabel and Kathleen.

Of course, the problems did not end there: this was the afternoon The Family Portrait was to be taken. Mother, father, sister, and two brothers were all going to be at the photographer's at three-thirty. She remembered her father's warning call that morning: "Don't let anything keep you away, Marlis. This is the third and last time we're going to try to get this picture taken. You remember your mother and I are leaving for Alaska tomorrow?"

"Of course, I do, Dad."

"So you'll be there?"

"I'll be there."

"Without fail?"

"Dad, don't worry. Amy will be here to cover the desk . . ."

But Amy would not be there to cover the registration desk when the two expected guest couples arrived. She also would not be cleaning the four rooms that had been occupied the night before.

And Mabel, the cook, would not be preparing one of her renowned breakfasts for these guests, *and* the food for tomorrow's meal was written on a shopping list, not sitting in the cupboard and fridge. There weren't even the usual extra coffeecakes and giant-size muffins in the freezer for emergency. Marlis would have to cook from scratch.

"When will I have time today to buy groceries?" she moaned out loud to no one as she slowly closed the freezer door, feeling as though it were one of her last acts on earth. She had a habit of muttering to herself. "The family fruitcake," her older brother liked to tease her. "It clears my thinking," she justified to anyone who caught her doing it and asked her why.

"The world is coming to an end," she muttered and sighed as she changed out of the sky-blue skirt and blouse she'd been wearing. Normally she dressed in skirts and jackets, nice dresses or pantsuits, because there were always people coming in and she wanted to make as good an impression as did the inn. But today was not a typical day—and it wasn't over yet.

Donning work jeans and an old plaid shirt of her brother's, she unenthusiastically put clean sheets on all the used beds, dusted the furniture, emptied the trash, washed the windows, put out pale-yellow towels that were very nearly the same color as her thick, shoulder-length hair, restocked the bathrooms with a local blend of herb and lavender soap and Kleenex and tiny elegant bottles of shampoo and hand cream and, though not finished, interrupted those challenging chores to dash down the stairs—tucking her shirttail in and hoping she didn't smell—in response to the repeated ringing of the silver bell on the registration desk. *I hope I haven't kept someone waiting*, she prayed on the run.

At the bottom of the stairs, braced as though to meet a charging bull, Marlis saw an unhappy man. A frustrated man. A tall, broad-shouldered, good-looking cowboy with dark, wavy hair and blue-black eyes that zeroed in on her as though she were the sum cause of every bad thing that had ever happened to him.

This hasn't been a good day for me either, mister, she felt like saying as she tucked some errant ends of her hair behind one ear. Instead, she mustered a cheerful smile that dimpled her cheeks and said, "Hi, I'm Marlis Kent. May I help you?"

The mouth of the statue moved. "If you have the time."

"Of course, I do," she assured him, sensing that he needed a thick raw steak, a brisk shower, and a soft bed—in that order. "I hope I didn't keep you waiting—"

"You did."

"I've been preparing rooms—"

"I need one."

"Then let's get you registered," she said, scooting behind the Queen Anne desk and flipping open the guest book, after she daintily removed a dusty cowboy hat which sat upon it.

"Later." The statue moved toward the stairs. "Are the rooms up there?"

His hand was on the railing, one size twelve boot on the first step, when Marlis said, "We will register you now, Mr.? . . ." Tired and hot and hungry she could understand. Total strangers sleeping in her beds she would not allow.

The man slowly turned around, his eyes narrowing as he stared at Marlis sitting primly and disheveled behind her antique desk. She stared back, grasping instantly that he was a man not used to being stood up to—in his world, whatever that was. But in her world she was the law, and she ran her inn with a firm though perfumed hand.

"Name, please?" she asked, holding her ground, and her pen poised.

A long pause, then "Grant Russell" came the name in a deep voice that rumbled through the tiny room. He walked to the desk, or rather ambled, the statue becoming a man with real arms and legs and other recognizable parts that moved in a sensuous way that Marlis couldn't help but notice.

She also noticed intelligent blue eyes studying her with interest from beneath a heavy fringe of dark lashes that any woman would kill for. Thick black hair repeated itself in thick black brows that were frowning less than before, though still frowning, as they slanted toward a wide but straight nose. His skin was tanned. His ears hugged his head. There was a mustache, neat and not too big, that nestled over his upper lip which pressed so wonderfully upon his lower one.

Marlis closed her mouth, which had begun to open.

"Don't you think we ought to call the owner?" the man questioned.

Marlis commanded her heart to stop fluttering, offered him a black Cross pen, and said in a voice that was as gracefully feminine as his was roaringly masculine, "I *am* the owner, Mr. Russell."

Grant Russell took the pen and felt the softness of her skin as their fingers collided. Even though she was dirty and disarrayed—what on earth had she been doing? And if she was the owner, *why* was she doing it?—he knew she was a woman he wanted to know. Well.

Instead of telling her how compelling her jade-green eyes were, he said brusquely, "You don't look like the owner of a place like this." He looked around the charming foyer with its two-hundred-year-old grandfather clock in one corner and shelf displays of silver and china, daguerreotypes and cornhusk dolls.

"But I am," Marlis assured him. With an embarrassed gesture of her hand that moved down her body, which Grant Russell had already assessed, and approved of, she added, "My housekeeper injured herself today. I got to do her chores. Lucky me."

"Is there only one housekeeper in Sutter Creek?" He signed his name with an authority that made Marlis think he did so often, and not just on beer tabs at the local bar.

"My backup woman wasn't available."

He handed her back the pen. "Does this happen often?"

Marlis heard the judgment in his tone and bristled. She was tired and testy and didn't need a cowboy to tell her how to run her business. She stood up, after glancing at the register.

"I see you're from Santa Barbara?" A pretty city she liked, in central California, on the coast. A former President lived there. Perhaps this cowboy worked on his ranch.

"Yup." He picked up his hat.

Normally she would have started a chatty conversation to get to know her guest, but she didn't really expect Mr. Grant Russell to be staying. He was hardly the type who frequented bed-and-breakfast inns, she decided. More the Motel 10-outside-of-town type.

"Would you like to know how much our rooms are?" she asked politely.

"Doesn't matter. I need a hot shower and a bed. If you've got 'em, I can afford 'em."

Only because Marlis had manners did she not grunt, "Oh, yeah?" Instead, she opened the top drawer of the desk and yanked a key from a square box. "I'll put you in the Big Bonanza." Big man, big room, she thought. Then a sly smile threatened to soften her mouth. It was also her most expensive. She looked forward to his look of shock when she told him. "It costs a hundred forty dollars a night."

"Fine."

Marlis blinked. "How long will you be staying?"

"Just tonight."

"Will you put this on your credit card—?"

"Cash." With strong hands he yanked an Italian leather billfold from the rear pocket of his hip-hugging jeans and took out a wad of bills that made Marlis blink again. He gave her a hundred and two twenties, and as he did their eyes met and held and in his was a challenge, fairly met by Marlis, who found his superior attitude annoying.

"Follow me," she said crisply.

To the ends of the earth, he thought, watching every sway of her hips as she preceded him up the stairs.

At the second floor she turned left, then left again two

doors down and into the Big Bonanza. It was called that because it was the biggest room in the inn and had the largest bed—a huge mahogany four-poster in which, supposedly, John Sutter himself, for whom the town was named, had slept. This was one of Marlis's favorite rooms because it was so masculine in decor with its rugged dresser and heavy rocking chair. It even had a potbellied stove in one corner that had come out of the office of the Forty-niner Gold Mine.

Marlis was proud of her lovely one-hundred-year-old inn, which she had bought from her parents who had operated it for many years. Each of her guest rooms had names like Claimjumper and Lucky Lady—reminiscent of the gold rush days that had exploded in 1848 and made Sutter Creek a vital part of the history of the Mother Lode.

She spoke over her shoulder, preferring no more eye contact with Grant Russell, giving him a quick history of the various pieces of furniture in the room while she opened the window, which looked out on the street, and rearranged the fresh flowers on the nightstand. She was aware of his eyes on her, those dark blue-eyes assessing whether she was round enough here and slim enough there. Typically male, she thought disgruntedly, to think the sum total of a woman was two of this and one of that and—

Whirling around to continue her explanation, she walked into a solid wall of chest. His chest. To keep herself from falling she grabbed his arms. At the same time, his large hands caught her waist.

"Sorry," she murmured, looking up, into softer eyes now that told her he was admiring something other than her furniture.

"I'm not," came the low reply. His hands tightened at her waist, and long pregnant moments heightened their breathing. His lips moved downward, close to hers, and then moved over to nibble on her ear.

The most sinful thought raced into Marlis's mind as her right thigh touched the side of the bed . . .

She pulled back, then squeezed around him, their bodies touching as she did so, making her way to the middle of the room, the safe middle of the room. "I must be out for a while this afternoon, but if you have any needs, I'll attend to them when I get back."

The slow, playful curl of Grant Russell's lips made Marlis aware of the unintentioned but intriguing suggestion of her words, and she blushed from peach to crimson before she hurried out of the room and down the stairs, nearly tripping on each one. She did not hear the slow expulsion of Grant's breath as he shook his head and softly murmured, "Whheeww."

On reaching the foyer, Marlis found three people waiting for her—a man, woman, and teenage girl.

"How long does a person have to wait around here for service?" the short, stocky man with balding head complained snidely.

"I'm sorry to have kept you waiting. I was showing another guest to his room."

The man gawked at her. "Is that what the hired help does around here? Where's the owner?"

Marlis straightened her shoulders and with her best smile answered, "I am the owner, Mr. . . . ?"

"Whitcomb. Julius, Abigail, and Tina Whitcomb. We want a room."

"Of course. Please forgive my appearance. My housekeeper was unable to come in today. I got to do her chores. Lucky me." Marlis moved behind her desk, her repeated joke no longer funny to her, but Abigail smiled sympathetically. Her husband just glowered. The daughter said nothing, for she was now examining a gilt-framed painting of John Sutter standing by the sawmill he had operated in 1846, just two years before gold was discovered in the area.

As Marlis was about to sit down, from the corner of her eye she spied something huge lumbering down the stairs. Glancing over, her shoulders snapped straight and her eyes bulged. There was Grant Russell, all six feet something of him, with no shirt on, his broad chest a forest of dark curly hair, muscles rippling everywhere, a set of keys dangling from his fingers.

"I forgot my suitcase," he explained, smiling for the first time since he'd been there. He turned to the new people on his way past them. "Nice place here, but expensive." Then he was out the door, the screen banging after him. Tina Whitcomb's dreamy eyes followed him. Her mother's expression was no less appreciative.

Julius Whitcomb turned to Marlis. "Just how expensive is this inn? I'm not a rich man."

Marlis sank down in the chair. "We're competitive with the other bed-and-breakfast inns in Sutter Creek. Would you like one room for the three of you, or a separate room for your daughter?"

"Separate," said the daughter, smiling at Marlis. She was about seventeen, with kinky dark hair tied back in a ponytail.

"One room," her father insisted. "Didn't you hear me tell the lady I'm not made of money, kid?"

The girl shrugged, but wasn't upset. She gazed at her father with a disinterested expression that told Marlis she lived in her own little world, and liked it that way.

Grant Russell exploded back into the room. With melting smiles for Abigail and Tina Whitcomb he passed behind them and proceeded to the stairs where he stopped, turned around, and leaned one strong, sinewy arm on the railing, the bare beginnings of a smile on his lips.

What is he waiting for? Marlis wondered, wishing he would go away. His half-dressed appearance was hardly a recommendation to Mrs. Whitcomb and her daughter that the Sunrise Inn was a respectable place.

"May I help you with something?" she asked him, hoping he could sense her irritation.

His smile broadened. "I have a question, but I'll wait till you're finished with these folks." The perturbed purse of Marlis's mouth tempted him to go over there and kiss it, right now, but propriety forced him to put off the experience till later, though not much later, he decided.

Marlis turned her attention back to the waiting family. "The Prospector Room will do nicely for your family, Mr. Whitcomb."

"How much will it cost me?"

"Eighty dollars a night."

A loud cough from the stairs was ignored by Marlis.

While Mrs. Whitcomb signed the guest register, Mr. Whitcomb, with a grunt, produced a Visa card from his wallet and extended it for payment. "Are you really the owner?" he asked.

"Yes, I am," Marlis assured him, taking the card and unsuccessfully trying to imagine him leaning over to sniff potpourri in a Victorian cranberry dish sitting on a Hepplewhite table.

"The Prospector is big and roomy, with a king-size bed and a double," she told him cheerfully as she got the key from the desk drawer. "The furniture is entirely nineteenth-century gold rush era."

"Does it overlook the street?" Abigail Whitcomb asked.

"No, ma'am, but it has a lovely view of our rose garden, at the side of the house."

"Oh, that's nice," Abigail sighed, pleased. "Roses are my favorite flower."

"Mine, too," Grant Russell agreed.

Marlis's jaw stiffened.

"And we get breakfast, too?" Whitcomb verified.

"Yes, indeed. From the best cook in northern California. Most of Mabel's fare is homemade." The words were already out of her mouth before Marlis remembered that the best cook in northern California was home with a strep throat.

"What's this best cook giving us for breakfast tomorrow?" Mr. Whitcomb asked.

He would have to ask. "The menu calls for southern ham, pineapple fruit boats, and blueberry muffins—twice the normal size—split and steaming with a thick pad of butter melting in the center." *I need a miracle, Lord, to pull that one off*, Marlis prayed.

"Sounds okay," Julius Whitcomb admitted with a shrug. Mrs. Whitcomb shook her head in agreement. Tina, the daughter, rolled her eyes and said, "I *love* blueberry muffins." She glanced over at Grant Russell, who silently mouthed the words, "Me, too." The girl giggled.

"And I love antiques," Abigail Whitcomb stated, beginning to explore the foyer with its pale-yellow walls and yellow-and-green carpet.

"Then you'll enjoy the house, Mrs. Whitcomb. Almost everything is from the eighteenth and nineteenth centuries. I'll be happy to answer any questions you may have."

"Don't forget my question," Grant Russell interrupted.

"Certainly not." The words were clipped.

Grant repressed a smile. She was a delight to tease because she was very much a woman in control of her emotions. He wondered how long it would take for him to break down that professionalism and expose the spitfire he was sure she was.

"Tomorrow we're going on a gold-prospecting trip for five days," Mr. Whitcomb said. "It's supposed to teach us everything from panning to sniping to dredging. Is it any good?" He pulled some paper from his shirt pocket and thrust it toward Marlis, who recognized it as the brochure for the business of one her friends.

Before she could take it, though, Grant Russell, in two strides, was beside the desk, and drew the brochure out of Julius Whitcomb's hands. "I took one of these a few years ago," he said. "It was a rip-off."

Marlis jumped to her feet and snatched the brochure from his hands, wishing this half-naked man would go drown himself in his shower.

"It's excellent," she assured all the Whitcombs. "I've taken it myself. I'm sure you'll enjoy it."

"We'd better, for what it's costing us."

Grant Russell shrugged his enormous shoulders but

didn't go back to the stairs. He just hovered around the desk, as though he were the host of the inn. Marlis's patience neared the snapping point.

"You're not listed in *Country Inns of California*," Mrs. Whitcomb spoke up, holding out the book in which every bed-and-breakfast owner in the state longed to be included. It was the Bible to the more sophisticated traveler who preferred spending his nights in the charming ambience of an old home rather than an impersonal motel.

"Not yet," Marlis assured the woman, "but we will be in the next edition."

"Really?" Grant Russell questioned.

As though he knows anything about it! Marlis fumed. She was stretching the truth a little, but had every hope it would happen. She had written to Kevin King, the writer of *Country Inns of California*, through his publisher, requesting that he visit Sunrise Inn. He had answered five months before with a courteous letter saying he would be happy to, but Marlis had not heard from him again.

In the meantime, she depended on word of mouth and the advertising she did in most of the major newspapers of California, and in some other parts of the country as well, to bring her customers.

"Your place looked so charming from the street," the wife went on, "with its white picket fence and the lovely green grass—"

"Abigail, you can ooh and ah later," her husband interrupted sharply. "Right now I'm tired. I've driven three hundred miles today and all I want is to get unpacked and relax. Picket fences and green grass I don't care about."

"Yes, Julius," Abigail responded meekly, lowering her head to stare at the floor while clutching her bed-and-breakfast guide to her chest.

Marlis finished the financial registering and handed Mr. Whitcomb his credit card. "Let me show you to your room." She moved to the stairs, with Grant Russell falling in beside her, his large, intimidating body touching hers at times as they walked up.

"After my shower I'll ask you that question," he told her, leaning closer.

Marlis moved away, recognizing raw male interest when she saw it. "Fine," she answered, "but I'll be working around the house."

"I'll find you."

It was a promise she was sure he would keep, but she'd be ready for him. If he thought he was going to have a quick roll in the hay with the local girl and then move on, he had another think coming. She had protected her purity from more than one predator, and she would continue to do so until she found a man she could love with her whole heart and for the rest of her life.

"Have a nice shower, Mr. Russell," she wished him caustically over her shoulder as they came to the top of the stairs and Marlis turned right with the Whitcombs.

Grant Russell watched them walk away, and the quickened beat of his heart told him he liked Marlis Kent. She was not a sweet and simple country gal waiting for a city slicker to warm up her life, and her bed. She was bright and intelligent, quick to challenge him, and might even have a sense of humor buried under that prim facade. If so, he'd find it, just as he knew he would learn everything there was to know about her, and enjoy himself doing so.

TWO

When Marlis left the Whitcombs' room, she glanced at her watch: two-fifteen. She had to be at the photographer's at three-thirty. "I'll really have to fly if I'm going to finish the housework, shower and change, and get over there on time," she said aloud to the empty hallway. But halfway to her room she groaned, remembering Mabel's warning from yesterday: "You'd better look at that oven. I've been having a dickens of a time keeping the pilot light on."

Marlis dashed through the rest of the chores, until all her rooms sparkled, ready for their next guests, then hurried to the kitchen. She dreaded cooking the way some people dread the dentist, "but if I have to do it, at least you must be working," she addressed the big white stove as she dropped to her knees and pulled down the door to the broiler. No pilot light.

Scrambling to her feet, she plunged her hand into a nearby drawer to find the box of matches and yanked it out when she felt a nail break.

"Darn!" She eyed the nail, which dangled by a thread. "I'll never have time to repair this before I have to leave."

Down on her knees again, Marlis struck a match and

leaned over the broiler door, reaching way to the back, leaning on one elbow, her nose almost inside the oven itself, her shapely bottom hovering high over long, slim legs encased in snug-fitting jeans.

"Once you're lit, don't you dare go out," she challenged the nonexistent flame. "Not today. And certainly not tomorrow. Just be good and—"

"Need help?"

The powerful male voice, so close behind her, startled Marlis from her intense concentration, and she crumpled onto the floor while twisting her head back to see if the voice belonged to whom she thought it did.

From her awkward position at his feet, Marlis looked up, past soft black leather loafers, neatly creased gray slacks, a blue-and-gray short-sleeved shirt, open at the throat, that clung to broad, muscled shoulders and well-developed arms that she had last seen naked. Grant Russell. Only he looked a lot different from the way he had an hour before. The rugged, sweaty cowboy was gone. In his place was Cary Grant's clone, clean and dashing, his sophisticated clothes screaming big city businessman despite the mountain-man breadth of his shoulders and chest.

Grant's strong hands reached down and grasped both her shoulders, and with little effort helped Marlis to stand up. "Don't you have a man around here to help you with things like this?" He gestured with his head toward the oven.

Marlis gave him a sassy smile while removing his hands from her shoulders. "I don't need a man," she informed him.

"Oh? Looks like it to me. The only thing you've accomplished is to break a fingernail."

Marlis looked him right in the eye. "I can fix it myself. I think the gas regulator is going out."

One of Grant Russell's eyebrows slid upward in surprise. It was the same reaction Marlis got from most people when they discovered how handy she was around a house. Through some quirk in her chromosomal makeup, she hated "woman's work" and relished, instead, fooling around with tools, always having helped her dad with repairs more than her brothers had.

"That could be serious," Grant said.

"When you have a houseful of people to cook for, yes, and I haven't got time to buy one before tomorrow. I just hope it keeps working through breakfast."

Grant cocked his head and squinted at her. "Are you the one who's going to be cooking those blueberry muffins?"

"Right."

"Didn't you tell the Whitcombs you have a cook?"

"Yes. But she's sick with strep throat."

"I see. And there's only one cook in Sutter Creek?"

"We've had this conversation before."

"No. Last time it was about the housekeeper. You have trouble keeping help, don't you?"

With a sigh of exasperation, Marlis dropped down on the floor again, and lit the pilot light, knowing Grant Russell was watching her. *Well, let him,* she thought. *That's all he's going to get from me: an eyeful.*

"Done," she said triumphantly, rising to her feet and giving Grant a look that dared him to say anything. He didn't. "I have to leave soon for an appointment, but didn't you have a question you wanted to ask me?"

"Yes. How many rooms do you have here?"

Strange question, she decided. She'd thought he was going to ask if she were married and had six kids, not that that probably mattered. A conquest was a conquest to a man like this.

"There are eight rooms available for guests," she answered him, starting to walk through the house. She had to hurry if she was going to get to the photographer's by three-thirty. "Two on the first floor, five on the second. And, of course, the Dog House."

"The what?"

Marlis laughed softly. "It's a toolshed in the back I've made up for last-minute arrivals."

"Or 'difficult' guests?"

She caught a glint of humor in his dark eyes. "Precisely," she shot back.

"And where do you live?"

Marlis hesitated. Did one tell the wolf where Red Riding Hood was? "On the third floor," she finally replied. "My apartment is what used to be the attic. Now it's just me up there, collecting dust."

Grant chuckled, and Marlis found herself smiling, too, and even wishing she didn't look as messy as she did. Not even her makeup was intact anymore. Most of it had worn off during the day of sweaty housecleaning, not that she cared particularly what he thought of her, but she always wanted to make a good impression for the inn and normally she looked as sophisticated as it did, in a country kind of way, but today she didn't. Not that it mattered whether she impressed him or not, but still there was a part of her that wished he could see her in an hour, when she'd have on the silky aqua dress with her hair shampooed, smelling sweet, and fluffed around her shoulders instead of dirty and pulled back in a casual ponytail . . .

Marlis took a deep breath, exhausted from her own thoughts, and from the fact they had climbed two flights of stairs rapidly and were now at the door to her room.

"Is that the only question you have?" she asked, pushing open the door and turning around to say good-bye. It was two forty-five.

"One more. Are you married?"

"No, I'm—"

"Then have dinner with me tonight. Seven o'clock. I'll pick you up here." He turned and started to walk away.

"I haven't agreed," she called after him.

He paused, then came back to her, his eyes capturing hers. "Why wouldn't you? You're not married. I'm not married."

"I have to be here for several guests checking in late this afternoon or early evening and," she paused before saying honestly, "I'm not sure I like you."

His eyes twinkled. "You will—by seven-fifteen."

This time when he walked away she didn't stop him, and later she would wonder why.

Pushed for time, Marlis showered and changed clothes as fast as she could, managing to get to the photographer's studio only a few minutes late. Her mom and dad were visibly relieved when they saw her and knew that finally the grand portrait was about to be taken. Everyone hugged everyone else.

Sondra, Marlis's older sister, who was born Sandra, but as she grew older and became more glamorous, changed the spelling of her name to Sondra, looked terribly chic, as usual, in a smart suit of black crepe de chine that accented the russet tones of her stylishly cut strawberry-blond hair.

"How do you do it with three kids tugging at your skirts?" Marlis wanted to know, proud of her sister's calm radiance.

"The love of a good man is the secret." Sondra winked at her. "You should try it sometime."

"Marlis is too busy playing Conrad Hilton," her brother, Bob, teased. He was always finding something cute to say to her. They were very close.

"Yeah, when *are* you going to get married?" her other brother, Willy, asked. He was a smart aleck, too, but a lovable one, and he eagerly gave her a peck on the cheek. "You're not getting any younger, you know."

"I'm not quite over the hill yet," Marlis retorted, throwing a pretend left hook at his strong jaw. "I have a few good years left."

"But you're no spring chicken, Sis," Willy asserted with a devilish grin.

"I'm springy enough to give you a rough time, though." It was amazing to Marlis that four children who had squabbled all of their growing up years could now be so close-knit and supportive.

"Will you join us for dinner, Marlis?" her mother asked.

"I wish I could, Mom, but I have to get back. There's no one to cover for me, and I have guests arriving." She decided not to admit she might be having dinner with one Grant Russell, cowboy or businessman, she didn't know which, but a decisive man who went after what he wanted which seemed, today, to be her.

"Oh, that's too bad," her mother said. "Are you sure you're not working too hard, trying to do everything yourself?"

Marlis groaned. "And who was my example? When you and Dad were running the inn, either one or both of you were over there every day that I can remember. I used to wish we could all live in it together."

"Your mother and I did, too," her dad spoke up. "But you four kids needed a place where you could relax and be yourselves, and not have to worry about breaking antiques and behaving well for guests."

"Are you saying we did not behave well at home?"

Everyone laughed.

"At least you and Mom are taking vacations now," Bob pointed out.

"We should have done it years ago, but we were too busy. Since Marlis bought the inn from us, we've been free to enjoy our retirement."

Her sister and brothers turned to Marlis and applauded.

"If there was ever an ideal place to meet Prince Charming," Sondra said, "it should be the Sunrise Inn. You must have a constant flow of eligible men through there."

Everyone guffawed and agreed uproariously with Sondra.

"Wait a minute, wait a minute," Marlis protested. "I am not running the Playboy Mansion of Sutter Creek. Most of my guests are respectable middle-aged couples or families with older children. There are few-to-none potential husbands who stroll through my door."

Until today. The words leapt to mind, as did a heart-pounding image of Grant Russell, the man who'd already nibbled her earlobe and was, no doubt, planning a dinner seduction at this very moment.

She hurried back to the inn as soon as the pictures were taken, and there found Grant waiting for her, again, in the foyer, his feet planted firmly on the floor, his arms across his chest.

"I have a complaint," he said, the seductive eyes and sexy grin gone, replaced by a scowl that suggested his complaint was something more serious than that he didn't like the color of the towels in his room.

"What's the problem?" Marlis asked, a tad dismayed that he wasn't noticing how lovely she looked compared to how she had that afternoon after a day of housecleaning.

"Follow me and I'll show you," he grunted, which Marlis did, optimistic that whatever it was, she could remedy it, or call in the National Guard, if need be, to help her.

He led her up to his room where the late-afternoon sun streamed through the lace curtains, bestowing a cheerfulness that Marlis particularly liked. Since he'd left the door open, she felt safe and turned to face him with a determined smile on her face. "What is the complaint you have, Mr. Russell?"

"There." He pointed at the four-poster bed, and Marlis saw the problem. Right in the center of the 1840's Virginia quilt, was the biggest, fattest cat she had ever seen. It was sleeping contentedly and hadn't even opened one eye when they entered.

"I'm surprised an inn of this caliber would allow pets," he chided.

"Oh, we don't," Marlis assured him. "I've never seen that animal before."

"Really?" The reply was derisive.

Marlis stabbed him with a glare that carried the message she did not like being thought a liar.

"We do not allow pets at Sunrise Inn." She said each word carefully, her green eyes dancing with irritation.

"Many people have allergies to cats, you know," he stated.

"Yes, I do know." Did he think she was stupid? Of

course she knew people had allergies. That was the very reason pets were never allowed in the house.

"I'll get rid of it," she announced, striding to the bed and scooping the white ball of fluff into her arms.

From being awakened so rudely, the cat quivered, then vaulted out of Marlis's arms.

"Here, kitty," she called, chasing it around the room until it dashed under the bed and she had to drop down on all fours to pursue it further.

Crawling awkwardly from the foot of the bed toward the head, impeded by the voluminous skirt of her dress, reaching out for the furry mass that cleverly managed to elude her, then scurried out the other side, across the room and into the hallway, Marlis felt like a fool. She balanced on both elbows and let out a gigantic sigh of frustration.

"He got away," Grant Russell pronounced dryly.

Marlis looked over her shoulder and found herself, once again, as she had earlier that day, gawking at the knees of the man's neat trousers. Moving her gaze to his face, she saw disdain in his expression.

"He has indeed," she agreed. "But I'll find him." Marlis felt worse about Grant's insinuation that she was negligent in her running of a bed-and-breakfast inn than that the stupid cat had outsmarted her.

"I'll check with the Whitcombs," she promised. "The cat may belong to them."

"Did you tell them no pets were allowed when they checked in?" His stare was condemning.

"Of course," she answered, but her confidence waned when she remembered how her attention had been distracted by the shirtless man standing on the stairway. Had she or had she not told them? "They did not have a cat with them today," she insisted, knowing that, at least, was true.

"People sneak them in," Grant informed her.

He's insufferable, Marlis decided. *How does he know what people like to do at bed-and-breakfast inns?*

"You sound as though you've had experience with this before," she replied crisply.

"I travel a lot."

"And often find cats on your bed?"

"Never before. I guess other innkeepers keep a closer watch on their guests than you do."

Marlis's nostrils flared in self-preservation and she wished for a second she were a cat herself, with long, sharp claws, the better to scratch his sassy mouth. The man had no manners. His suave good looks meant nothing compared with that.

"Would you like another room?" The frost in her voice chilled the temperature by twenty degrees.

"That won't be necessary, as long as the cat is gone— and will stay gone." The last words were more an order than a statement, and Marlis bristled.

"It will just take a minute to transfer your things—"

"This room is fine."

"If you're really sure."

"I'm sure."

They glared at each other across the Colonial rug Marlis had found in an antique shop in New Hampshire. A tiny war was declared.

Seeing a movement behind him—the cat—Marlis almost knocked Grant down as she flew out the door and scooped the troublesome feline into her arms, holding it tight enough to keep it imprisoned.

"End of problem," she announced triumphantly.

"For now," he answered, with a patronizing tone that sent Marlis's temper soaring. She was about to retort in a way she would later have regretted when the Whitcomb girl appeared.

"Oh, there he is," she shrieked with delight. "You found Muffy."

"This is your cat?" Marlis questioned.

"Yes. You didn't hurt him, did you?"

From the corner of her eye Marlis caught sight of Grant Russell standing with his arms folded across his chest, his interest apparent as he waited to see how she would handle the situation.

"No, Tina, I did not hurt Muffy. The problem is that I do not allow pets in the inn." Her need for firmness battled her understanding. She had had a cat herself when she'd been growing up. "Muffy was sleeping on Mr. Russell's bed," she explained.

"He likes soft places."

Marlis heard a throat being cleared behind her, as though to urge her on. She didn't need urging on. She knew her responsibility.

"That may be, Tina, but Muffy will have to sleep elsewhere."

"In our room?" Tina looked hopeful.

Marlis held out her arms, relinquishing the cat to his owner. "Out of the inn, I'm afraid."

"Where?"

"Anywhere. Your car will be fine."

Tina shook her head no. "Dad never allows Muffy in the car alone. He goes kinda berserk."

The cat, or your dad? Marlis could have asked. "Well, Muffy cannot stay here," she insisted.

"Dad'll be mad," Tina warned.

"Have him see me. I'll explain the rule and the reason for it."

Marlis looked down at her dress and saw with dismay long, white hairs clinging to it, but worse than that, some catches in the material from where the cat had torn it.

"Isn't Muffy declawed?" she asked Tina.

"Heck, no. He's got to be able to defend himself."

Marlis's mouth tightened across her teeth. "Tina, I do not want to see Muffy again. Is that clear? If you cannot promise me that, your family will have to leave."

"Who has to leave?" It was Mr. Whitcomb, walking toward them.

Marlis turned to face him and noticed Grant Russell now leaning against the door to his room, one foot crossed over the other, the toe of that shoe resting on the floor, his hands stuffed casually into the pockets of his slacks. *He's enjoying all this,* Marlis thought, the smug look on his face increasing her ire.

"I've just been explaining to your daughter, Mr. Whitcomb, that we do not allow animals in the inn."

"That's a silly rule."

"Your cat was found sleeping on one of my guest's bed."

"So?"

"So, Muffy must stay somewhere else."

"Hey, a nice little kitty like this can't cause any problems." Mr. Whitcomb chucked the cat under the chin, and his voice was friendly enough, but Marlis knew a challenge when she heard it.

Keeping her voice steady, and looking Mr. Whitcomb straight in the eye to show him she meant business, she repeated her warning. "That cat must go. Or you."

"Oo-ee, you're an uptight little thing, aren't you?"

Marlis successfully squelched the urge to give him a piece of her mind. "I'm an innkeeper who has to think of all my guests, Mr. Whitcomb, and I'll appreciate your cooperation." She managed to give him a smile.

"Okay, okay, we'll find a place for him. No wonder you're not listed in that fancy bed-and-breakfast guide, if a family can be thrown out into the night all because of a cat who likes to roam. Come on, Tina."

Father and daughter and cat went back to their room at the end of the hall, and Marlis turned to face Grant Russell.

"You're tough," he conceded, but Marlis was not flattered. She had skillfully handled a touchy problem, but she did not want to be thought of as "tough" because of it.

"I just did what needed to be done, Mr. Russell."

Marlis turned on her heels and walked briskly downstairs, and he didn't stop her, so she guessed that he no longer wanted to take her to dinner, which was fine with her. She was tired from her day's work and hoped the two scheduled couples who had made reservations months before would arrive early so she could go to bed by nine. And when she did, she wouldn't be dreaming about Grant Russell, either. He had plummeted from a ten to a zero in her ratings.

Looking back over the day, Marlis decided the only good thing about it had been the family portrait that had been taken. Everything else, including meeting Grant Russell, had been a disaster. And tomorrow didn't promise to be any better: she had to cook breakfast.

By the time seven o'clock came, Marlis's expected guests had arrived, were snug in their rooms, and she was hungry, so she was just getting ready to go down to the kitchen to raid the refrigerator for a light snack when a firm knock on her door surprised her. Even before she could get to it, the knock grew more urgent and a familiar voice called out, "Marlis, open up."

Her hand froze on the handle of the door. It was Grant Russell, there to take her to dinner after all, but she hadn't dressed for it, although she was wearing neat black slacks and a soft aqua sweater, her hair freshly brushed and makeup newly applied for her venture through the house, never knowing whom she'd meet. While she definitely did not want to go out with him, as she whipped open the door, she wished she'd remembered perfume.

Grant Russell loomed there in the dim light of the hallway, in the same clothes he'd had on that afternoon but with dark-rimmed glasses sitting halfway down his nose. His hair was disheveled and he was breathing heavily, gasping for breath actually, his eyes glassy.

"What's wrong?" Marlis questioned, alarmed.

"I need another room."

An attempt at a smile from him brought instant sympathy to her heart. The man was suffering. But why?

"I'm allergic to cats," he explained as his broad chest heaved up and down in an exhausting effort to breathe.

"I thought I wouldn't be affected . . . since the beast was only in my room . . . a little while, but I was wrong."

Marlis understood completely. Her aunt was allergic to cats, and she'd seen her several times in the throes of a reaction, her eyes watering and throat closing up, every gasp for air sounding like her last. It was nothing to take lightly.

"I'll move you to the first floor," she said, coming out of her room and leading him quickly toward the stairs, quelling a strong urge to put her arms around him in comfort, he looked so haggard, but a natural wariness won out. *No sense giving the wrong signals,* she instructed herself. *Treat him as you would any other guest.*

"What you need most is fresh air, unless you want to go to the hospital emergency room for oxygen," she said, as they started down. She suspected he'd been suffering for hours before finally coming to her for help.

He shook his head. "I'll be okay here."

"But outside on the back porch. It might be chilly. Do you have a sweater? I'll get it for you."

"Yes, in the first drawer . . . of the dresser."

They were on the second floor now, where his room was. "I'll be right back," Marlis promised, and turned to leave, but he caught her wrist.

"I'm sorry about dinner."

"That's okay."

"I haven't missed my one and only chance, have I?"

"Since you're leaving tomorrow, probably."

"Maybe I'll stay over another day." He pressed his lips into her open palm. "If you save my life," and his voice oozed over her like rich, melting chocolate, "you'll be responsible for it forever." His eyes made love to her.

Good heavens, she thought, the man is dying and he's still a predator. "That's an old Oriental fable that doesn't apply here in Sutter Creek," she managed to say before something happened to her tongue and vocal cords that kept her from saying another word.

She knew she should pull her hand away from his, but

she liked what he was doing to it, kneading it gently, exploring it, creating rivers of warmth that swam up her body and started nerves on fire that had never been on fire before.

You're just feeling sorry for the guy, she reasoned with herself, but she knew that wasn't entirely true. There was a powerful magnetism to Grant Russell that drew her to him with an invisible lasso, despite her desire to resist.

Finally pulling free of him, she said, "Wait here. I'll be back as soon as I find your sweater. Then you go outside while I change your things to another room."

"Yes, ma'am."

Marlis caught the twinkle in his eye that conveyed he was not used to being ordered about by a woman, but he obeyed meekly by letting her go, and she dashed into his room, found a soft blue sweater in a drawer of neatly stacked shorts and T-shirts, and returned to find him leaning on the stair railing, his head bent down, his breathing still ragged.

"Here you are." She handed him the sweater. "I'll join you outside in a minute. Would you like some coffee?"

His eyes roamed over her face with mute appreciation as he put on the sweater, and Marlis's blood did a tango to and from her heart.

"Coffee would be great. Thanks."

His lazy grin left her breathing heavier, too, and she turned away before he could see what he was doing to her. But it was too late. Miserable as he was, Grant Russell knew she was attracted to him. Step one accomplished. Step two would have to wait until he could breathe again. A man in his condition could hardly kiss a woman the way he intended to kiss Marlis Kent the first time.

The making of coffee had never been a particularly challenging task for Marlis, so while she waited for the water to boil, she thought of the man who was sitting outside on the swing just beyond her kitchen window. A person's possessions and how he arranges them reveals much about that person, but, contrarily, she hadn't learned much about Grant Russell when she'd moved his things into the Shady Lady room.

He traveled lightly, with only one suitcase and a garment bag holding several pairs of slacks and a few well-tailored shirts. His clothes were expensive, and his reading habits sophisticated, as the current best-seller by a former British prime minister on the nightstand attested. But other than that, and a bottle of masculine cologne sitting on the dresser, there was not much revelation about the man himself—except for the laptop computer in the closet. Whatever did he use that for? Marlis wondered.

Minutes later she stood in front of Grant, offering him an insulated mug of steaming black coffee. Its aroma drifted into the still night air, competing with the subtle fragrance of the many healthy rosebushes which surrounded three sides of the porch.

"You're an angel," he said.

And you're probably the opposite, she thought.

He was breathing easier, though still with difficulty, and her anger at him for pointing out the cat's presence, and making her feel incompetent, vanished in a sea of empathy. "Feeling any better?" she asked.

"Yep." He smiled. "Fresh air helps."

"I knew it would."

She gave him the warmest smile he'd received since checking in, which sent all kinds of male impulses into gear and made Grant wonder if it would be worth his dying breath to take those rose-petal lips with his own.

"I do apologize for the cat," she said, "and I'd better check on its whereabouts. I've been so busy today I haven't had time to be sure the Whitcombs did, indeed, put Muffy out of the inn. We don't want him wandering into your new room, do we?"

"Unless that would mean I'd get to stay in your room . . ."

" 'Fraid not. Next would be the Dog House."

She turned to go, but Grant jumped off the swing. "No, wait," he called, and the swing, returning from its backward journey, crashed into him, launching him off balance into Marlis's arms which flew up, instinctively, when she saw him falling toward her. His coffee cup sailed across the porch, not spilling anything on either of them, but clattering on the floor, coming to rest by the steps.

"Sorry," Grant breathed softly against Marlis's sweet-smelling hair. Her body was molded against his, and he felt every curve of it, and silently thanked the giddy swing for accomplishing what he had been figuring out how to do for himself.

She was one beautiful woman, this innkeeper: hard-working, independent, and intelligent. Talented in ways most women weren't. Caring, too. And soft in all the right places. He wondered if there'd been any serious relationships in her life.

Marlis pulled back, but he held her shoulders with strong hands. "I haven't had a chance to tell you how gorgeous you looked when you came back from your appointment this afternoon."

"Why . . . thank you."

"I was actually the beast, making you chase that cat in so beautiful a dress. Did he ruin it?"

"Damaged here and there, I'm afraid."

"Too bad."

He took off his glasses and set them on a nearby table, yet, to Marlis, he didn't look any more handsome with them off than he did with them on. They gave him a sophistication that blended nicely with the rugged physique that was also his.

He led her back to the now-quiet swing and they both sat down, one of his long legs starting the swing on a gentle movement back and forth and keeping it going.

The night sky beyond the roof of the porch moved slowly through a rosy dusk which blanketed the lush lawn and flower beds and narrow brick path that wound around the entire house in a subtle hue that urged a relaxation from the business of the day and called, instead, for a contemplation of sounds and movement that spoke of quiet evening and gray shadows.

Under the roof of the porch, the diminishing light created a romantic atmosphere that melded with the silence of the night, broken only by the constant chant in unison of the crickets, and an occasional indistinguishable noise from inside the house.

The mood became hypnotic, and Marlis did not move when Grant's right hand reached up and touched the soft waves of her luxuriant hair where it nestled upon her shoulder.

THREE

"I'm very, very sorry you're going through this," Marlis apologized in a whisper.

"Don't worry about it. I'll be okay." Grant's words caressed her.

"I've never had this happen before. I'm strict about not allowing pets."

"I'm sure you are." His fingers meandered to the back of her ear, then down her neck . . .

"I really should check on the whereabouts of Muffy and get you some more coffee, too."

"Later."

They sat in silence, Grant longing to pull Marlis into his arms, Marlis afraid he would pull her into his arms.

"Does anyone else in your family have such an allergy?" she finally asked, just as his arm moved across her shoulder and she felt the touch of his hand strengthen.

"My wife did."

Wife? Marlis turned suddenly to face him, breaking his touch. "She doesn't any more?"

"She died six years ago."

"Good heavens, not from . . ."

"No," he quickly assured her, "not from a reaction to cats. It was an accident."

"I'm sorry."

His arm stretched out behind her again, but Marlis stood up. "How about a walk?" Not waiting for a yes or no, she walked briskly off the porch and onto the brick path, pausing to wait for Grant to catch up to her.

"You're running away from me," he told her.

"Don't be ridiculous."

They started walking, hearing the movement of the nearby fir trees as the playful breeze danced through them and smelling the sweet fragrance of the grass that had been cut that afternoon.

"Why aren't you married?" he asked her.

"That's a personal question, isn't it?" she answered.

A low rumble escaped Grant's throat. "That's exactly what it is, lady. I want to know."

"Why?" Marlis turned to face him.

"Because you fascinate me." With the back of one hand he followed the curve of her cheek. "You're beautiful, intelligent, and compassionate." The hand slid through the thick tangle of her hair to rest at the nape of her neck, and his eyes never left hers. "But you're alone."

"A matter of choice," Marlis murmured.

"Mmmm, I don't think so. You've just never met a man who was your equal."

Marlis allowed her eyes to travel slowly over Grant's face, fully aware of what her heart was telling her at that moment—that she had found her equal, and he was standing with her now. Except that was absurd. She knew nothing about Grant Russell. Her body was dictating to her head.

"Perhaps I'm not the marrying kind," she suggested, for want of a better explanation.

"I don't think that's true."

Marlis had no idea how to answer his question, and didn't want to. There was no point in recounting her dating life in college, or explaining why she had decided not to marry Tim. Single men were scarce in Sutter Creek, and she had been too busy to worry much about the fact that she was reaching the age when most women had husbands, but she did not.

"Is there a man in your life now? Is that who you met this afternoon?"

Marlis smiled. "Actually, I met three men, and they all are special to me." She explained about the family portrait as they continued their stroll.

"Your folks used to own this place?"

"Yes. I helped out, as all us kids did, when I was growing up. Then after I graduated from college, I decided to work here for the summer before looking for a job in my field."

"Which was?"

"History. Having lived all my life in a place where some of America's most fascinating events took place, it was a logical choice. I wanted to teach."

"What happened to change your mind?" Grant's hand found Marlis's, and she did not pull hers away.

"My folks, who'd rarely taken a vacation in twenty years, decided to take advantage of their loving daughter's accessibility. They dumped the whole thing in my lap for three months and drove around the country visiting relatives. By the time they got back, I knew I wanted this place for my own, and they had decided it was time to retire."

"Don't you find it hard to run a bed and breakfast by yourself?"

"Most of the time, no. I have wonderful people who work with me and normally things go pretty smoothly." She groaned. "Today was not normal." Marlis recounted the ironic unavailability of all her employees at the same time, and ended with the assertion that she was far better with a screwdriver than a spatula.

"So you'd rather fix an oven than cook food in it," Grant summarized.

"Exactly."

"What may I expect tomorrow morning from this meal

you are being forced to provide for your guests, or should I check into the hospital tonight?"

Marlis laughed and her green eyes sparkled. "Tonight would be better. Then you'd be sure of a room, before all the others arrive."

Grant joined her laughter.

They had taken a small rocky path off the main one and now were standing in front of a pretty white gazebo with latticed walls halfway up, and fully open to the night air from there to the solid roof.

Grant walked inside, but Marlis hesitated. The moon spilled out of the heavens and washed the lawn around her with a gauze of fantasy, but she was trying to remain the realist she'd always been. Outside the gazebo, she could run away from the man who had now turned, and extended his hand, inviting her to join him. Inside the gazebo, she knew she'd be too close to him, to his charm, to the very manliness that lured her and frightened her at the same time.

"I won't attack you if you join me," Grant promised, seeming to read her mind.

Marlis slowly put her hand in his, then stepped inside the cozy structure. Someone inside the house turned on a radio, and dreamy music floated through the window and across the lush grass to engulf the couple now standing close, gazing at each other.

Without a word, Grant put his arm around Marlis and they began to dance, slowly, sensuously. His arms had actually ached from wanting to hold her. She was intoxicating and he was falling for her faster than he would have believed possible. After his wife died, he'd closed off his heart for years, eventually dating but never seriously caring for another woman—till now, till he'd met this funny, wonderful, unpredictable Marlis person, and she'd turned him inside out.

He bent to kiss her, but she backed out of his embrace, avoiding his intention.

"You asked me a very personal question before," she

said, leaning against a rounded pillar of the structure. "Now I have one for you."

Grant stuffed his hands in his pockets. They were trembling and he didn't like being out of control. "Ask away," he gave her permission. His breathing was still not normal, but it was vastly improved, although he wasn't sure now whether his shortness of breath was from the darn cat or the overpowering presence of this enchanting woman he was going to kiss very soon.

"What do you do for a living?" Marlis asked her question.

Grant seemed to ponder his answer before he said, "I'm a writer."

"Really? What do you write?"

Another pause. "Mysteries."

"And you're published?"

"Yes, which allows me to travel, which I greatly enjoy."

A writer. It fit him. Unusual, and a little mysterious, like he was.

"Do you write under your own name or a pseudonym? What are the titles of your books? Perhaps I've read one. Wouldn't that be something if I had?"

"Lady, you talk too much."

Without warning, Grant pulled Marlis into his arms, slipped one of his hands through her hair and tilted her head, capturing her lips in a kiss that meant business. His mouth played with hers a long time and his fingers caressed her chin and cheek and the silky side of her neck.

Fourth of July exploded in Marlis's head, and fireworks went off all through her body. She was stunned by the intensity of her reaction to this relative stranger, and for a moment tried to rally her resistance to him. But she couldn't. She just couldn't. Everything he was doing to her was producing one thrilling sensation after another, and she finally gave in, to him and to the moment, and kissed him back.

Grant had wanted to touch Marlis, to kiss her, almost

from the first moment he saw her, but he never imagined the physical and emotional impact her allowing him to do so would have on him. He was overwhelmed with desire and couldn't get enough of her. His arms, his mouth, his hands, all made her his, and he knew it was right, and good. He was there, at her inn, for deceptive purposes, but he had found truth in his deep and fascinating feelings for this woman he hadn't even known that morning.

He could have gone on and on, taking more and more of what she had to offer him, but Grant's rational side, and honorable side, began a recording in his head that said Stop. He had never been a man to enjoy a quick affair. He seldom gave his heart, but when he did, he gave it with a purity of purpose not many other men could match.

Wanting to keep the magic of what they had, he decided against taking too much too soon, and disentangled himself from the exquisite Marlis and whistled softly as he leaned back and just drank in the sight of her. She was all woman at that moment—eyes soft with longing, lips slightly swollen from his use of them. Her body was liquid as she began to sway to the music still playing on the night breeze, and he wanted her as he had not wanted a woman for a very long time.

"Marlis," he whispered, his voice husky and low, "you're bewitching me." He kissed her gently, briefly. "I don't want to be a gentleman and let you go"—*What kind of fool am I anyway?* he wondered—"but I want you to be willing to talk with me tomorrow."

Marlis smiled and planted a barely felt kiss on each of his cheeks. "Thank you, Mr. Russell, for your honorable intentions. I promise to speak to you tomorrow."

A soft chuckle came from his mouth that Marlis was now fascinated with and wanted to kiss again and again.

Grant took both her hands in his and silently kissed the backs of each one. "See what happens to a girl when she innocently plays Florence Nightingale?"

"How is my patient doing?"

With a groan, Grant swept her into his arms again and kissed her with a sweet passion. "What's your opinion?"

"He's alive and very, very well," Marlis confirmed with a giggle.

With their arms locked around each other's waists, they walked back to the house. Marlis showed him his new room and then Grant insisted on walking her up to her apartment. At the door he murmured, after a quick hug that sent tongues of fire over her sensitive skin, "Thanks for saving my life."

"You'd better see if you survive breakfast," she joked.

He chuckled. "I have confidence in you. What time is the big occasion?"

"Eight-thirty, sharp."

"I'll be early."

"You're brave."

He stepped back. " 'Til tomorrow." He gave a broad sweeping bow, as a dashing cavalier from an Alexandre Dumas novel would have done, and Marlis felt like a giddy schoolgirl on her first date.

Long after she had snuggled down in her bed, she felt the manly touch of Grant's lips on hers and his hands imprinting on her body. Thank goodness he had had the fortitude to stop before they had gone too far. Marlis was not used to showing such abandon and knew she would have regretted it had anything more happened between them.

"I like Grant Russell," she said out loud to the darkness of her room. "He makes me feel like a woman." She replayed in her mind every minute of the evening, saw the way he walked and moved his hands, heard his voice speak her name with tenderness and desire. She saw his strongly sculpted profile captured in the moonlight and felt the unique warmth of being in his arms.

Her daydreams melded into blissful sleep, but the next morning her real life became a nightmare.

* * *

"I can't believe it!" Marlis wailed, standing glumly in the middle of her kitchen. "I forgot to get groceries yesterday." It was seven A. M. She was supposed to be starting breakfast for her guests, but there wasn't any southern ham, or fresh pineapples with which to make fruit boats, or luscious blueberry muffins. All she had was the butter, and barely enough eggs to make a decent batch of scrambled, and if she used what tomato juice was available, the glasses would be only half full.

There weren't even any spare coffeecakes. Never, in the five years Mabel Foster had worked for Marlis, had she failed to have spare coffeecakes or muffins or *something*!

"It's all *his* fault," Marlis ranted, thinking of all the time she'd spent with Grant Russell the day before. Dishes and silverware clattered as she set the Chippendale pine table for eight. "I surely would have remembered to buy the groceries if I hadn't been thinking of having dinner with him, and getting rid of the cat, and then dealing with his reaction to it. If I hadn't been sitting on the porch with him, and walking in the garden with him, and letting him turn me to Jell-O in the gazebo, I know I would have remembered."

Ranting seemed to make things better, and Marlis ranted as she made coffee and tea, and searched for the fresh oranges she was sure she had seen just a few days before.

Things got worse when, from the corner of her eye, she saw a ball of fluff dash by the kitchen door. "Muffy!" she exclaimed, disgusted with herself for forgetting to check on the feline the night before, but not having time to now. She just hoped Grant wouldn't see him, or have another reaction to him.

"Thank goodness the oven is working," Marlis declared, "but I'll definitely have to replace that gas regulator today, if I can find one in town."

The retired couple from Kansas City were the first guests to appear—at eight-twenty.

"Hi," Marlis greeted them as cheerfully as a stomach

in turmoil would allow her to. "There are hot drinks on the sideboard, and a fire to warm your toes."

It was cold enough in the mornings, even in May, to have a blaze going in the big old fireplace, and Mrs. McIntosh sat on one end of the large stone hearth enjoying the warmth, while Mr. McIntosh examined the andirons in the shape of black owls and sipped coffee he didn't complain about. Marlis sighed with relief for that small blessing.

They asked her questions about Sutter Creek and the inn and the antiques that hugged the walls of the huge combination kitchen and dining room, which always reminded people of another era.

Marlis tried to answer their questions while breaking the eggs into a bowl and reaching for canned peaches. She hadn't found the oranges. It was hard for her to work and talk at the same time, and she hoped her answers were intelligible. She remembered to take the butter out of the refrigerator so it would be soft for the toast. Plain old toast. What would Mr. Whitcomb say when he saw plain old toast instead of the luscious giant-size blueberry muffins she'd promised him?

Fred and Grace Baldwin, a pediatrician and child psychologist who practiced together in Reno, Nevada, entered the kitchen with a cheery good morning for everyone. Marlis introduced them to the McIntoshes.

Grace perched herself on the other end of the stone fireplace and her husband poured them both some hot chocolate.

"Is there any whipped cream for this?" he asked.

"Sure," Marlis replied, yanking open the refrigerator door and seeing none, not even a carton of dairy cream Mabel used to whip up her own. In the freezer there was a tub of non-dairy topping, but it was frozen. Marlis slammed the door.

"Sorry, Dr. Baldwin. Seems we're out."

Mr. McIntosh and Fred Baldwin began discussing local fishing and the women asked about each other's vacations.

Marlis mixed the eggs and milk and oil together and put them on the stove. Then she turned on the water over the humongous sink to wash her hands again and halfway through the process the water dribbled to a stop.

"What now?" she mumbled to herself, opening the cupboard door under the sink to see if that's where the problem was. Finding nothing out of the ordinary, she returned to the faucet handle which she flipped on and off a few times. But nothing came out.

A howl from upstairs shattered the relative peace of the house.

"Excuse me," Marlis said to her guests and hurried out, knowing it sounded like Mr. Whitcomb bellowing triple forte. When she knocked on the door of his room thirty second later, having galloped up the stairs in record time, she heard beyond it words she wished she weren't hearing. Tina opened up to her.

"There's no water," she announced even before Marlis could ask what was the matter. "My dad's real mad."

So what else is new? Marlis could have said, but, of course, didn't.

"Tell your father I'll take care of it right away."

Marlis bounded down the stairs two at a time and dashed outside toward the shut-off valve. The minute she rounded the corner and saw water squirting all over the place, she knew what was the matter: a pipe had broken between the water meter and the house. Better outside than in, she thought.

Running to the garage where she kept most of her tools, then back again, Marlis crossed the lawn that was fast becoming a quagmire. Fixing a broken pipe was a piece of cake for her, but first she had to turn the water off. Her feet squished in the soggy grass as the force of the spray made it harder than she'd anticipated to get near enough to the valve to shut it off. Her hair and make up were ruined in ten seconds. Her new pink cotton jumpsuit was a shrinking mess.

"What in blazes is going on out here?"

Marlis recognized Grant's voice, and the frustration in it. She was struggling with a pipe wrench to turn the rusted valve which hadn't been used in years, but through the vicious inundation she saw him striding toward her, his arms swinging angrily by his sides. He was wearing only a bath towel.

One last turn did the trick. The water stopped, and Marlis gasped. She was totally soaked, and it was chilly outside, not to mention the fact that the water had also been cold. She began to shiver.

"Doesn't anything ever go right around here?" Grant yelled at her, totally without sympathy for the bedraggled, half-drowned woman he'd kissed only hours before. "I was in the middle of my shower," he raved, "when the water went off. Look at me!"

Marlis was looking at him in dismay. Water was dripping onto his face from hair that was standing on end, clotted with wisps of shampoo that clung to it like tiny misshapen marshmallows. She also was admiring him. He was built like a decathlon athlete with a flat, firm stomach and powerful thighs and biceps, not to mention that wide, muscular chest she'd seen before with its covering of dark, curly hair that was now wet and clinging together in little clusters. In frustration he brushed a lock of hair out of his fiery eyes.

"I'm sorry, Grant. The pipe broke."

"Don't you check those things? A house doesn't take care of itself, you know."

He was really mad. Those blue eyes were smoldering behind the dark-rimmed glasses.

"I do take care of this house, as well as anyone can," Marlis defended herself, her temper rising. "One can't control some things, that's all."

"A lame excuse."

She stepped closer to him. Her hair was hanging down her neck, plastered against her skin, some of it dangling around her cheeks. Her eyes were bloodshot from having gotten so much water in them, and her teeth were beginning to rattle. She wasn't feeling too kindly toward this spoiled little boy who wanted to make her feel guilty over something she shouldn't be feeling guilty over. All he'd lost was a relaxing shower. She had disgruntled guests, a broken pipe, and a breakfast that was probably burning . . .

"Burning. Oh, my gosh!" Marlis whirled around and flew back into the house, skidding into the kitchen. All eyes bulged when they saw the condition she was in, and she felt the tears stinging her eyes as Mrs. McIntosh hesitantly held up the frying pan.

"I'm afraid the eggs have burned, dear," she said with a sweet sympathy, and Marlis sank down on the hearth, feeling the delicious warmth, and cried.

"Is this the way you handle an emergency? By crying?"

Marlis jerked her head up, looking over her shoulder into Grant's eyes, and the tears stopped immediately. How dare he put her down in front of the others.

She stood up to her full five feet four and a half inches and glared at him. "It relieves the tension."

He snorted. "But it doesn't feed hungry people."

Marlis's gaze sped around the room. Sure enough, everyone was there. Hungry. Waiting for a breakfast that was ruined.

"What happened to the water?" Mr. Whitcomb growled. His wife tried to shush him, but he wouldn't be shushed.

"I had a mouth full of toothpaste when it quit on me." He strode up to Marlis and leaned toward her, his breath strongly evident that he'd been doing just that. "Have you ever tried to get toothpaste out of your mouth without water?"

"I'm terribly sorry, Mr. Whitcomb, but a pipe broke outside. As soon as I get it fixed, we'll have water again and everything will be okay."

"*You're* going to fix it?" he asked in amazement.

"Yes."

"Little lady," he sneeered, "what you need is a man around this dump. Then you wouldn't have busted water pipes and dumb rules that discriminate against people who love animals.''

Marlis was about to reply hotly when Grant stepped in.

''Go change your clothes, Marlis. I'll take care of breakfast.''

She turned to face him. ''The eggs are burned. There's not enough juice. The bread is probably stale since it's been out the whole time. And . . .'' She paused, her eyes scanning his half-naked body. ''As magnificent a specimen as you are,'' and he certainly was, ''you're . . . you're . . .''

''Not dressed,'' he finished for her. ''But I'll take care of that, too. Where are the blueberry muffins?''

''There aren't any.''

''Okay, get out of here and let me work.''

Marlis hesitated.

''These good people have to be on the road again soon,'' Grant reminded her of a fact she knew well enough while pushing her gently toward the door, ''and deserve the breakfast they've paid for.''

''You see,'' Mr. Whitcomb inserted his two cents' worth, ''that's the way a man handles things.''

''Yes, but . . .'' Marlis began.

''No buts. You change. I'll take over here.''

''We have to leave in an hour,'' Dr. Baldwin said, ''and we're not packed yet.''

''No problem,'' Grant replied with a winsome grin. ''You'll have eaten a hearty breakfast by that time. And a good one, I promise you.''

He gave Marlis a warning look that sent her scurrying up the stairs, determined to change in record time so she could get back to help him, before his towel dropped off.

One hour and seven minutes later she was sitting across the table from a fully clothed Grant, staring at him with undisguised adulation. All the guests had eaten, and gone, most of them understanding of the morning's disaster, except for Mr. Whitcomb who had asked for a refund of his money and had informed Marlis that he would never recommend Sunrise Inn to any of his friends, for which she was grateful, if they were anything like him.

"How did you do it?" she asked Grant, as if his answer were as important as the secret of the Sphinx. He was no longer mad at her; in fact, he was watching her with a grin on his mouth as she finished a giant-size croissant, warmed and filled with bacon, tiny shrimp, and melted cheddar cheese, which she washed down with freshly squeezed orange juice.

"Simple. The bakery down the street had the croissants, and the Golden Dollar Cafe was more than willing to provide the rest, for you. Donald Cavanaugh, the owner, thinks you're terrific."

"Mmm."

The beginnings of a frown creased his forehead. "Is that all you have to say, 'Mmm?' The man fell all over himself at the thought of helping you."

"He's nice."

The frown deepened. "That's all he is, nice?"

"Well, he's also considerate . . . and intelligent . . ." She was about to add boring, but changed her mind. Grant Russell didn't need to know about her personal life, and there was nothing to know about Donald Cavanaugh anyway. She had gone out with him a couple of times, but there was nothing there, no spark, no desire for more than platonic friendship—for her, at least. He accepted that friendship, though, on the premise that sooner or later she would find he was the best man for her. Today's rescue had raised him a notch on the ladder, but that meant he was only up to two.

"This is a gourmet treat," she said enthusiastically, taking another bite of the succulent croissant and its filling. "I'll have to remember the combination."

"It's fast and simple."

She gave him a certain look. "For simple-minded cooks like me?"

"For a beautiful woman whose day hasn't started off

very well and who doesn't intend to tell me anything about her love life.''

Their eyes met.

"There aren't enough words in my vocabulary to properly thank you for bailing me out,'' Marlis told him emotionally, really touched by his having done so.

"I left you the dishes.''

"Small price to pay.''

The quiet that pervaded the cozy kitchen now was a soothing antidote to the hectic past twenty-four hours, and Marlis didn't want to break the spell. The dishes could wait. She and Grant continued sitting at the table, drinking coffee. He was wearing blue jeans and a western shirt, unbuttoned, and Marlis wondered if the women had appreciated such a "hunk" fixing their meal. She tried not to ogle the breadth of his shoulders and the muscles in his arms.

The early-morning chill had dissolved into a comfortable warmth, and the fire in the fireplace was down to embers. Bright sunshine flooded into the big kitchen through spotless windows, and outside on the porch two birds chattered back and forth in a nest they'd built in the eaves.

"How much do I owe you for the food, Grant?''

"Don't worry about it.''

Marlis shook her head no vigorously. "I am not going to let you pay for breakfast for my guests! Wasn't it enough that you cooked it for them?''

"Okay,'' he relented. "May I see a smile on that pretty face of yours? If you frown any more this morning, there will be permanent wrinkles where there shouldn't be any.''

Marlis gave him her best smile.

"Payment in full,'' Grant announced.

The phone ringing kept Marlis from replying. She jumped up to answer it there in the kitchen.

"Marlis, it's Amy.''

"Hi. How's the wrist?''

"Not too good. I won't be able to work for a few days."

"Don't worry about it. Just come back when you can. I sure miss you. You're worth your weight in gold. In fact, I'm giving you a raise."

The stunned silence on the other end of the line gave Marlis immense satisfaction. She liked to share her profits with her employees, and Amy certainly deserved to be included.

"Gee, thanks, Marlis."

"You're welcome, kiddo. I look forward to seeing you real soon."

Grant poured more coffee for both of them when Marlis came back to the table. "Someone's getting a raise?"

"My housekeeper."

"The one who wasn't here yesterday, whose work you had to do?"

"Yes. She's a jewel."

"In need of polishing, I'd say. Is she generally undependable?"

Now Marlis did scowl. "Grant, the girl broke her wrist. I'm sure she didn't do that on purpose."

"No, of course not. Hey, I'm sorry I yelled at you out there," he apologized. "It wasn't your fault the pipe broke."

Marlis surveyed him from the corner of one eye. "No, it wasn't. I maintain this house very well, Mr. Russell. I practice preventive care."

"Apology accepted?" There was sincerity in his eyes.

"Sure. How are you feeling after your allergic reaction? Did you get any sleep last night?"

"Very little," he admitted.

Oh, no, she groaned silently, *he hasn't had another run-in with Muffy, I hope.* "Grant, that's too bad, but you seem to be breathing all right now."

He reached out and laid his hand over hers. "I didn't lose sleep because of my reaction. I couldn't sleep from thinking of you."

"Me?" Marlis whispered, astonished.

"I wish I didn't have to leave this morning, Marlis," he said in husky tones.

Marlis's heart rose and sank.

"I'd like to stay around and get to know you better," he added. "Maybe save you from another disaster."

Marlis gazed deeply into his attentive eyes. "You might be back this way again, someday." She felt a peculiar pain in the pit of her stomach. She didn't want him to go.

His hand squeezed hers. "Plan on it," he promised.

He didn't want to go. He wanted to stay here with her. There was something about this unlucky innkeeper that tugged at him to stay. What was it? It had to be more than physical beauty, because California was filled with beautiful women. It wasn't her intelligence; he'd dated more than his share of book-smart and street-smart girls.

Maybe it was her caring . . . like she'd cared for him last night. Or her understanding . . . like she'd understood about her housekeeper's inability to work. Maybe it was her pluck. Man, she had looked adorable, standing in that puddle of water outside the house that morning. She had looked fetching in her "housecleaning garb." She had looked downright delectable in that aqua sweater last night, soft, desirable, belonging in his arms.

A certain current sparked between them as his mind photographed every detail of Marlis Kent and he leaned across the table, cupped her face in one of his big hands and kissed her softly on her lips. "Don't forget me," he whispered.

"I won't," she promised, knowing the Sunrise Inn would be sadly empty without him.

FOUR

The broken pipe was fixed. A new gas regulator kept the oven pilot light burning steadily. Amy was back doing the housework. Mabel was cooking in the kitchen, after a stern reprimand for having insufficient supplies on hand, and Marlis was doing what she liked most to do: caring for her guests and running the business.

The month's bills were stacked neatly on her antique oak rolltop desk and she was writing checks one day when she heard a knock at the door of the tiny den just off the parlor that she used for an office.

Looking up, she saw with pleasure that it was a friend of hers, Steven Alexander, who owned a bed-and-breakfast inn two blocks away.

"Steve, come on in. What have you been up to?"

"The same as you, from the looks of your desk. Paying bills." Steve was a short, chubby man, somewhere in his thirties, with rust-colored hair and a smooth, fair complexion. He sauntered over to a chair beside Marlis's desk and plopped down in it. "How's business?"

"Pretty good." Marlis put down her pen and gave him a generous smile. "By next month I should be fully occupied just about every weekend, and half so during the week. I can live comfortably on that."

Marlis and Steve had known each other for two years, ever since he'd moved to Sutter Creek "to get away from the big city," he'd explained then. In the beginning they had dated a couple of months, and Steve had fallen in love. But Marlis had never gotten past the initial bloom of interest. Steve had even proposed, pointing out how much they had in common, but had soon accepted graciously the reality that Marlis didn't return his feelings. Now they were just friends, but good ones.

"So, what's been happening around here?" he asked, leaning over to pick up the statement from the florist for the fresh bouquets that Marlis put in each room every few days. She scowled at him playfully and snatched it out of his hands.

"Don't ask. Things are okay now, but there was a day . . . two days actually . . ."

Steve's eyebrows shot up. "That bad?"

"Worse."

"Problems with employees?"

"Yep."

"And guests?"

"Aren't you perceptive."

Steve grinned. "We all have bad days, Marlis. Don't let it worry you. You're a clever, hard-working, conscientious lady who knows this business," he flattered her, which he did often with the greatest of sincerity and respect. "You'll survive, no matter what comes up against you."

Marlis shrugged her shoulders. "I guess." Until recently, making a success of the Sunrise Inn had been the main goal of her life. Now it didn't seem quite so important, and Marlis knew why: Grant Russell, a man with broad shoulders, terrific blue eyes, and a personality that angered, frustrated, confused, and attracted her. He'd dropped into her world, turned it upside down, then left with only a vague promise that he'd be back.

"Did Kevin King spend a night with you?" Steve

asked, stretching his short legs forward and slouching in the chair.

"*The* Kevin King, who writes the bed-and-breakfast guide?"

"The very one. He stopped in at my place a week ago. I assumed he'd be going on to yours, or had already been here."

Marlis sat straight up, her eyes widening with amazement. "Did you know he was coming or did he just pop in?"

"I didn't know who he was until the next day. I nearly choked on an orange slice covered with honey and coconut when he told me at breakfast."

Marlis smiled. Steve was a marvelous cook, as his size forty-six waist testified. "Well, how did it go?" she asked, breathless with friendly envy.

"Fine. Before he left he complimented me on the excellent service, pointed out two or three things he'd particularly liked, including my famous Swedish-pancake breakfast, and said he'd send me a proof of his write-up before it goes to press, in case I wanted to add anything. The next book's due out in six months. He was a real easygoing guy."

"How marvelous for you, Steve."

"I agree. King operates anonymously under the guise of an ordinary traveler, so he won't be given preferential treatment."

"That makes sense." Marlis's heart stopped beating. Oh, no, he couldn't have been Julius Whitcomb, could he, posing with his family? She recalled with a shudder the overbearing, criticizing, challenging chauvinist who had left her inn with toothpaste in his mouth, promising never to recommend her to anyone. Naw, he couldn't have been . . . could he? No! "Steve, I want to be in that guide book. I've got to be. It's vital if I want to grow. I wonder why he didn't come here?"

"Can't say. Sure is a good-looking fella. Belongs in the movies, if you ask me, even if he does wear glasses.

All that dark, wavy hair, and the bluest eyes I've ever seen on a man.''

Marlis died, in agony, as the truth dawned. Travels a lot, laptop computer, a writer . . .

"What kind of a car did he drive, Steve? Do you remember?''

"How could I forget? It was a red Porsche.''

"Ouch," Marlis sobbed, covering her face with both hands. On the morning Grant had left, she'd accompanied him out to his car, remarking to him how smart-looking it was. One didn't see many red Porsches in Sutter Creek.

"What's the matter?''

Marlis jumped to her feet, her stomach suddenly a mass of knots. "He was here, Steve. Right here.''

She raised her hands to heaven in a sign of helplessness. "Everything went wrong. I mean everything! First of all, Amy wasn't here, and I spent most of the day cleaning up after four couples, so I was dirty and sweaty and didn't hear him ringing the bell at the registration desk, and I hated him standing on the stairs, in front of prospective guests, with no shirt on, and then the stove went out and I was seeing to that instead of buying groceries for the next day because Mabel hadn't gotten them before she took sick, and I was on my hands and knees on the floor and had broken a fingernail and he thought I was incompetent. Then a guest snuck a cat into the house which decided to sleep on Grant's bed. That's what he called himself, Grant Russell. How was I to know he was allergic to cats? He pounded on my door that evening, bleary-eyed and barely able to breathe, so I made him coffee and we sat out on the porch and walked in the garden and ended up in the gazebo . . .''

Marlis finally took a breath as a pink tinge began at her neck and raced up her cheeks. The story was bringing back delicious memories of arms holding her and lips vigorously sampling hers.

"What happened in the gazebo?'' Steve asked. "It didn't burn down, did it?''

"No," Marlis sighed, although she remembered the fire that had raced through her body when Grant touched her.

"The next morning I had to cook breakfast," she continued, leaving out the racy details of her sensual encounter with Grant, "because Mabel was sick, and I burned the eggs after a water pipe broke outside, and Grant got caught in the shower—"

"Hold it, hold it. I get the picture."

"Can you believe it?"

"Frankly, no. Not from Sunrise Inn. You're the epitome of cool, professional service."

"Tell that to Grant Russell." No wonder he didn't use a credit card when he paid for his room, she suddenly recalled. The deceiving beast.

"He used another name when he stayed with me, but it has to be the same guy. Did he have a laptop computer with him?" Steve asked.

"Yes."

"Did he give you a hard time? I mean, with all that happened?"

"Unfortunately, yes. 'Do you only have one housekeeper in Sutter Creek?' he asked once, and later he . . . yelled, 'Doesn't anything ever go right around here?' "

Steve groaned.

"I thought he understood," Marlis went on. "He even cooked breakfast for my guests when I ended up soaked from the broken pipe."

"Are you serious?"

"And went out and bought groceries to do so when I ruined what I was fixing and didn't have enough to start over."

Steve shook his head. "Can he cook?"

Marlis sighed. "Yes."

"And he never told you he was Kevin King? Not even when he left?"

"No. He said he was a writer, but neglected to mention the minor detail that he is famous for writing the most prestigious guide to bed-and-breakfast inns in the state of California.''

How could he have held me with such tenderness and kissed me with all that passion and not told me the truth? Marlis wondered as tears formed in her eyes. Unless he didn't mean it. She began to form an unpleasant idea. *Was his attention to me another test—to see if I would get romantically involved with a guest? If so, I certainly failed it. I wasn't at all professional in my dealings with him.*

Marlis remembered thinking, not long after Grant had arrived, that he was interested in more than a simple night's lodging, and that *more* was her. She had resisted him, been cool to him, even told him she didn't think she liked him. Still, he'd won her over with his smooth manners and good looks and persistent pursuit of her, even when he'd been devastated from the effect of the cat—which went a long ways toward disarming her.

There was no denying she had responded to him on a physical level. How could any woman not with his gorgeous build and those teasing blue eyes and strong hands and rich voice? He was so . . . so . . . masculine and tempting, like a five-pound box of Godiva chocolates that you know you shouldn't eat but just can't help doing.

Hadn't she tried to resist him in the gazebo? Yes. She'd listened for all of four seconds to the warning voice in her head and then had stepped totally out of character and given herself to him.

Marlis paced the small room, humiliated with the ease of his conquest of her. She relived the nightmare of comic coincidences that had sprung up during his visit and all the frustration and anxiety of that thirty-hour period became vivid again, and was now doubled with the certain knowledge that Grant/Kevin King thought as little of her as he did her bed-and-breakfast inn.

"The only reason I can think of, Steve, why he didn't admit he was Kevin King is because he's not going to include me in his next edition of *Country Inns of California* and didn't want to humiliate me by telling me so.''

"I hate to say it, kiddo, but that makes sense." Steve stood to his feet and put out his arms to Marlis, who went willingly into them. She needed a shoulder to cry on, and whose better than someone who was in the same business she was and understood its ups and downs.

"Why, why did this happen to me?" she moaned. "If an inn isn't in that book, it's considered second class, and you know I run a first-class place here, Steve."

"Of course, you do. Everything about you is first class, Marlis. I've always thought that."

Steve held her away from him and gazed at her with a woebegone look on his face. "I wish there were something I could do. Hey, what if I wrote to the guy and explained that you're a friend of mine, and that normally the Sunrise Inn is a fantastic place—"

"Thanks, Steve," Marlis cut him off, "but I doubt that would change his mind. He saw what he saw. I had my chance, and blew it royally. He'll never waste his time by coming back. There are too many other inns to check out."

Steve shrugged his shoulders. "I'm sorry, Marlis."

"I know you are." She sank down in the desk chair and stared at the bills, but they soon became a blur through the tears that blinded her.

A week later the phone rang half a dozen times before Marlis grabbed it off the hook with a breathless "Hello?" She'd been outside weeding the flower bed. Why hadn't Amy or Mabel answered? she wondered. Keeping potential guests waiting while the phone rang and rang and rang was one of Marlis's pet peeves.

"Hi, yourself. This is Grant Russell."

"Grant?" The incredulity in her voice brought a soft chuckle from the man.

"You sound as though you never expected to hear from me again."

"Well . . . uh . . . I . . ."

"I love it when a woman is overcome by my presence."

"You're not exactly present."

"No, I'm not, am I? How are you?"

"Fine." She was recovering from the momentary shock of hearing from the one person she was sure would never contact her again.

"The water pipe?"

"Fixed and holding like a charm."

"Mabel?"

"Cooking every day and freezing coffee cakes at night."

"Amy?"

"Is this is a test, or what?" Marlis began to resent the cheerful voice on the other end of the line. She felt like telling him right then and there that she knew who he was, the sneak, and ask him why he hadn't told her the truth about himself the morning he'd left. Just the thought of him making notes on all the faux pas she'd committed when he'd stayed there burned her inside. The fact that he was merely doing his job, and what had happened had happened not through any fault of his, didn't do much to ease Marlis's crushed feelings over not being included in his forthcoming bed-and-breakfast guide.

"You sound a little down, Marlis," he said. "Is everything all right?"

"Couldn't be better, Grant. I've had a full house the last few nights, and with summer almost here, I'm expecting most nights to be the same. Problems are gone with the wind. Sunrise Inn is the smoothest-running place a person can lay his head at night."

She stopped, realizing she was giving him a grand sales pitch, and hating herself for doing it. For having to do it. She could tell him all day long how great things were going, but that wouldn't change his mind. He had been an eyewitness to her supposed ineptitude. Futhermore, she was demeaning herself by bragging so. Sunrise Inn was an elegant establishment she was extremely proud of, and she didn't need to grovel at the feet of any writer, no matter how revered, to prove that fact.

So, if she wasn't listed, she wasn't listed. She could still hope to flourish on word of mouth from satisfied guests. That was what she had done in the past, and that was what she would continue to do. Grant Russell could go jump in Sutter Creek, for all she cared.

"Are you home now, or still on the road?" she amazed herself by asking politely.

"I'm in Fresno, then it's Monterey and San Luis Obispo before I head back to Santa Barbara."

With only the slightest of pauses Marlis inquired, "Gathering research for your next book?"

"As a matter of fact, I am."

That meant he was finding absolutely wonderful inns to write about, and knowing that hers was not one of them stabbed Marlis deep.

"I wish you luck on your book. You never did tell me what you've written in the past."

"My mind was on other things." His voice was wistful and Marlis almost believed it really had mattered to him, the pulse-pounding interludes they had shared. But it couldn't have; it was just part of the game he played.

"Well, I'm sorry to cut this short, Grant, but I have a zillion things to do." There was a decided crispness to her announcement, and Marlis knew that if she didn't hang up soon, she'd end up saying something she'd regret later. "The bell is ringing at the desk. That means there are more people coming in. Nice to talk to you."

Without even waiting to hear his good-bye, Marlis plunked the receiver down on its cradle. Her heart was racing and her hands trembled as she removed the gardener's apron full of tools from around her waist. That man affected her even on the telephone.

"I just won't think of him anymore," she muttered as she washed her hands in the kitchen sink.

"Who won't you think of?" Mabel asked, coming out of the pantry with a bag of whole wheat flour in her hands.

"The devil," Marlis retorted.

But saying she wasn't going to think of Kevin King any

more and pulling it off were two different ball games. There were at least four hundred and eighty-three times during the day when the man's winning smile or muscular arms or heart-stopping kiss came to mind. With each tender memory, Marlis purged the unwanted thought and breathed easier, until he surfaced again, drifting over and over through her mind like a bad dream that refused to go away.

Why had he deceived her? she pondered again that night as she turned for the umpteenth time from one side to the other in the crumpled bed where she was getting no sleep at all. Part of her yearned to see him just one more time; another part promised to smash his cowboy hat, give him nails for breakfast, and round up every cat in northern California and sic them on him if he ever set foot in Sunrise Inn again.

Her less violent wish came true unexpectedly a few days later when, running lightly down the stairs on her way to the kitchen for lunch, she saw Kevin standing by the desk. He was wearing loose-fitting black slacks and a polo shirt of cerulean blue that showed to advantage the well-formed muscles of his chest and shoulders, and which accented the gorgeous blueness of his captivating eyes that were now riveted on her beneath scowling brows. Marlis nearly fell down the remaining three steps when she saw him.

"How long have you been there? Why didn't you ring the bell?" she questioned him, in frustration that, again, he wasn't getting punctual service. Yet she was delighted he was there, actually there, just a few feet from her, and she could touch him if she wanted to. And she definitely wanted to—before she killed him.

"I don't like to be hung up on." His mood was menacing as he moved toward her.

"Did I do that?" She backed up.

"You know you did, and I want to know why."

He was right in front of her now, and she couldn't run away, for the heels of her shoes were smack up against the stairs. He reached out and grabbed her shoulders. "Tell me what's wrong, Marlis. When I left here, I had the distinct impression that you liked me a little more than you would a snake in the grass."

What an appropriate analogy, Marlis thought. "I did like you. I do," she amended. "I was just busy that day."

Suddenly his mood changed, became soft and tender and his big hands moved to cup her face and tilt it up. "I had to see you again. I've missed you like blazes." His head lowered toward hers, and a delicious warmness flooded over Marlis in anticipation of the kiss she knew was coming.

Could she honestly welcome him, knowing now that he was not who he had pretended to be? She wanted to believe his romantic feelings for her were genuine. Surely he wouldn't be faking that, for the way he was looking at her now spelled "I want you" in no uncertain terms. Still, was she being a fool to show feelings for him again? Was he laughing at her?

"I haven't been able to stop thinking about you," he whispered into her ear, relishing the scent of her, the silkiness of her skin, the fullness of her lips. He kissed her, gently at first, but then with a growing urgency that said it all: he wanted her, he needed her. She had stuck in his mind like a delicious fantasy, and he'd hurried through his business in record time to get back to her.

Marlis trembled from his onslaught, and his hungry mouth on hers devoured her doubts and reignited the fire he had begun in the gazebo. His hands were strong and possessive as they moved over her back and captured her waist, crushing her against him in a desire she knew had to be real; he wouldn't have come back otherwise.

"You look like a dream," he said, raising his head and gazing at her with blatant longing, his fingers locked behind her waist. "You smell good, too, like you just stepped out of a bath."

"As a matter of fact, I did," Marlis admitted. Her hand reached up and touched his cheek. *He cares for me; I know he does*, and she ignored the sick feeling in the pit of her stomach that warned her to be careful.

"Can you believe some people?" the shrill voice of Amy pierced the room behind them. "Marlis, I found a dozen pieces of gum stuck to the dresser in the Prospector Room. Who was in there anyway?"

Grant dropped his hands and stepped back. The corners of his mouth tightened in annoyance at the interruption.

Marlis was not pleased, either. Amy was always where she wasn't supposed to be,. and not where she should be. "A couple from Seattle had that room," Marlis answered the meaningless question. "Get some ice to remove it."

Amy swept past Marlis and Grant, seeming not to notice what she had interrupted.

"And who is that?" Grant asked, feeling the vibration in the wooden floor as the husky girl lumbered by and staring at her mannish-cut bright red hair. Because she was tall, close to six feet, her weight could not be called fat, but she was a b-i-g woman, just the same, and an unhappy one. She looked as though she never smiled.

"That was Amy."

"Ah, the housekeeper. Working today, I see."

"Yes."

"And enjoying every minute of it."

Marlis laughed, then whispered, "Amy looks tougher than she is. She's a hard worker and handles my delicate antiques with a care you might not expect."

"You're right. She impresses me more as the bull-in-the-china-shop type."

Marlis couldn't resist reaching up and with one finger, tracing Grant's lower lip. "Enough about Amy. Let's talk about you. I'm surprised you're here," she admitted.

He pulled the palm of her hand against his mouth and kissed it. "You didn't *know* I would come back?"

Marlis shrugged. "And put your life in jeopardy in this place?"

He chuckled. "I'm not worried, because you take very good care of your guests."

"Do I?" Marlis stared at him, trying to detect if he was complimenting or mocking her.

"In fact, Miss Kent, I would like a room, please? Minus cat. And gum."

Marlis smiled. "Of course, Mr. Russell. And may I assure you we're fresh out of cats." She wondered when he would tell her who he really was.

"Excellent. What kind of breakfast may I expect?" he asked with a perfectly straight face, wishing it would be served in Marlis's bed, not in the dining room with a bunch of strangers.

"Tomorrow morning we'll be having a delectable ham quiche, cinnamon chocolate chip coffee cake, pear almondine—"

"Am I cooking or are you?"

Marlis snickered. "Mabel is!"

"God bless Mabel. She'll deserve a kiss for that, but I think I'll give it to her employer instead."

Kevin swept Marlis into his arms again and kissed her slowly but thoroughly and she responded, for which he was very glad. She *had* hung up on him, and her voice had been tight. Something was wrong between them, and he was going to find out what.

Marlis enjoyed Kevin's kiss, glad he did not hurry it, but took his fill of it, leaving her satisfied, and happy. *Surely he must be back to give me another chance*, she thought.

"I'll get settled," he announced, planting a tender kiss on her right cheek, "and then I'll come down and we can get started." He kissed her other cheek.

"Get started with what?" Marlis asked with a grin.

His exuberance spread from his face to his body as he reached for her shoulders and shook her gently. "I'm taking some time off and spending it here with you. You need help in organizing and running the Sunrise Inn. Key, please."

Whistling cheerfully, not quite in tune, he bent down and grabbed his overnight bag, then vaulted up the stairs, the key Marlis had given him without a word dangling from his little finger. He could hardly wait to continue their relationship. Marlis Kent was becoming very important to him.

Marlis stared at his retreating figure in silent disbelief, and then the seething began. ''What did he just say?'' she exclaimed out loud. ''He's going to help me organize and run this inn?''

She stormed across the foyer and into the parlor which, fortunately, was empty at the time. Standing in the center of the lovely Persian rug, surrounded by unique furniture from previous centuries, Marlis clenched her fists until her nails left imprints on the palms of her hands and the color on her cheeks approached crimson. Even taking long, deep breaths and glaring at her favorite painting on the wall did not dispel her fury.

''How dare he? That pompous know-it-all! That chauvinistic pig! That miserable excuse for a man!'' The silent furniture offered no reply. Marlis planted her legs firmly on the floor as though preparing to face a charging bull, folded her arms determinedly across her chest, and waited.

FIVE

In ten minutes Kevin came downstairs and found Marlis waiting for him in the parlor.

"Ready, darling?" he greeted her enthusiastically, not even noticing the smoke that was pouring from her nostrils or the searing blaze of her jewellike eyes.

"I am not your darling, Grant Russell, and I'm definitely not ready to do anything with you!"

The stunned expression on Kevin's face pleased her.

"You're upset. Mind telling me why?" He reached for her, but Marlis backed away.

"With pleasure, *Mr. King.*"

One of his dark eyebrows lifted, followed by the other. "So, you know who I am."

"Not because you thought enough of me to tell me yourself."

"What I think of you, Marlis, as a woman, has nothing to do with the reason I didn't confess to being Kevin King."

Marlis began to pace the room, with Kevin following.

"I much prefer you in my arms than ready to claw my eyes out," he said gently.

"Cling to the memory," Marlis retorted. "It won't happen again."

She threw herself down on a Hitchcock chair and Kevin sank onto a Victorian sofa of scarlet velvet across from her.

"Because I didn't tell you I was Kevin King?"

"Partly, and also because you have the unmitigated gall to suggest I need help in operating Sunrise Inn."

"Not just help—*my* help."

Her scathing stare would have withered a less confident man, but Kevin leaned forward, clasped his hands together, and leaned his elbows on his knees while giving her a slow grin. "You don't want my help?"

"I don't need it just because a few insignificant things went wrong when you were here before."

"Which was why I didn't tell you I was the evil man who observes insignificant—and significant—happenings in California's bed-and-breakfast establishments. You would have been humiliated."

"True, but none of those incidents were my fault."

"A good proprietor has to be able to handle all inevitabilities."

"And you don't think I did?"

"Do you? Honestly now?"

"Yes, I do." And she meant it.

Kevin sat back, so darned in control that Marlis felt like slapping him, just to shake him up.

Kevin looked at this woman he had decided brought the sun up and made the moon come out and was amazed at this side of her that protected her reputation like a tigress. He had chosen to remember the soft and sweet-smelling woman who had melted in his arms, the vulnerable woman who had been grateful for his assistance at breakfast. The capable innkeeper who had stood up to Julius Whitcomb and the dexterous female who could fix a broken water pipe held less charm for him.

Of course, he admired all the abilities she needed to run a place like the Sunrise Inn, but he was attracted far more to the liquid jade of her eyes and the tempting curves of her body and the compassion she had shown for his reaction to the cat. He liked a woman to be a woman, and he had thought Marlis Kent was all woman. Now, though, he saw before him a creature determined to do everything her way. How foolish, when she had him to help her.

"First of all, honey, you shouldn't have been doing the housework yourself," he began patiently. "You couldn't monitor what your guests were bringing into the house—like the Whitcombs' cat."

"My housekeeper had broken her wrist."

"You told me that before."

"And when I tried my other lady, she wasn't home."

"You should have a dozen backups."

"Sutter Creek is a small town."

"Sacramento isn't. They have temporary help agencies there."

Marlis gasped. "That's thirty-five miles away. Besides, I'm not trusting the cleaning of the priceless antiques in this house to a stranger."

"Even if it means providing better service to your guests?"

She had to ponder that one. He was maddening, and so impossibly logical.

"The same solution applies to your cook," he dared go on.

"I have a perfectly wonderful Irish woman who fills in for Mabel."

"Who was in Ireland, if I recall."

Marlis sighed. "Yes."

Kevin suppressed a laugh, and she hated him for it.

"Is there no one else in town who can cook for you?"

"I've never needed anyone else. This is the first time neither Mabel nor Kathleen were available."

"A good innkeeper must anticipate—"

"Yes, yes. Could we drop this, please?" she snapped.

"Sure. Now about the water pipe—"

"Forget it!" Marlis jumped to her feet, her hands plastered to her hips. "I don't want to talk about water pipes, faulty stoves, cats on your bed, or any other complaint you may have. If this is the worst inn you've ever been in, and I'm the most incompetent innkeeper, why on earth did you come back?'' She glared at him with all the venom she could muster. Who did he think he was, tearing her apart like that?

Instead of jumping to his feet, too, to carry the argument further, Kevin leaned back into the sofa and stretched both arms across the back of it. He looked so sure of himself, so comfortable in her parlor, that Marlis wanted to scream.

''Don't you know why I came back?'' he asked her, his eyes compelling hers to return his gaze.

''To enjoy yourself at my expense?'' Marlis snapped.

''You certainly jump to a lot of erroneous conclusions, lady,'' Kevin said lazily. ''First of all, I think Sunrise Inn is a fine bed and breakfast, and you are a capable proprietor who will someday be exceptional.''

''And to get from capable to exceptional I need you?'' Marlis did not try to hide the cynicism in her voice.

''We all need advice now and then, Marlis. I can help you round off the edges.''

The volcano began to gurgle deep inside her. ''What if I'm not interested?''

He stood up slowly, all six feet three inches of him. ''Why wouldn't you be? I'm not going to charge you anything.''

''Imagine.''

He shook his head as though he were listening to a pouty teenager. ''Look, you're a novice in this business. How long have you been running the inn?''

''Five years.'' She bent over and began to straighten some magazines on a nearby table.

''You're a beginner. I've been in it for twelve.''

''In it? As in writing your B&B guide?''

''In it, as in owner. I have three inns of my own: one in Sacramento, one in Huntington Beach in southern California near Los Angeles, and another in Santa Barbara, where I live.''

Marlis stared at him. "Three? You own three?"

He nodded yes. She was speechless.

He moved closer to her. "I'm sorry if I came across as putting you down. I didn't mean to." Her perfume drifted through his nostrils and triggered fresh desire for her.

Marlis caught the scent of his after-shave and fought to keep her temper hot against this insufferable man.

"You're doing a terrific job here, you really are, for someone so new to the business." His voice was soothing. "The imported Swiss chocolate on the nightstand before bedtime, the sheets turned back, soft music on the radio, a night light glowing reassuringly—all nice touches."

"Th-thank you," Marlis managed to stammer.

He stretched out an arm and captured a handful of her hair in his fingers. He played with it tenderly. "But they're not enough. You have major problems, and a lack of experience."

He leaned down over her face. "I'm willing to share my expertise with you."

His lips hovered tantalizingly over hers, and Marlis's eyes became huge saucers of blue-green confusion. She was losing the battle, but she didn't want to, even when his lips pressed upon hers lightly, softly, urging from her a kiss in return. Her heart betrayed her and fluttered rapidly and the rest of her body followed suit with the nicest sensations dancing here and there.

Her hands had somehow come to rest on the rock hardness of his chest and they became her only ally. She pushed with all her might away from him, an act that took him by surprise and almost sent him crashing into the seventy-five-year-old piano.

Their eyes locked in a deadly duel for supremacy. Actually, for Marlis, it was more a case of survival. The man was getting to her, and if she didn't want to end up playing student to his professor she had to set him straight right now.

"Look," she said in as firm a voice as she could muster with the thrill of his lips still tingling on hers, "I appreciate your gallant offer to save me from myself, but to use an old expression, I'd rather do it myself."

"Does that mean you won't have lunch with me?"

"Correct." *He isn't angry with me,* she thought. *Why isn't he angry with me? He must think I'm behaving like a spoiled brat.*

"No one to relieve you?"

He never gives up. "I prefer to eat at the desk."

Kevin acquiesced with a genuine smile and a hand sweep around the room. "This is nice."

"Changing the subject won't change my mind."

"I'm trying to give you an honest compliment on your decorating."

Marlis squinted her eyes as she studied his face. Was he being honest? She allowed her eyes the pleasure of taking in the combination parlor and library that was cozily furnished with pieces she'd hunted all over the country for in order to create a soft, lived-in look. Guests were free to play the piano, as they were games from a nearby cabinet, or chess on an Early Georgian mahogany table. There were hundreds of books in the floor-to-ceiling bookcases, and for those who just wanted to sit and relax, tall windows curtained with exquisite cream-colored lace allowed in lots of sunshine and fresh air. A sigh of renewed appreciation fell from her lips. "It is nice, isn't it?"

"It could be improved, though," Kevin said.

Marlis would have stabbed him right there had she not minded getting blood on the old and valuable carpet.

"Make yourself at home, Mr. King," she spoke in icicles. "I have work to do."

The chuckle that she heard from him as she stiffly exited the room didn't change her opinion of him. He was an egotistical, pompous, self-centered chauvinist, and as best she could, she was going to ignore him for as long as he chose to stay there.

Her being included in his important book was now out of the question, so what did it matter if she refused both his advice and his lunch? She didn't need Grant Russell and she didn't need Kevin King, either.

Marlis was not able to carry out her plan of indifference because Kevin disappeared shortly after their spirited discussion and didn't return till nearly five o'clock—not that she was keeping track of him, of course. She was writing a personal letter at the registration desk when she heard whistling from outside. It was Kevin, coming along the side path. He pulled open the screen door with two fingers and stood before her, laden with three paper sacks that looked heavy.

"I'm sorry, sir," she said sweetly, "we don't allow pets here."

His eyes danced mischievously. "Glad to hear that, ma'am. Entertainment for the evening." He gestured with his head toward the sacks in his arms.

"Entertainment?" Marlis was curious and stood up, planning to peer into the tops of the sacks, but Kevin backed away, making it clear that whatever he was about was none of her business.

With a huffy toss of her shimmering blond hair that reflected the sunlight still streaming in through the wide window beside the desk, Marlis sat down and picked up her pen.

"How many guests do you have tonight?" he asked.

Marlis began writing and mumbled something.

"I didn't hear that."

"None. So far. But I'm sure there will be some soon. I've only had a totally empty house seven times in five years. Pretty good, huh?"

"Excellent."

She waited for his qualifying downer, but none came.

"I'll be in my room," he said, too cheerfully for her

to be comfortable with, "if you should need me for anything."

"I won't."

"Don't be too sure."

He walked off, up the stairs, and Marlis thought for more than a few minutes about him, and what he had in those mysterious sacks.

By seven-thirty Marlis decided no one would likely be checking in, which meant the inn would be empty—except for a certain man whom she would have expelled had she been strong enough and brave enough.

"A quick bite of supper and a good book is the best way to spend this evening," she told herself, except that she wasn't hungry. So she opted for the book. Going into the quiet and darkened parlor, she turned on a floor lamp nearest the library, which created a romantic gauze of softness that should have eased her troubled mind, but didn't.

Marlis was a brave woman who didn't mind staying in her lovely house alone, except that she wasn't alone. The cause of her troubled mind was just one floor up—an exasperating, opinionated man who also happened to have captured her heart and feelings like no other ever had. She wanted to like him; she didn't want to like him.

She was heartsick that her beloved Sunrise Inn had not made a better impression on this respected professional writer but too proud to accept his help, which she knew was unnecessary, in running it better.

Taking out a dog-eared copy of a James Fenimore Cooper book, Marlis settled down on the sofa, thinking to read for a half hour, then get herself something to eat. She wasn't aware of Kevin's having come into the room until he'd been standing there several moments, watching her. When some inner sense made her look up, she started.

"Intellectual as well as beautiful, I see." His velvet

words floated across the grayish light and lodged in her heart. "You belong in this room."

"You mean I blend well with the antiques?"

"In a way you do." He came closer and sat down in the chair she'd occupied that afternoon. "There's something old-fashioned about you."

When Marlis started to protest, Kevin held up a hand. "I mean that in the nicest way," he quickly added. "You remind me of an era when people were gracious and observed amenities, when gentility was a quality to be admired."

"And women were properly subservient to men?"

He chuckled and shook his head no. "When women were not afraid to be women."

His bold eyes fastened on her face and Marlis could not look away, even though she desperately wanted to. "I am not afraid of men, Mr. King. Least of all you."

"Good. Then you can start calling me Kevin, and accept my invitation to dine in my room."

She stared at him. "Dine in your room?"

"Yes. Everything is ready."

Marlis frowned. "The paper sacks?"

"Inelegant wrappings for all that was necessary to provide you with an elegant dinner you deserve."

"For doing what?"

A boyish grin spread his mouth. "That remains to be seen."

Marlis looked down at her book, pretending an interest in it that was no longer there. "I'm really not hungry, Mr. King. But you go ahead without me."

He casually brought his right ankle to rest on his left knee. She was the most exasperating and challenging woman he had ever known, but the contest was only beginning. "It's a shame you won't join me. I'll have to think of some excuse to explain it to Steve Alexander."

Marlis's eyes flew up. "What does Steve have to do with this?"

"He's catering the dinner. The things I brought in earlier were the accoutrements. The food should be here in," he extended his right arm and studied an expensive gold watch, "about ten minutes. I think it's too late to call and cancel, don't you?"

Marlis slammed the book down a little harder than she should have on the seat of the velvet sofa and rose quickly to her feet. "What are you up to now?"

Kevin stood, too.

"When I stayed at Steve's inn," he said, "I was very impressed with his service and food. I asked him to prepare an intimate supper for us."

"Intimate supper?" Marlis gulped, wondering what Steve must be thinking. "I hope you didn't use those words when you asked him."

"Exactly those words, I believe, since they most accurately described what I had in mind." Kevin's blue eyes were round orbs of innocent skulduggery.

Marlis plunked her hands onto her hips. "What you had in mind, I'm afraid, is not going to come about." She marched toward the door with her head held high, but didn't get far. Kevin caught her by the arm, and pulled her back against him. "Won't you even come and see what I've done? Just for you? I think you'll like it."

"I won't like it because I don't indulge in intimate suppers with my guests or with men I hardly know," she asserted, feeling acutely the pressure of his fingers on her flesh and her body resting against his.

"You know me," he whispered, lowering his head until his lips were in her hair. "You can't have forgotten the time we spent in the gazebo," he murmured.

"My memory, sometimes, is faulty," Marlis said weakly, hating herself for being so vulnerable to his physical temptations. But somehow she pulled away from him and proceeded out into the foyer, with Kevin close behind her.

"Steve will be disappointed," he told her. "He's going to a lot of trouble to provide a special evening for you."

"He'll understand."

"Will he?"

He hit a sensitive nerve. Marlis had sampled Steve's cooking before, and it was superb, an evidence of the special talent he possessed and the care he took with every meal. And, if he knew he was cooking for her, she was sure he'd go to extra lengths. What she hated was the idea of him thinking something was going on between her and Kevin King.

"He's in love with you, isn't he?" Kevin asked.

The question caught Marlis unaware. "Why do you say that?"

"Because the minute I mentioned your name his eyes lit up and a dozen different menus were on his tongue."

"We're friends."

"Good friends?"

There was no way Marlis could deny it, and Kevin saw the answer on her face.

"Don't disappoint him."

Marlis straightened her shoulders. "I'll come up and see what you've done, then I'll take some of the food when it's delivered. But I will not share dinner with you in your room. When I tell Steve how wonderful everything was, as I know it will be if he's done it, I'll be able to speak the truth. I'll also tell him I ate alone."

She spun around and moved up the steps, as stiffly as she could, knowing Kevin King's eyes were watching her as she did.

So far, so good, Kevin told himself, as he watched the gentle sway of Marlis's hips moving in front of him up the stairs. He hadn't meant to insult her by offering his help, but since the damage was done, he'd do whatever necessary to change her mind about him. And he knew he could, if she'd just give him the chance.

She was not going to get away from him, he'd determined, but he knew that would take some doing, for he'd already met two men in Sutter Creek who would eagerly have put "Mrs." in front of her name, but had lost her.

What Marlis saw when she entered Kevin's room took

her breath away. A large card table had been draped by a white linen tablecloth upon which sat some of Steve's best English bone china—the set he'd gotten in the Cotswolds. There was a small bouquet of pink rosebuds in the center of the table, flanked by two silver candle holders in which pink tapers flickered enchantingly in the lowered light of the room. *Why did I install dimmer switches in all my rooms?* Marlis berated herself, knowing that if she tried to turn the lights up, one very large male hand would prevent her.

Defeat, but it was only a battle, not the war. "It's lovely." She breathed the compliment softly, picking up a sterling silver fork and admiring its patina.

"For a lovely lady."

She whirled around, expecting to find a victorious smirk on Kevin's face. Instead she was met by a contemplative expression that almost made her feel guilty of suspecting him of anything more than simply wanting to do something nice for her. She was no fool, though. Lurking beneath that Boy Scout facade of his was a mind which, she was sure, was most adept at planning seductions.

"I wish I had known what you were planning," she said, looking away. "I could have saved both you and Steve a lot of trouble."

"It was no trouble at all. It's given me pleasure."

Marlis felt the net slipping over her head, and groped in her mind for what to say next.

Kevin solved her dilemma. "We'll leave the door open," he offered, "and I promise not to touch you all evening, if that will ease your mind. All I'm asking for is your company."

With an offer like that, wasn't she going to appear an insensitive ingrate if she turned him down? Marlis reasoned. "I'm afraid the answer is still no, Mr. King." So, she was an insensitive ingrate. That was better than giving in to feelings she didn't want to give in to.

They both heard pounding on the door downstairs.

"That may be Steve with the food," Kevin surmised.

"Or a potential guest," Marlis added, happy for the interruption. "I'll go see." She hurried from the room.

It was Steve, carrying covered trays of food from which wafted delectable odors that made Marlis's stomach rumble in joyful anticipation. She flung open the door for him.

"Come in, come in," she cried.

"I have more out in the truck." His eyes gobbled her up. "Wait till you taste the strawberry mousse."

Marlis's face dissolved into lines of anguish. "Steve, I had no idea what Kevin King was planning. I'm not going to share an intimate supper with him."

Steve set the trays down on the desk and faced her. "Why not? He's a nice guy." He looked disappointed. "You'll be missing my spiced crabmeat crepes."

"Is that what you fixed?" Marlis groaned, having had them before, and knowing what a delight they were.

"And my special spinach salad with homemade hot bacon dressing."

"Mmm."

"Freshly baked orange juice muffins."

"With your own homemade honey spread?"

"Of course. Hey, don't look so worried. It's not as though you'll be totally alone with him. There are guests just across the hall."

"There are no guests."

"Oh? Oh."

"I hate to have wasted your efforts, Steve, since I know what a marvelous chef you are, but I'm not comfortable being with him. Besides, he insulted me this afternoon, so I hardly want to have dinner with him."

Steve shook his head back and forth. "You can tell me the whole story tomorrow. In the meantime, just see the situation as a bonus for me. He gave me a great compliment by asking me to perform this little service. He is, after all, Kevin King, highly respected author—"

"I know, I know."

"Besides, he paid handsomely for this meal. You should be flattered."

"You think so?"

"I do. So, eat with him or don't. That's your choice. Whatever you decide won't change my feelings for you." His smile was warm.

"Oh, Steve. You're wonderfully understanding." Marlis put a hand on his arm and squeezed it.

"Ah, here's our splendid meal," Kevin called out from the stairs, "getting cold."

Marlis spun around and was more than a little happy to see a jealous scowl on the man's face. *Isn't that nice,* she thought. *I really shouldn't let him think there is something between Steve and me, but if it will keep the wolf from my door, why not?*

With a wickedly gorgeous smile, she bounced toward Kevin. "Steve's made my favorite crepes. Isn't he a sweetheart?"

Sweetheart grabbed up the trays and trotted up the stairs. Marlis followed, a smug smile of victory lying across her lips. Kevin King trudged last, a little of the wind knocked from his presumptuous sails, Marlis thought with satisfaction.

If she thinks I think there's something between her and Steve, she's mistaken, Kevin decided. *Steve's gooey adoration is too clearly one-sided, not to mention the way Marlis responded to my lovemaking in the gazebo not many nights ago. But what a woman!*

Within ten minutes Steve had brought in the rest of the dinner, arranging the food on their plates and leaving extra portions and the dessert on the dresser.

"Enjoy," he urged, flicking his eyes anxiously from Marlis to Kevin and back to Marlis again.

"We will," Kevin promised.

Steve somehow managed to balance all the trays in his arms and Marlis hurried downstairs ahead of him to open the door.

"I'll talk with you tomorrow, Steve. Thanks for everything."

"Have a good time," he called over his shoulder.

With slow step, Marlis made her way back upstairs, wavering between having dinner with Kevin King and not.

"Well," she sighed, moving to the table, surveying the culinary masterpiece Steve had created with her in mind, "Steve's outdone himself this time."

"He's a talented man."

"In many ways."

She looked boldly into Kevin's sensuous, attentive eyes and almost lost her nerve, but not quite. "I've decided to eat in my room, Mr. King," she announced. She took a deep breath and held it, waiting for either a tirade or a charming attempt to persuade her to change her mind. Neither was forthcoming.

"I understand," he said lightly, as he sat down and picked up his salad fork. "You're afraid to be alone with me." He took a bite of the spinach salad and murmured his satisfaction.

"I am not!" Marlis denied hotly, letting out the breath. "That's for teenagers." She snatched her salad and dinner plate, one in each hand, and a fork, and strode out the door and up the stairs. When she reached her apartment, she grumbled softly because the door was shut, as it should be, but it meant she had to put the china down on the floor to let herself in.

Some time later, having finished her salad, and beginning to pick at the crepes, Marlis wondered out loud, as was her habit, "Am I the year's biggest fool for refusing to eat alone with Kevin King? After all, there's one or two things about him that I admire, and there's no denying I'm attracted to him physically. But his patronizing attitude and galling suggestion that I need his help in running this inn—well, that's too much to overlook. Now, if he'd kindly offered a few suggestions, without making me feel so incompetent, I would have accepted his advice, wouldn't I have? After all, he is an expert in the field. I'd be foolish not to take advantage of his knowledge."

Marlis stared down at her plate and realized she had already eaten one of the crepes and hadn't even tasted it.

Darn him! Now he was spoiling her dinner as well as her peace of mind.

Still, she rationalized, *he is a guest in my house, and he did arrange this lovely meal for me. Should I add ungraciousness to all the other faults he finds in me?*

Marlis debated what to do for several more minutes before picking up her plates and going back down to Kevin's room where she paused in the doorway, struck again by the romantic aura of soft music, flickering candles, and the most compelling presence of all—Kevin King himself.

"I thought I'd join you for dessert, at least," she offered him a crumb.

He looked at her with surprise. "I'm sorry, Marlis. I thought you'd want that alone, too, so I took it upstairs and put it beside your door. Didn't you see it?"

Marlis's face reddened. Had he heard her foolish talk about him? Ranting about how she was attracted to him?

Setting the plates down on the table with a little thump, she fastened her large, flashing eyes on the man she was liking less and less as time went by. "On second thought, I think I'll skip dessert," she said. "If you're finished, I'll take these dishes down to the kitchen so Steve can get them tomorrow whenever he likes."

"I'll help." Kevin stood up.

"That's not necessary."

"I know. but I don't want you thinking I'm one of those men who won't deign to lift a dish." His eyes sparkled. He wasn't angry, or even a little bit miffed, and Marlis was wary, because she'd seen his temper that first day when he'd been waiting for her in the foyer and when he'd been caught in the shower when the water went off. What was he up to, with this unflappable disposition?

"My, my," she said, "you do dishes as well as cook? What a find."

"I hope you'll think so."

"Don't concern yourself with what I think of you," she retorted.

"Oh, but I must."

"Why?"

He came around the table and kissed her without touching her. "Because we're falling in love."

SIX

"Falling in love?" Marlis scoffed. "You've fallen out of a tree." She bravely looked into his eyes and instantly knew she shouldn't have. Desire, longing, passion all raged in those dark-blue circles that held her to him as though they were a steel vise. "If anything, you're falling in lust,". she suggested.

"I won't argue with that."

"That's not enough for me."

"What do you want?" His arm snaked toward her waist.

"Don't you touch me," she warned him, backing up slowly. "You promised you wouldn't."

"Under duress."

"A man never betrays his word."

He pursued her, only inches away, his look conveying what he wanted, his body taut and hungry as it advanced on her retreat. "There's no point in fighting what we both know is happening," he said. There was a dangerous huskiness in his voice and Marlis wondered if he were a man who could control himself. At the moment her knees were growing weak, and if he didn't stay away from her, she'd have enough of a time controlling herself, let alone a hundred and eighty pounds of solid male on the prowl.

"Nothing is happening between us," she insisted, still backing up in tiny steps.

"Yes, it is. You can't deny it."

"I can." Her legs hit the bed. There was nowhere else to go. He was so close to her she could feel the warmth of his body, hear his shallow breathing, watch the heightened movement of his muscular chest. She sank down on the bed, on her back, and he followed her, still not touching her, but lying beside her, leaning on his left elbow, his eyes moving over her body slowly, sensuously drifting from her widened eyes to her parted mouth down her throat over the swell of her breasts across her flat stomach along her thighs. "Stop . . . please," she pleaded.

"I'm not touching you," he said so softly she barely heard him. But he was. With those compelling blue eyes he was branding every inch of her as his.

With a will of its own, Marlis's hand lifted, hesitated in midair, and then trailed over his cheek. He shuddered. Her fingers eventually found their way into the thickness of his soft hair and she groaned, her eyes closing then opening to gaze full on him. His lips separated. Her breathing quickened.

"Touch me," she invited.

An iron arm imprisoned her waist and drew her slowly against him, under him, the pounding of her heart crashing in her ears, her resistance melting in the wake of his overpowering appeal. He bent and kissed her, softly, tenderly, murmuring her name as his lips took hers. His muscled arm tightened, and then gentleness fled.

Kevin's kiss became possessing, a fiery, pulsating demand for more and more. A powerful hand plunged into her hair and held her head firmly while his tongue probed the moist interior of her mouth, tempting her to join in the dance, to give in to him, and Marlis felt herself on a roller coaster of desire that was taking her she knew not where. One of her hands clutched the knotted muscles of Kevin's shoulder then slipped inside his shirt to caress the forest of dark hair that awaited her fingers.

The telephone rang. No, it was a ringing in her head, some primitive warning that things were going too far too fast. Marlis ignored it and kissed Kevin again, their bodies meshed in an embrace of delicious entanglement, their hands wandering over each other, caressing.

She knew she must stop, mustn't she, but he was the one who, with a loud sigh, let her go and gradually sat up, running one hand through his disheveled hair. Leaning back on one hand, he looked down at her and shook his head slowly from side to side. "Girl, what are you doing to me?"

Marlis sat up, catching her breath, touching her lips where she could still feel the vibration of his mouth moving over it. She gave him a heated look. "We are *not* falling in love."

"Yeah, right."

In thoughtful silence they made two trips to the kitchen with the remnants of the dinner. Kevin washed the dishes while Marlis dried, and pondered the man beside her.

He was sophisticated and mysterious. Angry one minute, cool the next. Determined and unflappable were two words that aptly described him. And dangerous. Dangerous because there was no future with him.

She had a bed-and-breakfast inn; he had three. Their lives could never mesh permanently and Marlis did not want an affair. She had grown up in a family that believed in marriage first, then you live together and have babies. Some people reversed that order, she knew, but she would not be one of them. And she had no idea where Kevin stood on such matters, although the fact that he had been the one to stop their lovemaking hinted that he wasn't quite the roaming predator she had at first thought.

"Thanks for your help," she said when they had finally finished. She was careful not to look at him. Those eyes had power over her.

"The night is still young," he quipped.

Uh-oh, he's having second thoughts about letting me go, Marlis figured, and she decided the sooner she distanced herself from him, the better. She walked briskly out of the kitchen, through the foyer, and up the stairs.

He followed her.

"Are you leaving tomorrow?" she asked, hoping he'd say yes, hoping he'd stay forever.

"Nope. You and I have work to do."

"I don't want to work with you."

"Even if I promise you'll like it?"

They reached the second-floor landing and Marlis turned to face him. "I won't like it. I won't like it. There. Do you understand now that I won't like it?"

"Yes, you will."

Marlis's eyes widened in dismay. Didn't he ever give up?

"We'll start tomorrow morning with your policy of hiring employees," he declared.

"No."

"And then in the afternoon work out a maintenance schedule for the house."

"No, no."

"Discussing the meals should take a little longer—"

"Kevinnn!" Marlis ground out his name between her teeth. "I do not want or need your advice on how to run Sunrise Inn."

He smiled, undaunted. "You haven't heard everything I have to say."

"I don't plan to."

"Did you know that you're stubborn?"

Marlis glowered at him, resenting the humor he was finding in all this. "I am not stubborn, but you are insensitive and overbearing. Give your advice to someone who really needs it."

His hands reached out and grasped her shoulders. "You're the only one I want to give it to."

Marlis gently pushed his hands away. "I'm declining your kind offer, then," she said.

"You don't really want to do that."

"Yes, I do."

"Let me convince you—"

"No, Kevin . . ." she began, but never finished the order, because his lips slanted across hers in the gentlest of kisses that sent a flash of quicksilver racing along every avenue of her bloodstream.

"What were you saying?" he questioned, barely lifting his lips from hers. But he gave her no chance to respond before he put them down again in a series of quick, breathtaking attacks that Marlis wanted to stop, and finally did, determining to be strong.

"You can't win every argument by kissing me," she told him.

"Mmm . . ." He snuggled his face in her hair. "Why not?"

"Because there is more to life than this," and she surprised Kevin by slipping her arms around his neck and her fingers into the curly hair at the nape of his neck where she tugged and played and kissed him fervently until he groaned against her lips, and then she stepped back.

"You are exciting to play with," she said, with a more determined glint in her eyes than he had ever seen before, "but that doesn't mean I can't think straight when I'm around you. I know who I am and what I am, even when you're kissing me. You can't bend me to your will just by taking me in your arms."

Kevin frowned. "Is that what I'm trying to do—bend you to my will? I thought I was generously offering help."

"You are forcing something on me I do not want."

His mouth tightened against his teeth, and Marlis saw a muscle in his jaw quiver. He had gotten the message.

"I guess there's nothing else to say then but good night," he said sharply.

"Yes," she agreed, knowing she was right to set the rules in her own house and her own life.

"Marlis, we're alone here," Kevin said, his sapphire eyes cold as they glanced over her mussed golden hair and parted mouth. "Don't lock your door tonight." To the quick intake of her breath, he added without humor, "You don't need to lock your door, for I promise you won't be awakened in the middle of the night by an amorous guest unable to control his longing for you."

Marlis looked skeptical. "You'll keep this promise as well as you kept the last one?"

"Hey," he said, throwing his hands up in defense. "Who touched whom?"

With a rush of guilt, Marlis cleared her throat and silently accepted the blame—but she'd been backed into it. Being on a bed with a man as obviously experienced as Kevin King wasn't a sport she was used to playing. She didn't know the rules, and she darn near had lost the game because of fouls—his sensuous eyes and mouth and caressing hands.

But now she was winning. She was glad she had stood up to him and told him she couldn't be swayed from what was good for her just because he aroused all kinds of desires in her. "Good night, Kevin," she said firmly.

"Miss Kent."

Kevin meant to go. He was angry with her for not appreciating what he was offering. He was angry with himself for hurting her feelings when he had never intended to. He knew he should go, but he just stood there, taking in every tantalizing curve of this woman who was driving him crazy. Every inch of his body craved her. That was a fact. But something held him back and he wondered what that was. The silly promise he had just made—not to break down her door and join her in her warm bed and make love to her—was wreaking havoc with his male hormones. Cold showers had never been his favorite pastime.

"Is there something else?" Marlis asked, straightening her shoulders, uneasy under Kevin's appraisal but determined to hold her ground. Because they did not see eye to eye on important matters, it would be hazardous to let their relationship grow, for it could only do so in a physical way and she would not subject herself to that alone.

She wanted to fall in love, to *be* in love, but the kind

of love she was looking for would have to have a whole lot more to it than just male/female attraction.

"No, there's nothing more to be said, is there?" Kevin stated. He turned and trudged down the stairs, his hands in his pockets, thinking that this woman was impossible to figure out. Why wouldn't she allow him to help her? Why did she tie him up in knots wanting her? He had come to Sunrise Inn to do his job. Just that, and nothing more. Instead, he had looked into a pair of emerald eyes and lost his heart.

All loss and no gain, he concluded, entering his room and flopping down on the bed where the impression from Marlis's body still showed in the bedspread. He reverently laid his hand on it. *She doesn't want me here. I threaten her independence, but I don't mean to. My only motive is to help her.*

He laid there staring at the ceiling, deciding what to do next. One thing he knew for sure: he was not giving up Marlis Kent even though he knew she was trouble with a capital T.

When Marlis awoke in the morning and recalled the events of the night before, she cringed in her bed, overcome with dismay that she had given in so wholeheartedly to Kevin—again. That was not like her. She was normally self-controlled and rarely let physical desire supplant rational common sense.

Sure, there were many things she liked about Kevin, but what she disliked led her to conclude he was trouble with a capital T, so why tempt herself with an involvement that would only hurt her in the end?

When she saw him later in the kitchen, just finishing his breakfast, she poured herself a cup of coffee and sat down across from him, expecting there to be a lot of tension between them, but still intending to boldly tell him there would be no more romantic . . . uh, what should she call them? . . . episodes between them.

"Good morning," he said warmly, his eyes wrapping

her up in them. "Mabel is one fantastic cook. You were wise to hire her."

What? She had done something right? His praise surprised her, as did his attitude of casual friendliness. She wasn't sure what to make of it, so all she said was, "Thanks."

"She *made* me take another helping of her cinnamon chocolate chip coffee cake. That vanilla glaze is perfect with it—mild but tasty."

"I like it, too."

"She saved you some."

Marlis smiled. "She'd better have."

The object of their conversation bustled up to the table and set a plate down in front of Marlis with hardly a glance at her. Mabel was tiny, barely five feet tall, had snow-white hair and a round face with rosy cheeks. Marlis thought if Mrs. Santa Claus really existed, she must look just like Mabel.

"Thank you, Mrs.," she used the nickname by which she sometimes referred to her cook.

Mabel nodded, but her full attention was on Kevin. "Can I get you anything else, Mr. King?" she asked breathlessly.

"Well, that pear almondine was delicious—"

"Say no more." Mabel's face was wreathed in a smile that put wrinkles over every square inch of it as she hurried away.

Marlis gave Kevin a shame-on-you look. "You've just made a friend for life," she told him.

"Mabel is quite a gal."

"That she is."

"Adores you."

"Hmph," Marlis retorted. "You wouldn't know it from the reception I just got. You seem to be the star attraction today."

Kevin poured coffee from a silver pot into Marlis's cup. "Mabel thinks you're the next best thing to motherhood and apple pie," he told her.

"Really?" Marlis took a sip of the hot brew.

"Yes. And she doesn't understand why you don't want to marry Steve Alexander."

Marlis coughed violently and barely caught her mouthful of coffee in her napkin before spraying it all over Kevin. "You two have been discussing me?" she asked when she was under control.

"Discussing? No. I've been listening. Mabel's been telling."

"Uh oh." Marlis rested her chin in her hands. "Mabel is like a second mother to me, and thinks she's been appointed to be sure I'm happy in life."

"At least you'll never starve with her around."

"What did she say about Steve and me?"

Mabel returned with a chilled plate of pear almondine and placed it before Kevin as though he were royalty. She waited while he took a spoonful and gazed up at her with admiration.

"Do you give out recipes, Mabel? I just may put this in my next book."

"You might?" Mabel was all atwitter, grinning like a silly goose and bobbing up and down like a cork in a bathtub.

After she went back to her kitchen to clean it up, Marlis said, "I'd like to know what that woman told you about me. Wouldn't want you getting wrong information."

Kevin leaned over and picked up her right hand. When Marlis tried to pull it away, his fingers tightened their grip and kept his hold. Then he kissed her middle finger. "She said Steve is in love with you, which is what I thought." He kissed her index finger. "You and he used to date, but don't anymore." He nibbled on her pinkie. "There was a man you almost married once whose name was Tim. She didn't like him and was glad when you called it off."

Marlis was blushing four shades of red.

Kevin turned her hand over and slowly kissed the center

of her palm. "Mabel thinks it's high time you found your-self a man and had some babies."

Marlis jerked her hand free. "Mabel thinks she knows what is good for me, and I appreciate her concern, but let me assure you I am in no great hurry to settle down and raise a family. I enjoy being independent. I enjoy operating this bed-and-breakfast inn. And I enjoy . . ." She stopped suddenly as a visual image of Kevin kissing her last night on the bed actually made her skin tingle.

"What do you enjoy?" he prompted her.

Marlis stared right at him and said nothing.

"Well, it sounds as though you have your life well planned and under control." Kevin finished off his pear almondine, wiped his mouth on the napkin, then turned and gave the okay sign to Mabel who was watching him with undisguised adoration from the sink. She giggled again, and Marlis stood up.

"Sorry I can't stay to watch you two admire each other to death," she said in a voice that was slightly higher pitched than usual. "I have some painting to do." She'd decided not to bring it up last night. Why warn him there would be no more scintillating moments between them when she was going to be sure there wouldn't be, and he was probably going home today anyway, since she had made it perfectly clear she was not interested in his ideas for restructuring the running of the Sunrise Inn.

"You're an artist?" Kevin asked.

"No. I'm painting two of the rooms upstairs while they're vacant."

"You don't hire that sort of work out?" He sounded amazed.

"Why should I? There's nothing to painting a straight wall."

Kevin grunted. "I guess you are an independent lady. Mind if I help?" He pushed the chair back and stood up.

"I'd rather do it alone," Marlis said. "You're a guest, after all."

"Yes, and no. I'm taking a short vacation to be with you."

"Which is thoughtful, but unnecessary." Marlis lifted her chin. "I can paint the rooms by myself, thank you, just as I can run this inn by myself."

"I'm beginning to see that. You're full of surprises, Marlis Kent. Still, I'd like to work with you. Then we can get to know each other better and I can tell you why our . . . episode on the bed last night was a mistake."

Marlis popped the lid off the gallon of flat vinyl paint with a screwdriver and began vigorously mixing it with a twelve-inch paint stick. She didn't know whether she was angry or humiliated by Kevin's statement that their love-making the night before had been a mistake. She'd like to remind him that he was the one who had put together a romantic dinner to seduce her in his room. He was the one who had practically forced her down on the bed. Where did he get off saying what happened next was a mistake?

She poured some of the Cream Silk paint into a pan and moved the paint roller through it. The wallpaper on two of the four walls was a lovely combination of cream and lilac as were the curtains, and bedspread, and various accessories scattered over dresser and reading table. Marlis was particular with colors, and had gone to three stores, two of them out of town, before finding the exact shade of cream she wanted for this room.

Stepping up on the ladder, she rolled the paint over the wall, starting in the left corner and working down. "We are going to talk about this," she pronounced out loud, meaning she and Kevin King, "as soon as he gets here."

The phone began to ring—once, twice, three times, four. Marlis scrambled off the ladder, grumbling. The rule of the house was that if she did not answer by the third ring, either Amy or Mabel were to do so. Both had been carefully instructed on what to say and how to take messages. Neither, apparently, was near a phone. The question was why? This was Mabel's baking day, and Marlis had seen Amy go by the door just minutes before carrying a fresh supply of towels for two of the rooms.

Too hastily Marlis dropped the roller into the paint tray, and some of paint slopped over onto the drop cloth she had wisely put on the floor. Some also got onto her left shoe.

In the hallway she grabbed up the phone on the sixth ring. "Hello? This is the Sunrise Inn. May I help you?"

"Kevin King please."

Talk about cream silk, Marlis thought. The female voice on the other end *was* cream silk. Very cream silk.

"May I tell him who's calling?" she asked. She didn't have to know, of course, but her curiosity was aroused.

"Yes. Amanda Stuart."

"Just a moment, please, Ms. Stuart."

Dashing across the hall to Kevin's room she found the door open, but he wasn't there. Nor was he in the parlor downstairs, or in the kitchen wangling some more pear almondine from Mabel. Where could he be? He'd said he was going to help her paint.

"I'm sorry, Ms. Stuart, but Mr. King must be out. I can't locate him."

"Oh." There was such dejection in the voice that Marlis could tell they knew each other well. "Would you ask him to call me, please? As soon as possible. I'm in Santa Barbara. He knows the number."

"Of course," Marlis agreed, thinking meanly that perhaps Kevin King was like the proverbial sailor with a girl in every port—only in his case was it a woman in every bed, in every inn along his way?

She had barely been up on the ladder for two minutes, when the man himself walked in. He was wearing blue jeans that were obviously new, and a western shirt open at the throat, with the sleeves rolled up to the elbows exposing the same thick hair that covered his chest. *Gads*, Marlis thought, *even his forearms are gorgeous!*

"I didn't bring clothes appropriate for painting walls,"

he explained with a smile, gesturing toward the jeans, "so I had to run out and buy a few things."

"You shouldn't have bothered," Marlis remarked with coolness, concentrating on the wall before her while deciding Kevin looked great in everything in wore.

"I promised I was going to help, and here I am," he said.

"You don't want to get paint on your nice new clothes."

"I don't mind."

"This won't take me long."

Kevin gave in, leaned against the door, and crossed his arms over his chest, staring at the stubborn woman. She was being her usual independent, exasperating self, but looked tantalizing doing it. Wasn't there anything she wore that she didn't look cute as heck in? he pondered. He would have whistled his approval, but knew he'd get a paint roller in the mouth if he did.

After a length of silence that piqued her curiosity, Marlis glanced over at him. "What's the matter?" she asked him. "Don't tell me you have no advice to give me?"

"Nope, none. I was just watching you . . . work."

The appreciating gleam in his eye did not escape her notice, all the way across the room.

"You're adept," he said. "I can see why you don't hire a professional painter when you can do it just as well. And look at the money you save."

"Yes," Marlis agreed, scampering down the ladder to put more paint in her tray. She felt uncomfortable with the way Kevin was scrutinizing her, his vivid, assessing eyes moving from the scruffy jeans she was wearing to the long man's shirt that was tied in a knot around her hips, to the western wrangler's scarf, a red one, that held her hair off her face. She looked a mess, she knew, but, after all, painting is a messy job, and not the time for high fashion.

"You had a phone call," she said, when pouring the

rich creamy paint into the tray reminded her of the rich, creamy voice of Amanda Stuart from Santa Barbara.

"Oh? Who was it?"

"Amanda Stuart." Marlis had turned around so she could see the reaction on his face. She wished she hadn't. His eyes brightened and he broke into a broad smile.

"Amanda? I'll call her right away." He almost tripped over his own feet getting out of the room, which left Marlis dejected. Whoever this Amanda Stuart was, she certainly knew how to make Kevin move. Not that she cared a hoot, Marlis told herself. She hadn't wanted his help anyway.

Ten minutes later he was back, whistling.

"Did you reach her?" Marlis had to ask, although she could have guessed the answer. He was beaming.

"Yep." He offered no explanation. "You've finished one wall already," he said with admiration as Marlis was just putting a few touches in the corners with a three-inch brush. "You're fast."

Marlis guessed that was a compliment. "Thanks."

"Are you doing the trim, too?"

"Yes."

"With a semigloss paint?"

"That's right."

"Want me to do that while you work on the other wall."

"No thanks." Marlis climbed down from the ladder and set the paint roller in the pan. Then she took a handkerchief from her pocket and wiped the perspiration from her forehead and upper lip.

Kevin walked over to her. "I'm a good painter. I won't mess up your lovely room."

But you're messing up my lovely life, Marlis felt like yelling. Instead, she looked up at him and asked the question that was burning in her mind. She had to ask it. "Why did you say last night was a mistake?"

Kevin took the handkerchief from her and wiped a spot of paint off Marlis's forehead. This put him within touching distance, which he wanted. "Because I lay awake half the night thinking about it," he said, "and almost broke my promise to you that I wouldn't come pounding on your door to continue our—"

"I see." That was not the answer Marlis had been expecting. She had thought he was going to say he'd been wrong, that they weren't falling in love but were only physically attracted to each other, as she'd suggested. Or that their body contact had proven to him that he wasn't really interested in her after all.

"I'm a relatively decent guy, Marlis, but you're more temptation than a normal man can resist. You should never have kissed me the way you did!"

Marlis's mouth fell open. "I didn't try—"

"I know that. You just responded to me the way I'd hoped you would. You proved that I was right when I said we were falling in love."

Holding the ends of the scarf with both hands, he reached it around her neck and used it to pull her toward him. "Would you mind demonstrating your considerable ability again?" He leaned toward her.

Marlis put both her hands on his chest to stop his advance. "I don't give home demonstrations, sir."

"Not even if I finish painting this room for you and do the other one, too?"

"I'm afraid not. I prefer to do my own work. Why don't you find something else to occupy your time."

"I'd rather stay here and ogle you."

"Kevin . . . please."

He released her. "All right. If you're going to insist on being conscientious, I should be, too. I brought some pages from my latest book that I need to go over."

"Your mystery?"

A guilty look exploded over Kevin's face. "Not exactly a mystery," he admitted.

"The next edition of *Country Inns of California*?"

"Yes. I'm sorry I bent the truth a little—"

"A little? You told me you write mysteries. That's

hardly the same as a guide to quality bed-and-breakfast inns.''

"Well, in a sense it is a mystery. Who will be included this time? Who won't?''

His words stabbed at Marlis's heart. Her Sunrise Inn was one of those which would not be included. She couldn't stop the tears from springing into her eyes.

"Marlis, forgive me. That was thoughtless of me.''

Marlis ran past him and into the hallway. Dashing up the stairs, she almost got to her room before a pair of strong hands stopped her, whipped her around, and gripped her shoulders.

"Look at me,'' he demanded when her head was bent over and tears were tumbling from her eyes onto her paint-splattered shoes. He shook her a little.

Because he had her arms imprisoned, Marlis couldn't wipe her face, so she was humiliated that he was seeing the tears that were wetting her cheeks, but she couldn't help crying. She worked so hard. So hard. It wasn't fair to be excluded.

"I'm sorry this inn gave me a bad impression the last time I was here,'' Kevin said gently. "I'd give anything to change that. I'm not a cruel man, Marlis. But I do make my living by being honest. People deserve that when they're going to spend good money for a night's lodging. Over the years I've earned the public's trust. That's important to me.''

"As it should be,'' Marlis agreed in a tiny voice.

"You do a great job of running the Sunrise,'' he said soothingly.

"Do you really think so?'' Her eyes darted up to his face.

"Yes, I do. And with my guidance, you will do even better—''

Marlis jerked herself free and brushed the tears from her face. "I thought we'd been over this. I don't need your precious guidance.''

"How can you say that? Chaos ruled this place the last time I was here."

Marlis's mouth opened in a gasp. "I'd hardly say chaos."

"What would you call it?"

"A few minor inconveniences."

Kevin grunted. "Being caught in the shower with no water is a minor inconvenience?"

"Well . . ."

"Burning up breakfast?"

Marlis glared at him. "All right. I'll concede to minor chaos. But those things were just coincidences, not regular occurrences."

"The Whitcombs won't be back, will they?" Kevin planted his muscular arms across his chest in that ruling potentate stance which aggravated Marlis to no end.

"My gain." She straightened her shoulders and crossed her arms the same way.

"Amy takes advantage of you."

"She does not."

"Mabel needs to be more conscientious."

"I've already spoken to her."

Silence, while a staring match went on between them.

"Fine," Kevin snapped.

"Yes, fine," Marlis also snapped.

He turned and marched across the hallway and down the stairs without another word. Marlis wished there was something nearby she could grab and throw at him. Something she didn't mind breaking, of course.

SEVEN

Marlis finished the one room she'd been painting and started the other. She was already regretting the quarrel she'd had with Kevin. Perhaps she was being petty in not taking his advice. After all, would it hurt to listen to what he had to say? If she continued to alienate him, she'd never get the Sunrise Inn into his bed-and-breakfast guide, and whether or not she liked the man who wrote it, being included in its prestigious pages was practically a guarantee of success. As a businesswoman she should put her personal feelings aside and do what was necessary for the good of her inn.

As soon as I finish here, she told herself, *I'll find him and apologize.* This made her smile.

"I'm glad you haven't forgotten how to do that," a voice announced from the door. It was Kevin, and from the look on his face Marlis could tell he'd been doing his share of soul-searching, too. He sauntered over to her. "I want to apologize, Marlis, for coming on so heavy-handed. I know I insulted you, and I'm sorry. My only excuse is that I become zealous in my cause to make every bed and breakfast the very best it can be."

Marlis's smile broadened in amazement that Kevin was

apologizing. That was an ability neither of her brothers had. They were stubbornly opinionated and rarely changed their minds once they made them up. Marlis had always felt it took a really self-assured person to admit being wrong. Kevin had just admitted he'd been wrong.

She came down the ladder and wiped her hands on a rag. "Thanks for understanding how I feel," she said, locking her eyes to his sincerely repentant ones.

"Friends?" he asked, holding out one hand.

With only momentary hesitation, Marlis slipped her small one into his. "Friends," she agreed.

He squeezed her fingers, then lifted them slowly to his lips. "Where's a brush?" he asked. "I am going to help."

"You don't have to—" Marlis started to say, but was stopped when a determined pair of lips planted themselves on hers in a brief kiss that was sensual but tasted good nonetheless.

"Where is it?" Kevin asked again. "If you don't tell me, I'll just keep kissing you until you give in."

Marlis remembered her vow not to let that ever happen again, so with a reluctant sigh, she produced the trim brush and pointed to the can of semigloss paint intended for the wooden trim around the doors, windows, and baseboards of the room. "Work before pleasure is what my daddy taught me," she said.

"A wise man," Kevin pronounced. "We'll save the romance for dinner."

"Not another meal in your room prepared by Steve?" Marlis questioned, realizing that to vow not to let Kevin touch her again was one thing and carrying that out was quite another.

Kevin shook his head back and forth. "In the nicest restaurant in town, if you will honor me with your company."

Marlis pursed her lips together. "Let's see how working together goes, and whether or not we're speaking to each other at dinnertime."

Having dinner with him doesn't mean we have to end up in each other's arms, she decided.

With a deep, throaty laugh, Kevin started on the wood trim at the window, spreading the paint in smooth, even strokes. "I'll whistle while I work," he threw at her over his shoulder, "then maybe I won't get myself into trouble."

"Good idea," Marlis agreed, going back to her own work with renewed vigor. Dinner with Kevin King in a public restaurant? Yes, she should be able to handle that.

* * *

The next hour and a half flew by happily as Marlis and Kevin worked together, sometimes in silence, sometimes conversing about their lives. The one-dimensional man who wrote a book for travelers broadened into a man who had divorced parents, both living in Spokane, a married sister in Kansas City, loved dogs, hated spaghetti, and had read every volume of Will and Ariel Durant's *The Story of Civilization.*

From Marlis he learned more of her family, her love of country music, her favorite period of history—the eighteenth century—and that she feared earthquakes, but not enough to leave California.

By the time they finished dinner that night at a restaurant built in 1885, where the food was good but not nearly as delicious as what Steve Alexander had prepared for them the night before, they were friends, because they had moved beyond the general facts of their lives and now knew more intimate details of each other such as favorite colors, most memorable vacations, political philosophy, and, perhaps the most important discovery, they both reveled in warm chocolate chip cookies, fresh from the oven.

"One difference in our upbringing," Kevin reiterated as they walked, in the cool of the summer's night, along the creaky wooden sidewalks of the town's main street, "is that you've lived in Sutter Creek all your life and my family never lived any place longer than four years, which is probably why I love to travel." To Marlis's affirmative nod he added, "My father was a teacher who moved from campus to campus in search of new challenges. My mother was talened in flower-arranging and never had a problem finding part-time work in local shops, so it didn't matter to her that we moved so often.''

"Didn't you mind, though, being uprooted from school and friends?'' Marlis could not imagine going through that as a child.

"Actually, no. My father made it a great adventure. Always ahead there were exciting experiences and wonderful people, he told us. I believed him, because that is what we always found.''

"You found it because you expected to.'' Marlis admired that positive thinking.

When they paused in front of an antique shop to gaze at cut glass and mining tools, old books and photos, Kevin took Marlis's hand. When they stopped to admire the ornate balusters, turned posts, and balconies of the western-looking buildings along Main Street, he slipped his arm around her waist.

By the time they arrived back in the inn, had passed through the old gate in the white picket fence, and were wandering slowly beneath the shadowed grape arbor toward the side door, a multitude of stars sparkled down on them from the clear sky, and in the unique quiet Marlis was not surprised when Kevin turned her to face him, drew her into his arms, and kissed her, gently at first, then with more and more intensity.

"Mmm,'' he murmured, "now this has been what I call a perfect evening.'' He kissed her eyelids and the tip of her nose and the sensitive side of her neck, and Marlis clung to him and reveled in his expertise in making every nerve in her body come alive beneath his touch. She had no memory of the vow she had made that morning.

Out of nowhere, a huge gray-and-white mass of fur nearly knocked them down as it galloped past, chased close behind by Amy's husband Mike and then Amy herself. The dog's fur had been wet, and soapy, and both

Kevin and Marlis's slacks were now covered with hair that clung stubbornly to the material.

"Amy, what are you doing?" Marlis shouted to her, grabbing the girl by the arm to halt her pursuit.

"Oh, I'm sorry, Marlis. We wanted to give Hercules a bath, and you know we live in an apartment, but the car wash where Mike usually takes him was closed, so I thought for a change, Hercules would like to romp on nice clean grass instead of smelly cement."

The Old English sheepdog, one of the biggest Marlis had ever seen, had reached the closed gate, and since he couldn't get through, bounded back the way he'd come. Playful as a pup, he jumped up on Marlis, knocking her backward into Kevin's arms. A huge slobbering tongue whipped out of a gigantic mouth and lapped Marlis's cheek while she tried to fight him off, getting thick soapsuds on her hands and arms and more dog hair and water down the front of her batiste blouse.

"Amy, get that dog out of here!" she ordered her housekeeper.

Kevin and Mike grabbed for him, Amy staying clear, trying to keep from breaking her wrist again, but without a collar to hold on to, it was impossible to calm the animal down.

Suddenly, though, Hercules stood still; then he shook himself vigorously, sending water and soapsuds flying everywhere, especially on Kevin, with one especially large blob landing right on the end of his nose.

"Amy!" Marlis yelled.

"Hercules!" Amy yelled.

"Marlis!" Kevin yelled.

"Come on, big boy," Mike shouted, running toward the backyard, and Hercules happily followed. So did Amy.

Kevin caught his breath and swiped at the soap on his nose. "That girl should never have been allowed to bring that dog onto this property."

"This is the first time she's done it, Kevin," Marlis tried to explain, but he was in no mood to listen.

"What if we had been guests?" he gestured dramatically with his arms toward her.

"But we weren't, and—"

"You could have been sued."

"I doubt that—"

"Nowadays? Let me tell you, it would be a sure thing. That monster could have knocked someone down, injured him, and sent him to the hospital. Believe me, Miss Innkeeper, you would have been sued royally."

"Kevin, you're blowing this all out of proportion—"

"Stop right there." Kevin held out his hand as though he were directing traffic and preventing an oncoming car from proceeding into the intersection. He got suddenly quiet. "Marlis, I was beginning to think I was wrong about my first opinion of Sunrise Inn. You almost had me convinced that all those things that happened during one twenty-four hour stay were, as you claimed, out-of-the-ordinary mishaps. Now I know better. You have no control over your own inn—"

"Now just one minute," Marlis spoke out to defend herself, but was cut off by Kevin's continued tirade.

"Things happen here, potentially dangerous things, because there are no rules, no discipline with your staff."

"That is not true."

"Yes, it is. Amy should have never even contemplated bringing that disastrous dog onto this property. What if he'd knocked down an elderly person? What if he'd dug up half your lawn?" Kevin's eyes blazed like those of a fiery orator making a crucial point. "Undoubtedly he has pooped on your grass, and tomorrow some unsuspecting guest will step in it, and then—"

"All right already. Blame me if you must. I suppose I deserve it because I never specifically told Amy not to bring Hercules here. That's because I never thought of a reason why she would. It's as simple as that." Marlis was getting tired of always explaining herself to this man who had changed from a charming dinner companion to a conscience who was giving her a headache.

"Efficiently running a bed-and-breakfast inn is not a simple task, as many people discover when they try it and fail."

"I am not failing—"

"When you are dealing with the public you have to anticipate every problem and prevent its happening."

Marlis's hands slammed down on her hips. "Mr. King, I am tired of being lectured to as though I were a mindless stump of wood. Thank you for your evaluation of my ability—or inability, should I say?—to run a bed and breakfast successfully. Thank you for the dinner. Thank you for your company, which I shall now leave."

With a defiant toss of her head, Marlis stomped down the stone path to the end of the grape arbor, turned left, and climbed the two steps to the back porch. Flinging herself down on the wooden swing, she massaged the soapy water into her skin, and gave a quick prayer of thanks that Kevin King was taller and heavier than she was. Otherwise she would have wrung his neck, right there in the grape arbor, uncaring of whether or not he'd sue her for doing it or, if he died, she'd be convicted of murder.

Her breath was rapid and the fire in her cheeks was spreading onto her forehead and into her scalp. It didn't matter that he was right, that there might have been serious injuries from this episode, it was that he was so rigidly unsympathetic with life's little happenings, although one could hardly call a soap-laden Old English sheepdog of over a hundred pounds a little happening.

She felt the swing sink as another body eased itself onto the other end. She knew it was Kevin.

"I want to be alone," she stated, staring straight ahead.

"I understand."

Marlis whirled so quickly to face him she nearly fell off the swing. "No, you do not understand. You never understand. Who do you think you are, coming into my house and into my life and criticizing everything I do?"

"I know how you feel," he said quietly.

"Ha!" The word was expulsed with a breath of exasperation. Marlis turned away from him and eyed the pretty baskets of pansies and petunias that hung from the four corners of the porch. They were just one of the really lovely attractions of the Sunrise Inn which she had brought into existence, or nurtured. Every room in the house carried her touch, as did the gardens and the grounds. But, oh, no, the great Kevin King couldn't see the good; he only focused on the bad.

"If I hurt your feelings back there," he said, reaching out to play with a tiny curl that lay at her temple, "I'm sorry. Don't let this come between us, Marlis."

"It already has." She stood up abruptly and started for the back door, but he caught her wrist.

"Business is business," he stated firmly, "and what we feel personally for each other is something else." Marlis looked him right in the eye with such an icy expression, Kevin was sure he was about to receive the death penalty.

"You're right, as usual," she said with a barely controlled rage, "but I'm just not sophisticated enough to think that way. When you criticize me, and my inn, I take it personally."

"Marlis . . ." Kevin called after her as she stomped into the house.

The phone was ringing. Reaching for the receiver on the kitchen wall, she answered with as cheerful a "hello" as she could muster.

"Is this the Sunrise Inn?" a honeyed woman's voice inquired.

Great. Now she wasn't even answering the phone properly. Maybe he was right. Maybe she wasn't a good innkeeper.

"Yes, it is. How may I help you?"

"Do you have a Mr. Kevin King staying with you?"

Marlis took a quick breath and held it. Here was another silken voice, like the one that morning, but a different person.

"Yes, Mr. King is just outside. May I tell him who's

calling?'' She did it again—being nosy when she shouldn't have.

"Susan Roberts. He knows me."

I'll bet, Marlis thought, wondering if the man had left this number with every gorgeous female from San Francisco to San Diego.

Going to the screen door she called outside. "Telephone for you, Mr. King."

Kevin was at the door in two giant strides, and when he came inside he imprisoned one of Marlis's hands in one of his. Though she tugged, Marlis could not break free of him and he pulled her over to the phone with him.

"This is Kevin King," he said into the receiver. "Susan? Hello. Am I glad to hear from you." Without another look at Marlis he let go of her hand and his total concentration was with the woman that Marlis just knew had long ebony hair and sexy dark eyelashes.

She wanted to cry. In fact, she did cry, exactly a minute and a half later when she slammed the door of her apartment behind her and sank down on the bed. Not that she blamed the two sultry-sounding women for succumbing to Kevin's charms. Hadn't she done the same, idiot that she was?

The man who brought out in her the opposite emotions of admiration and animosity did not come to her room that night. She had thought he might when he finished talking with Susan. He must be tired of apologizing, she decided.

* * *

Falling restlessly in and out of sleep, Marlis finally greeted the morning in less than a good mood. She hoped Kevin would be gone before breakfast, but no such luck. There he was, in the delicious-smelling kitchen, downing thick, golden pancakes with blueberries and macadamia nuts on top when she walked in.

"Marlis," he called out to her.

The other guests greeted her, too, and she went to each one and chatted a few minutes with them. By the time she was at the far end of the big table, where Kevin was sitting, he was scowling. *So, what else is new?* she thought.

Three empty chairs beside and across from him showed that a few guests had already eaten and were gone.

"Good morning," she murmured, only the strongest of determinations keeping her from asking if he had enjoyed talking with sexy Susan last night.

"Well, I'm being spoken to," he said.

"I always speak to my guests."

"And enemies?"

"I was taught in church to love my enemies." The words were out before she thought of their implication in the present circumstance, and she lowered her eyes to avoid the amusement she knew would leap to Kevin's eyes. She heard it in his voice, though: "What an interesting concept."

There was a pause and then he said, "I hope you're not painting this morning." He finished the last bite of one of Mabel's great creations.

"No," Marlis admitted.

"Good, then grab a pencil and some paper and meet me outside in the gazebo."

Marlis frowned. "Why?"

Kevin leaned across the table. "So we can discuss you-know-what."

Marlis's mouth slowly dropped open and her blood raced redhot through her veins. "Are you saying you expect me to listen to a list of your complaints?"

"Complaints is a harsh word. I prefer suggestions."

"Forget it."

"This is strictly business, Marlis."

"I thought I explained my feelings on that last night."

"You did, but this is morning, and I knew you'd change your mind."

"I haven't. Besides, I have to be away from the house most of the day."

"Running away?" The grin on his lips was almost tempting enough for her to slap off. But she was a civilized woman, after all, and one did not handle one's problems with violence, even though the thought of it, on him, was not that repulsive.

"There are some gentlemen I am meeting," she informed him.

"Men? As in plural?"

"Yes."

"Is this a business meeting?"

"No. It's strictly pleasure."

Kevin scowled, and Marlis pranced out of the kitchen, forgetting she had not eaten a thing.

"Hi, Miss Kent."

"Hi, guys."

"Hooray, she's here."

"When do we go?"

A dozen excited, fidgety, rambunctious six-to-nine-year-old boys were waiting for her outside the church when Marlis drove up.

"Is everybody ready for our outing?" Marlis called out as two of the boys threw themselves around her legs and hung on.

"Yesss," came the enthusiastic roar from the crowd.

"Do you have your pans?"

"Yesss." Little hands held up old pie tins given by mothers for the occasion.

"I don't have a pan." A familiar deep voice from behind her startled Marlis and she whirled around to see Kevin standing a few feet away looking sexy in blue slacks and a matching short-sleeved shirt that showed impressive biceps. "Why do I need one?"

Marlis glared at him. "You don't."

"But everyone else has one."

"That's because they are going to be panning for gold. You'll be busy doing something else, I'm sure."

"No. My time is your time."

"I don't want your time," Marlis said sweetly and turned her attention to a six-year-old redhead named Jason who was tugging on the sleeve of her pink western shirt that was tucked into loose-fitting jeans. "Miss Kent, is he," he pointed at Kevin, "going with us?"

Marlis tousled the ragged hair of the boy. "No, Jason, he isn't."

Kevin squatted down on the sidewalk in front of the boy. "But I'd sure like to." He leaned over and whispered loudly into Jason's ear: "Where are we going?"

Jason's friend, a skinny boy with two front teeth missing, spoke up. "Miss Kent is taking us up the creek to look for gold."

Kevin looked astonished. "Not real gold?"

"Yes," the two children shouted excitedly in unison.

"That sounds like fun."

"Yeah. You wanna come along?"

"Sure, if Miss Kent doesn't mind." Kevin stood up and gave Marlis an innocent, hopeful look.

"Miss Kent does mind," she pronounced. "This is an outing for the Sunday school class my brother teaches, which is for boys ages six to nine, which you obviously are not." Marlis almost laughed at that remark. No, Kevin King was definitely not a boy, not with those broad shoulders and that devilish gleam in his eyes.

"Are you going to handle all these kids by yourself?" he asked, looking at the exuberant boys anxious to get going.

"Sure."

"Do you think you can?"

Marlis sighed and glared at the man. "Are you suggesting that since, in your opinion, I cannot run a bed and breakfast properly, I also am not qualified to take some little boys panning for gold?"

"Are you? What do you know about gold?"

Jason spoke up. "Miss Kent knows more about gold than anyone in Sutter Creek."

Marlis grinned and patted the boy on the head. "Thank you, Jason." She looked at Kevin. "Slight exaggeration."

"That's what our teacher, Mr. Kent, says," Jason said.

"My brother, Bob," Marlis clarified.

A car pulled up to the curb with Sondra, Marlis's sister, driving. The passenger door flew open and a dark-haired charmer ran as fast as he could to Marlis. "Auntie Marlis. Auntie Marlis," he hollered, throwing himself into her arms when Marlis bent down and scooped him up.

"Hi, Ricky." She gave him a resounding kiss on his cheek. "How's my favorite nephew?"

"Yuk," the youngster exclaimed, wiping the wetness from her lips off his skin as Marlis put him down.

"That's not what I'd say if you put your arms around me and gave me a kiss," Kevin spoke up.

"We'll never know," Marlis shot over her shoulder.

"Is this help for the day?" Sondra quipped, strolling up to Marlis and eyeing Kevin with undisguised interest. "Remember, I told you I thought you were crazy to take on this many kids at one time."

"I've done it before, Sondra, and no, Mr. King is not going along. He's just here to . . . to . . ."

Sondra leaned over and whispered into Marlis's ear, "Does it matter why he's here, just so long as he *is* here?"

Marlis gave her sister an exasperated look. Sondra never gave up hoping she would find the man of her dreams. Well, Kevin King had turned into a nightmare and, therefore, was not marriage material for family scrutiny.

She introduced her sister to Kevin.

"Not *the* Kevin King," Sondra gushed, batting her gorgeous green eyes which almost matched the gorgeous green pantsuit that hovered enchantingly over her gorgeous body. Marlis felt like a scuzzball in comparison. "Why, our family digests every edition of your famous bed-and-breakfast guide," Sondra assured him.

"Thank you," Kevin answered.

Before her sister could interview him for the position of brother-in-law, Marlis took her arm and began leading her back to her car. "Thanks for bringing Ricky by. We're going to have a great day."

Sondra managed to pull herself away from Marlis long

enough to look back over her shoulder at Kevin. "Where on earth did you meet him?" she wanted to know.

"Details another time, Sis. Right now, I have to get these kids under control and then be on our way."

"I want those details," Sondra insisted, shaking a beautifully manicured finger in Marlis's face.

"Promise."

They gave each other a quick hug and then Marlis turned to the business at hand. "Okay, kids, we need to get going. There's a lot of adventure waiting for us out there. Does everyone have extra tennis shoes and pants?"

The boys yelled that they did.

"And your lunch?"

More yelling. Some held up bulky sacks. One little boy's sack broke and a banana, a peanut butter sandwich, and a Snickers bar fell on the sidewalk. His friends laughed.

"Do you have the soda pop?" Ricky asked.

"I sure do. It's in my van, along with a great big box of chocolate chip cookies."

"Hooray," went up the chorus.

"Did you bake—" Kevin started to ask.

"Mabel," Marlis growled.

"Then I'll have some, too."

With a sigh of frustration, Marlis turned to face him. "Mr. King, although you are a guest of the Sunrise Inn, this is not a guest activity."

"But you need help."

"I do not."

"To handle a dozen boys this active? I think you do. Besides, I've never panned for gold, but have always wanted to."

Marlis's eyes slanted nearly shut. "Right in front of me, in the foyer of my inn, you told Julius Whitcomb you had been on a trip and it was a rip-off."

Kevin swallowed hard. "Slight exaggeration? I'd still like to go with you and the boys."

Marlis shook her head no. "There's a company right

up the street that will take you on an expedition by the hour, the day—or even overnight," she added the last hopefully.

"Yours will be better."

"Kevin . . ."

"If I promise not to lecture?"

"No."

"I'll just help with the boys. They need a male role model."

"No."

The group started panning for gold along Sutter Creek a few miles from town.

"Are we going to have fun today?" Marlis asked as she waded ankle-deep into the cool water and shivered a little.

"Yes," the boys shouted exuberantly.

She turned around to face them, and Kevin, on the shore. The man had come, despite her objection, and was now watching her intently—*the better to see whether or not I really know a fig about panning*, Marlis thought grimly.

She didn't want him there. He was distracting, and it wasn't fair to the youngsters. This was their day, not a day for Kevin King to pursue Marlis Kent.

"Are we going to find any nuggets today?" she questioned.

"No," answered some.

"Yes," answered others.

"Now, wait a minute," Marlis said, pushing her fourteen-inch green thermoplastic gold pan into the moving water and scooping up half a panful of sediment from the bottom of the creek. "There's still a lot of gold in this part of the country. Most of it is buried in the ground, in what we call lode or vein deposits. But some of it lies along the curves of slow-moving streams and creeks and rivers—in places just like this one, where we are right now. These are placer deposits."

She had the boys wade into the creek and thrust their pans into the bottom, as she had done.

"I don't have a pan," Kevin called out from the bank, standing alone.

"I'm sorry," she shrugged.

"May I use yours?"

"I have to use it to show the boys what to do."

Little Jason sloshed through the shallow water to Kevin and held up a rusted pie pan. "I'll share with you, mister." His bright blue eyes and chubby cheeks gave him an angelic appearance as he generously offered what he had.

Kevin laid one hand firmly on the boy's shoulders and gave him a big smile. "Thanks, pal. I'll appreciate that." Then he took off his shoes and socks, rolled his pants legs up over muscular calves, and waded in to join the group scattered in front of and to the sides of Marlis. "Stand right here by me, Jason," he said to the boy, "then we can see everything Miss Kent does." The youngster almost fell face forward into the creek in his anxiety to obey. He had found a hero to worship.

EIGHT

Marlis addressed the group. "Okay, kids—and man—now that you have dirt and sand and gravel from the bottom of the creek in your pan, I want you to hold that pan just below the surface of the water. See? Like this." She held hers level with one hand. "With your other hand break up any large clumps of dirt."

The boys and man obeyed although some of them, including Jason, let out wails when their pans, not held tightly enough, tipped too much and the dirt slipped out.

"Let's fill those pans up again," Marlis instructed.

Kevin supervised Jason doing that, then moved back and forth through the water, helping Marlis with the other boys. Once or twice their eyes met, her attitude, at first, skeptical that he was doing this for any other reason than to be near her, but then realizing, finally, that he was actually enjoying himself being with the children.

When all the boys had accomplished the task, Marlis said, "Now bring your pans up to the surface carefully and slosh the water in one side and out the other."

This was hard for most of them to do, but after several tries they began to get the hang of it.

"With your pan under water, hold it with one hand and

tap the side with the other. This causes the gold to settle to the bottom because gold is much heavier than the dirt and sand."

The boys tapped away.

"Have you ever heard your folks say we are living in the Mother Lode?" Marlis questioned.

A lot of little heads nodded yes.

"Do you know what that means?"

A little blond boy with very large ears yelled, "There are lots of loaded mothers around here?"

The others thought that a good answer, and Marlis giggled out loud. "It's true, there are lots of mothers in northern California, but the term Mother Lode refers to a belt of gold one mile wide and a hundred and twenty miles long that lies along the western slope of the Sierra Nevada Mountains. And we're living on that belt."

"Wow."

"*Golly.*"

"Whew," came the surprised replies. Even Kevin King's eyebrows shot up. "A hundred and twenty miles long?" he exclaimed.

"Yep. All right, team, now we get down to the serious panning, and this is what is tricky and takes practice." Marlis leaned over so they could see what she was doing. "We want to get rid of all the useless stuff—the dirt and sand. To do that we take the pan out of the water, then tip it forward and put only the front of it back under. If we very gently move the pan in a circular motion, gently, gently," she admonished as some of the boys moved too much and lost all their sediment, "then the water will separate the dirt from any gold that's there and float it out of the pan but leave the gold behind." She did this for several minutes until the pan was clean except for some minute sand in a recessed pocket at the front. "Sorry, folks, no gold. So I'll try again."

Marlis demonstrated the technique, and the boys imitated her. Kevin worked with Jason until he began to do it right. Then the boy insisted Kevin try. Marlis watched with interest as Kevin panned several times but came up with nothing. He was, though, good with his hands and wrists—which she already knew. He swirled the pan in a counterclockwise motion with real finesse, leaving Marlis with no other conclusion than that there was nothing the man could not do once he put his mind to it.

"Your pan is different than ours," Kevin said to Marlis. "Why?"

"It's specially made for gold panning. See, there's a pocket in the front with grooves that catches the gold better than if it were flat." She demonstrated while he watched, which attention made the hairs on the back of her neck tingle. Skillfully she washed a panful of dirt until tiny flecks of gold were seen in the riffled pocket.

"These can be picked up with a magnet," she said, producing one from a front pocket and a tiny plastic bottle which was partially filled with water. Getting the tip of her finger wet, she pulled the gold flecks off the end of the magnet, laid her finger on top of the opening of the bottle, turned it upside down, and received applause from Kevin and Jason when the water sucked the gold fragments into itself.

"You're really a pro," Kevin stated with definite admiration, which included acknowledging how good she was with kids. The boys adored her, and she had no trouble keeping them in line. There probably wasn't anything she couldn't do if she put her mind to it, except figure him out. He knew she was having trouble with that.

"The flecks add up, but the real fun is in finding nuggets," Marlis told them all.

"Have you?" Kevin asked.

"Sure."

"What did you do with them?"

"Sold them to local jewelers to make into jewelry. There are a number of prospectors around here who do that."

"Miss Kent, Miss Kent" came an excited cry from

the big-eared blond boy. "I think I found gold. Hurry. Look."

Marlis moved through the water quickly and peered into the boy's dented pan. "Mark, you did. You found gold. That's a nice little nugget."

Marlis reached into the front pocket of her jeans and pulled out tweezers and another plastic bottle. Putting some water into the bottle, she then lifted the gold piece from the pan and dropped it inside, screwing on the top.

"Everybody!" she yelled. "Mark found gold. Come and see."

The creek was noisy with a dozen pairs of boys' legs splashing to see what their friend had.

"This gold has been here a long, long time," Marlis told the group. "People didn't know there was any in California until what year?"

"I know, Auntie Marlis," Ricky spoke up first. "It was 1848."

"Very good, Ricky. Does anyone know where?"

Puzzled looks were exchanged until Jason said, "Wasn't it somewhere near here?"

"Right you are, Jason," Kevin congratulated him with a slap on the back. "It was at Coloma, California, which is only about thirty-five miles from Sutter Creek. On January 24, 1848, James W. Marshall found gold in the gravels of the American River. That started the famous gold rush we hear so much about."

"Wow!" Jason exclaimed. "You're smart, Mr. King."

The other boys agreed, and even Marlis gave him his due.

"Do I get a reward, teacher?" Kevin inquired, with a wicked grin that left no doubt in Marlis's mind that the reward he wanted was her.

"I think I have an extra candy bar in my lunch sack," Marlis told him. "Will that do?"

"Sure," Kevin agreed good-naturedly. "What else could a guy want?"

What else indeed? Marlis contemplated, glad it was time

for lunch. Maybe if Kevin concentrated on eating instead of on watching her, she'd have a little peace. Her system had been racing ever since she'd first seen him on the sidewalk in front of the church. That was a bad sign. It meant she was out of control, and in her whole life she'd never been out of control where a man was concerned.

"Come on, kids, let's eat."

Though hard to believe, the boys were far more interested in continuing their panning than they were with eating. Now that one of them had actually found a nugget of gold, each one wanted to best him. They were competitors, all.

Kevin helped Marlis spread a huge blanket down on the soft grass and invited himself to join her. She didn't object because, to tell the truth, she wanted to be with him.

"You're wonderful with the boys," she told him while taking Mabel's marvelous lunch of chicken legs and fresh fruit salad out of the ice chest. She offered him some, along with two chocolate chip cookies, all of which he hungrily accepted.

"I'm a boy, too," he shrugged off the compliment.

"It's more than that," she laughed. "You're patient with them, and really care that they succeed."

He cocked his head and studied her seriously. "Which surprises you since you thought all I enjoyed in this life was criticizing."

"Guilty as charged," Marlis agreed, gulping and staring down at a piece of melon she had just stabbed with a plastic fork. Then, peeking up at him, she added, "I wish I didn't feel that way, but . . . how else can I when you are so intent on 'teaching' me how to run the Sunrise Inn?"

He smiled a little, not offended. "Not teach, Marlis, *help*. There's a difference between those two words."

"I suppose."

"I enjoyed helping the boys this morning, and not because I want them to think I'm something great."

"And with me?"

"I'll do anything I have to to stay around you, even if it makes you angry." He took a bite from a cookie and chewed it slowly as his eyes traveled sensuously over her body, from soaked tennis shoes and slacks to the manly shirt which could not hide the curves beneath it, to the hollow of her throat, over her mouth, and up to the tiny gold hoops in her ears. He couldn't have excited her more if his hands had done the roving instead of his eyes. "Besides," he went on, "if I stay around you long enough, I may end up really rich."

Really rich? Marlis thought. "What do you mean?" she asked.

"Anyone can see you know your gold panning. Do you have a mine of your own somewhere?"

"No," she laughed, "but I enjoy hunting for the stuff."

"What do you do besides panning?"

"A little sluicing, some dry washing, occasional crevicing, and dredging."

Kevin grunted. "The lady's an expert."

"I try."

"So, where's your fortune?"

"That's a personal question, isn't it?"

The grin spreading over his mouth was like a magnet. Marlis almost leaned over and kissed him, hard. "There's nothing I like better than asking you personal questions," he responded.

The enticing conversation was interrupted by three of the boys who came looking for some chocolate chip cookies, which Marlis promptly gave them, along with words of encouragement to keep trying and that dimpled smile that changed every plan Kevin had ever had that did not include Marlis in it. He was out of control, and in his whole life he'd never been out of control where a woman was concerned. It scared the heck out of him. The trouble was, Marlis seemed quite able to keep him at arm's length when she wanted to. His primary goal today was to see that she no longer wanted to.

"So, when you sell the gold you find to local jewelers,

what do you spend the money on?'' Kevin asked, munching on another cookie, knowing he'd have to work out a little longer tomorrow to pay for this indulgence.

"The inn, of course."

"No pretty necklaces or rings for yourself?"

"The Sunrise is more important."

"Wrong. Definitely wrong."

"Auntie Marlis, come quick." It was Ricky, shouting.

Marlis and Kevin dropped their food and dashed to the creek, thinking there was an emergency, that someone had been hurt. But it turned out to be the nicest of emergencies.

"I found some, didn't I?" Ricky held up his pie pan with all the hope in the world shining in his eyes.

Marlis grinned from ear to ear. "That you did, my darling, that you did."

Ricky's war hoop almost pierced their eardrums and the other boys dashed over to have a look, some of them still panning in the creek, others from the bank where they'd been eating. Jason stood off from the rest with his head down, kicking restlessly at the ground with his dirty, wet tennis shoes.

Kevin walked over to him. "What's wrong, sport?"

"Nothin'."

Kevin squatted down beside him. "I'm your buddy, remember?"

"Yeah."

"So what's the problem?"

A big tear started in Jason's right eye and slithered down his pudgy cheek, darkening as it collected the morning's dirt along its path. "I haven't found any gold," he mumbled. Kevin glanced up at Marlis who had just come up to them, wondering what was going on.

"Hey," Kevin said, "we still have time. Maybe we'll be lucky."

"Naw, I'm never lucky."

"Okay, then, we'll stick to it until we do find something."

Marlis intervened. "That's a nice wish, Mr. King, but Jason needs to know that sometimes we just can't find what we're looking for." She glanced up at Kevin as the words seemed to be for the two of them rather than Jason. "Especially if it's gold," she continued, kneeling down on the ground beside the boy and taking both his hands in hers. "The important thing, Jason, is that we have a good time together trying. Trying is really what counts, even more than success."

"But I promised Miss Dorothy I'd bring her a big nugget." His lower lip jutted out in a pout of disappointment.

"Who's Miss Dorothy?" Kevin asked Marlis.

"The social worker at the orphanage."

"Orphanage?"

"Yes, Jason's parents died two years ago in an accident."

Marlis could not believe what she saw next: Kevin's eyes filled with tears and the muscles along his cheekbones quivered. He grabbed Jason by both shoulders and almost shook him. "Listen, fella, you and I are going to find that nugget if we have to stay here all day. Let's go."

"But what about your lunch?" Marlis asked.

"Save it for later." Kevin took Jason's hand and led him toward the creek. "My partner and I have some serious panning to do," he announced over his shoulder.

Marlis shook her head in wonder. Would she ever understand that man? There was an intensity in his living that was admirable, and perhaps was the reason he was so bulldogged when it came to working with her at the inn. He saw a problem, and he fixed it. Simple as that.

His response to learning that Jason was an orphan touched her deeply. Any man who could be moved like that was a real man in her eyes. Macho was fine, when you were being attacked by a street gang. Decisiveness was great when you needed a leader. But give her a man with sensitivity to the needs of others and you had a man she could love. Love? Good heavens, what was she saying? Love Kevin King? Ridiculous. Admire? Sure. Respect? Absolutely. But love? No way.

At three o'clock twelve tired boys agreed it was time to go home.

"Who brought Jason?" Kevin asked when they were all back at the church.

"One of the mothers."

"I'll take him back."

Marlis smiled warmly. "You don't have to do that."

"Yes, I do." The look she received from Kevin's clouded blue eyes stopped her from arguing. Hidden behind the dark-rimmed glasses his expression was somber. "I'll see you back at the inn. How about dinner? I'll cook."

"Okay."

Kevin took Jason by the hand and led him to his red Porsche. They made quite a pair, one so big and one so little; one so wise and one so innocent. Marlis wondered what was going on in Kevin's mind. He was really taken with the little tyke.

Every room was filled at the inn that night, even the Dog House, and all from reservations. Marlis personally signed in the last two couples and then called Mabel to let her know there would be twenty-one for breakfast.

"Will that handsome Mr. Kent be there?" Mabel wanted to know.

"He should be."

"Do you think he's handsome—in a distinguished kind of way?"

Any kind of way, Marlis could have said. "He's very attractive, yes."

"And he's so thoughtful."

"I suppose."

"And . . . and . . ."

"What, Mabel?"

"Rugged. Masculine."

"I understand your drift."

"I'm making my special ham loaf. When I described it to him this morning he said his mouth watered just thinking of it."

"Is that what he said?"

"Yes, and he loves fresh strawberries."

"Don't we all?"

"But he likes his long-stemmed and dipped in powdered sugar."

"Mabel, you never serve your strawberries with powdered sugar."

"I will tomorrow, for Mr. King."

By seven o'clock Marlis figured Kevin had forgotten about their dinner date since he hadn't even called to say he wouldn't be there. *Oh well,* she sighed, *I might as well eat by myself and do that bookwork I've been putting off.*

She went to her office and dawdled an hour and a half over a project that should have taken her forty minutes. Her mind kept slipping into another realm where the focal point was a tall, dark man with compelling blue eyes and a smile that made her tingle. When she heard the side door open and close around eight-thirty, she didn't get up to see who it was. She was miffed at being stood up, and didn't feel like a confrontation. At ten o'clock she went to bed.

At breakfast, Marlis was surrounded by guests who were a talkative bunch and very interested in the history of Sutter Creek, which she gladly recounted for them. Mabel's breakfast was raved over by everyone, as was the beautiful Sunday-morning weather.

"A great day for a picnic," a lawyer from Florida declared.

"Mabel will pack you a basket, if you like," Marlis informed him. The man and his wife decided they would.

"This is the cheeriest kitchen I've ever eaten in," a schoolteacher from Minnesota exclaimed. "I love the way the sun floods into the room. It makes a person so appreciative of life."

Marlis agreed even though her mind was not really on the beauty of the sun and crisp air but on the fact that Kevin was not there. What had happened to the man?

Mabel was greatly disappointed, and it showed in her downcast expression. Marlis was disappointed, too, and wished she weren't. She didn't want to be looking forward to starting each day with the man at her table, because someday soon he would leave and then she'd be lonely. She knew she would.

All the time she was getting ready for church she wondered where Kevin was and what he was doing. She had expected him to pressure her again, today, to let him expound his ideas for running the inn and she had decided she couldn't avoid the conflict any longer. Perhaps if she got it over with, he'd not bring up her "failings" again, and they could just enjoy a few days together before he drove off in his fancy sports car to pursue his career and she went on with hers.

There were lots of visitors that day at church, from all over the country. Some of them were staying at the Sunrise Inn, and Marlis smiled at them when they were introduced to the congregation. The hymns were uplifting, the reading of the Scripture inspiring.

The people were standing, singing the last hymn before the sermon, when Kevin King made his way through the pew until he was next to Marlis.

"Good morning," he whispered, leaning over so his voice would not carry. Then he began to sing, in a rich, deep baritone that showed he knew the songs.

Marlis was shocked to see him there in his sophisticated sports jacket and open-necked shirt, and even more surprised when he took her hand as they were being seated, and held it all during the pastor's message, even though she tried to tug it away.

Looking across the aisle, she saw her sister Sondra watching her. A few rows behind, her brother, Bob, was eyeing them, too. She and Kevin would never get out the door without going through a family inquisition.

After the service, sure enough, Bob and Sondra hurried up to them.

"Marlis, aren't you looking stunning in that blue dress," her sister gushed. "Hello, again," she said to Kevin.

Bob introduced himself before Marlis could, and the men shook hands. As if he had a script, Bob quizzed Kevin on where he was from, what he did for a living, how long he was staying, and whether he was a sports fan. Marlis could have strangled him.

Finally, after a reasonably polite interval had passed for the men to speak, she tugged on Kevin's sleeve. "I'd like you to meet Reverend Cole."

"Sure. Hope to see you both again," he said warmly to Sondra and Bob, who gazed at him with approval, then nodded that approval to Marlis.

She introduced him to her pastor and to several of her friends who stopped them on the way down the sidewalk toward Kevin's car, and in the eyes of each person there was the silent question: Is this man special to you? She wanted to say, *Yes, he is, not that that matters much since he'll be gone in a few days and I'll probably never see him again.*

"I'm glad you're still speaking to me," Kevin said as they walked home. "I have no excuse for last night except that I got involved in some business and the time got away from me."

"That's all right," Marlis said. "I understand." And she did, sort of, even though she was curious to know what kind of business would have detained him so.

"I should have called you, but it just wasn't possible." His smile could have melted the butter Mabel used for her Belgian waffles, and the sincerity of his apology assured Marlis that he hadn't meant to treat her casually, so she decided there was no point in being hurt.

Mabel was overjoyed when they walked into her kitchen. She had just finished the dishes from that morning's breakfast and was checking supplies for the next day's meal.

"Oh, Mr. King. You missed my ham loaf," she exclaimed.

"I know, Mabel, and I'm sorry about that. Did you have the strawberries, too?"

"Yes, sir. The biggest I've seen for a long time. I served them with powdered sugar, just the way you like them." She beamed, and behind his glasses Kevin's eyes rolled heavenward in an expression of disappointment over the delight he had missed. "You wouldn't happen to have any left, would you?" he asked hopefully.

Mabel's tiny mouth spread from ear to ear. She leaned toward him and said, "There's a bowl in the refrigerator I saved—just for you."

"Great."

"Would you like them now?"

Kevin glanced at Marlis.

"Go ahead," she said. "You have plenty of time before we get started."

His look became puzzled. "Get started?"

"Yes," Marlis said sweetly. "Didn't you want to talk with me about the Sunrise Inn?"

Kevin squinted at her, as though that would explain her surprising suggestion. "It's not necessary," he said.

"Oh, but it is," Marlis insisted.

Kevin held his breath. He would never understand this woman. She had fought him like a mother tiger protecting her cubs, in this case, her inn, refusing to budge in her declaration that she did not need his advice. What had changed her mind? he wondered.

He leaned over and kissed her on the cheek. "Are you really sure you want to do this?"

"Yes."

When Mabel brought the huge bowl of strawberries and powdered sugar, he gave her an enthusiastic kiss, too, which sent her into a silly chatter about what she was serving the next week for breakfast, hoping Mr. King would like every single thing.

"I think we'll take these out to the gazebo, Mrs.," Marlis

said, knowing that was the only way they would not have to listen to the woman's infatuated conversation.

"Good idea," Kevin murmured, scooping the bowl off the table and grabbing two napkins from a nearby holder.

"Good-bye, Mabel love." He gave the older woman an affectionate gaze and she smiled adoringly at him and held the screen door open as they passed through.

Kevin remembered the white-latticed gazebo with fondness, for it was here that he had first kissed Marlis and had taken a step over the line he had carefully drawn for himself for years where women were concerned. No serious involvement was the name of that line. It was now obliterated by the sparkle of Marlis's eyes and the sheen of her beautiful thick hair and every detail of her nature that made her unforgettable.

The gazebo could seat about eight, and had bright orange-and-white cushions (*Funny I don't remember that*, Kevin told himself with a smile. *I wonder what I was thinking about instead?*), the orange matching the shade of climbing rose that ran rampant on its outside and gave off a delicate aroma.

"They're called Joseph's Coat," Marlis explained.

"Very pretty," Kevin commented, snipping off one flower and slipping it into her hair, behind her left ear. He wondered if she knew the significance of that placement: right ear, available; left ear, a taken woman. His woman. "You'll have to sit next to me to eat these strawberries," he instructed, setting the bowl down on one side of him and patting the cushion on the other side, as a signal for Marlis to sit there.

"I can handle that," she agreed.

"I'm glad you can, because I can't wait any longer to do this." He pulled her into his arms and kissed her long and meaningfully. "There," he breathed out slowly, cradling her head along his shoulder and holding her close, "that's better. I can only be with you just so long, Marlis Kent, before I want you in my arms."

With a sigh, Marlis abandoned her vow not to let him touch her, and enjoyed the moment, but couldn't quite bring herself to tell him she felt the same way.

Kevin picked up the bowl of strawberries and put them in his lap. Then he dipped a good-sized one into the powdered sugar and brought it to Marlis's lips and held it there as she bit into it. Some powdered sugar remained around her mouth and slowly, with his tongue, he licked it off while his fingertips feathered her bare arms.

Marlis trembled from his touch and groaned when his lips moved over hers and settled a kiss on her that was gossamer light. Then she fed him a luscious strawberry, her eyes never leaving his.

The sensuous ritual went on, without a word said aloud, but volumes were spoken by their hearts, until all that was left were a dozen long stems in an empty bowl.

"Now, what did you want to say to me?" Marlis asked in a voice husky with emotion.

Kevin responded by throwing himself prone along the cushions and lying his head in her lap. Reaching up, his left hand captured the back of Marlis's head and pulled it down until their lips met in a kindling kiss of fire. "Tell me every detail of your life," he murmured against her mouth, "and don't leave out the men."

"Kevin . . . I thought you wanted to talk about the inn."

"Not now. Do as I ask, woman, or I'll punish you."

Marlis grinned. "And just how will you do that?"

"I'll make you listen to my life's history."

"I'd like that, Kevin."

"Would you?" He took off his glasses and dropped them onto the floor of the gazebo and kissed her again, long and hard. "I'm going to like getting to know you," he said against her cheek. Then he laid his head back down in her lap and said, "Start with the minute you were born."

NINE

The balmy Sunday afternoon drifted on as Marlis revealed the days of her life and Kevin countered by sharing his. They found things to laugh about and others that made them sad. Kevin did not mention his marriage until Marlis brought it up.

"Belinda was a sweet girl. Quiet. Introspective. She loved to read and sew."

"Did you have any children?" Marlis asked, thinking perhaps he had a son or daughter, which would explain his easy way with the boys the day before.

"No. We'd only been married two years when Belinda was thrown from a horse while riding with a friend. Her neck was broken."

"Oh, Kevin, I'm so sorry."

He sat up and gazed into space. "It took me a long time to get over losing her. I thought I would never love again, until . . ."

He glanced at Marlis, then looked away quickly. "Anyway," he said with vigor, as though shaking off the dusty memories, "that was a long time ago, and this is too beautiful a day to be haunted by ghosts." He turned to Marlis. "Why don't we go somewhere?"

"Oh, no, you don't," she countered. "I finally got up the courage to listen to your lecture on how to make my bed and breakfast a better inn, and now you're going to give it to me—without charge, you said."

"Uh, why don't we skip it?"

"Absolutely not. You've eaten more than your share of Mabel's strawberries, so now you can repay me by sharing your expertise."

Kevin picked up his glasses from the floor and slid them on. "I don't want us to argue," he said.

"Neither do I," Marlis assured him. "Just be gentle with me."

He caressed her cheek with two fingers. "I would never be any other way," he promised.

Once they got into it, there was no arguing—just a frank discussion between two businesspeople about how a successful bed-and-breakfast inn could be run. Marlis liked some of Kevin's suggestions, and others she did not. He approved of some of her practices, and others he did not. What came from the exchange was a new respect for each other, and a tolerance for their differences.

"I've never heard of anyone giving their employees a percentage of the income from the inn," Kevin said, amazed at the idea.

"I do that because I want Amy and Mabel to work for me a long time. Having to constantly train new people cuts down on overall efficiency, don't you think?"

"Definitely."

"While their regular wages are adequate, and competitive with what other B&B's in this area are paying, I reward their conscientious contribution to encourage both better work and loyalty."

"And do you get it?"

Marlis laughed softly. "From Mabel, almost always. Amy was marvelous until she got married. Now the attraction to her husband seems to be greater than her attraction for dusting."

"Still, it's an idea worth thinking about for my own

inns," Kevin surprised, and flattered, her by saying. What he did not say, though, was that he was going to put the Sunrise in his next edition of *Country Inns of California*. Marlis was disappointed.

Leaving the gazebo after several hours, they changed into casual clothes having decided to spend the rest of the day in Volcano, a former boom town from the gold rush days, located twelve miles away, "from which over ninety million dollars in gold was taken after it was discovered here in the 1850s," Marlis explained when they arrived at the quaint tree-lined town that now claimed only eighty-five inhabitants. "It was mainly a placer and hydraulic mining center."

"Where are the supermarkets and fancy motels?" Kevin asked as they drove by vacant and dilapidated buildings of another era and the few small shops that now catered to a low-key tourist trade.

"There aren't any," Marlis said with a smile.

"I like it," Kevin chuckled, stopping the red Porsche for a big black dog who was asleep in the middle of the narrow street and only got up, stretched, and plodded slowly to the side of the road after a toot from the car's horn.

Driving from one end of town to the other only took about thirty seconds, then Kevin parked the car in front of the St. George Hotel at the end of Main Street.

"The hotel was built in 1862," Marlis told him as they got out, "and it used to be in the middle of town."

Kevin looked to his right, at the woods that now stood where half the town had been. "Times change," he observed. "Can we eat here?" He gestured at the grand old building.

"Sure, if you like."

"And spend the night?"

Marlis clicked her tongue on the roof of her mouth. "And I thought you came here to learn some history."

They walked along the uneven cobblestoned sidewalk of Main Street, and Kevin took her hand. "There used to be more than five thousand people who lived here in Volcano's heyday,'' Marlis explained as they gazed at the limestone ruins of the Wells Fargo office, the brewery built in 1856, and the Hale Sash and Door Factory with its sturdy stone front but no roof, each building a gaunt reminder of a day when they had flourished and been important.

"There used to be seventeen hotels here, twenty-four saloons, and several breweries," Marlis recounted. "Churches, a public school, two bakeries, a public hall and theater, a fire company, a lending library, and a debating society."

Kevin looked around at what was now almost a ghost town. "That's hard to believe." He stopped, and listened to . . . the summer quiet. "But something that's been so alive can never really die, can it?"

Even as he said the words, Kevin wondered if the same would be true with him and Marlis. Their relationship was growing. It was alive. But would it stay that way? He knew the one thing Marlis wanted was to be included in his next bed-and-breakfast guide but he wasn't sure he could give her that. Then what would she do? Could she separate Kevin King, the man who wanted her so much it was driving him crazy, from Kevin King, the writer who controlled the fate of her inn?

"You've captured the essence of this town," Marlis told him. "It is life. Even if I'm the only person walking down the street, I still feel that any moment I'm going to hear a whoop of joy and see some grinning miner cavorting toward me, holding up a sack of gold nuggets he's just discovered."

At the far end of town they came to the local cemetery.

"What are we doing here?" Kevin asked, pausing at the gate.

Marlis tugged him inside. "Don't you love to read gravestones?"

He grunted, looking at some of the stones that were very old and run-down. "It's not one of my hobbies, no."

"But they're so interesting."

"To a history buff like you, maybe . . ."

"Look, here's one for a gunslinger who was shot while robbing a saloon."

Kevin leaned over and peered at the almost unreadable inscription that gave the birth and death of one Zachary Grant. "Is this the highlight of your tour?" he asked, but Marlis didn't hear him. She was moving from grave to grave, commenting at each one. It was as though she had known the people.

Finally Kevin took hold of her arm. "I don't want it said that this is how Kevin King shows his girl a good time," he quipped, and he led her out of the cemetery, receiving some resistance, and down the uneven steps to the street where Marlis pulled him to a halt. "Your girl? When did I become that?"

He smiled like a panther who had just eaten his fill. "The first day I saw you, right there in your foyer, when I was mad as blazes and you calmly put me in my place. Then in the kitchen at the inn, when you were trying to light the pilot light, and your shapely bottom was in the air—"

"That's not when you decided," Marlis groaned.

"Well, no, it was a few seconds later, when you pulled your head out of the oven and I saw the smudges of dirt on your nose—"

"My nose did it?"

"And your dirty-blond hair pulled into that silly pony-tail—"

"Silly?"

"Or maybe it was when you stood up and said in a shaky voice—"

"Wait a minute. What shaky voice?"

"The one that quivered when you spoke to me. I knew you liked me, so I decided to like you, too."

"Oooh, you conceited beast." Marlis punched him on the shoulder.

"Don't fight me, woman, or you'll lose."

"Says who?" Marlis challenged, punching at him now with both hands.

Kevin grabbed her wrists and whipped them behind her back, imprisoning her against him. "You were saying?" he mocked.

Marlis squirmed to get loose, but her softness was no match for the hardness of his well-muscled body.

"Stop wriggling, Miss Kent, or you'll get more than this," and he kissed her with increasing intensity until Marlis surrendered and moved her arms around his waist and hugged him tightly. She didn't even care that they were behaving like lovestruck teenagers on a public street. Of course, there was no public there to see them, except for the lazy black dog who had come upon them, laid down at their feet, and was now asleep.

At that quiet cemetery, on a craggy hill where there was no other sound than the wind whistling around scrubby trees and cracking tombstones, Kevin came to a jolting realization that he knew was going to change his life: he could not live without Marlis Kent in his arms.

Walking through Volcano, he had felt that the almost-deserted town mirrored his own condition—lifeless. Since Belinda's death, he'd put all his energy into his work. It was easier to deal with filling a blank page with words, and an argumentative editor, and the emotionless details of keeping three bed and breakfast inns functioning than to allow himself to feel again.

But Marlis had exploded into his life, filling it with her vitality, compassion, understanding, beauty, and yes, lusty physical desire that, along the way, for him, had evolved into a deep, rich love he was never going to let go of. All he had to do was persuade that stubborn, exasperating, absolutely wonderful woman that he was the only man for her.

How am I going to do that? he pondered, as Marlis showed him the Chinaman's Shop, a store that dealt in mineral specimens, pre-Columbian artifacts, and unusual gifts—"It's been here since the 1850s," she told him—*when she thinks I'm critical, overbearing and insensitive?*

"I want to get you a souvenir," Kevin said.

"You don't have to do that," Marlis protested.

His eyes roamed appreciatively over her frothy green sundress with its cinched waist and tiny straps spanning bare shoulders and arms. "I know, but I'm going to anyway. You wait outside."

It only took Kevin a few minutes to speak to the store owner, then he joined Marlis.

"What is it? Tell me."

"You need to develop patience, my dear," Kevin teased her. "Where's a good place to eat? I'm starved."

"There's the Jug and Rose just down the street."

"Take me to it. We'll pick up your surprise later."

They ambled half a block to a charming restaurant where a few local people were eating and chatting with the waitress and had a sandwich. While Marlis enjoyed a last glass of sun tea, Kevin left her and returned five minutes later from the Chinaman's Shop with a brown paper sack in his hand which he handed to Marlis without comment.

"Kevin King, what are you up to?" She reached into the bag and took a blue velvet jewelry box from it that held, she saw, when she opened its lid, a small, odd-shaped gold nugget strung on a lovely 14-karat-gold chain. Marlis took in a breath of wonder. "This is exquisite, Kevin." She held the piece of gold in the palm of her hand to examine its uniqueness. "You aren't intending to give it to me, are you?"

"Yes."

Marlis stared into his sapphire eyes. "I couldn't possibly accept, as wonderful and generous as your gift is."

"Why not?"

"It's too expensive."

"I only bought the chain. The nugget I found."

"You did? When? Where?"

"This morning. I picked up Jason at the orphanage early

and we went panning together. Actually, that's where I was last night, too. He was so disappointed yesterday when he didn't find anything that I wanted to give him another chance. So I took him back to the place where you'd taken the kids. We didn't find anything last night, and the time got away from me, and then I really did have some business to take care of, which is still no excuse for standing you up for dinner."

His look was so repentant that Marlis could not help but say, "That's okay. You were doing something far more important." And she meant that.

"This morning, though, we both were lucky and found the gold."

Marlis was amazed. "You mean he actually found something?"

"Yes. It wasn't as big as this piece, but it was enough to satisfy him. I was going to stay out longer, but he got all excited about going back and showing Miss Dorothy."

Tears formed in Marlis's eyes. "Kevin, what a thoughtful thing to do for that child."

"Hey, put away the hero's award." He took the necklace from Marlis and undid the clasp, then placed it around her neck. "A woman as beautiful as you needs to have gold next to her skin, and since whatever gold you find goes to buy things for the Sunrise Inn, I thought it was about time you had some for yourself."

When Marlis started to protest again Kevin said, "All you have to do is say 'Thank you.' "

"It's really lovely. Thank you. I'll wear it till we get home. Then you must take it back," Marlis insisted as he helped her to her feet and they left the restaurant.

"You'll wear it the rest of your life," Kevin said gruffly, "or answer to me."

There was a strange look in his eyes that Marlis could not fathom, although it might have been caused by the same thought she had just had: Would he be with her the rest of her life, to be sure she did wear the necklace?

* * *

When they got back to the Sunrise Inn, Amy handed Marlis a list of calls that had come in. One of them was for Kevin, from Amanda Stuart. When he heard that, he excused himself and hurried away, leaving Marlis with an abandoned feeling that was only eased a little when she placed her hand around the golden nugget that dangled from the necklace he had given her.

Looking over the rest of the calls, she was alarmed to see one from her sister, Sondra. "Bob's in the hospital." That was all it said.

"Amy, did my sister say what's the matter with my brother?"

"No, Marlis."

"I wonder how serious it is."

Marlis dashed to the nearest phone and grabbed it up. She heard Kevin still talking with Amanda Stuart. "You're the only one I thought of both yesterday and today, Amanda. You're the perfect woman." His emphasis on the word *perfect* made Marlis's heart lurch. She gently replaced the receiver on its cradle even though she wanted to slam it down instead. Kevin King was a womanizer of the worst kind. He romanced them long distance as well as in person. The cad.

"Amy, take care of the inn. I'm going to the hospital."

Marlis ran up to her room, grabbed her purse and keys, and was just going out the door when Kevin came into the foyer.

"Hi, beautiful," he addressed her.

With a venomous look, Marlis slammed the gold necklace, which she'd taken off in her room, into his hand. "Give it to someone else," she snapped as she flew out the door.

"Marlis!" Kevin called after her, but she didn't stop. Her brother was hurt, and family came before strangers who could not be trusted.

Bob looked at her with glazed eyes and accepted her kiss of concern. "Are you okay?" she asked.

"Now that they sliced out my appendix, yes. It was touch and go there, the doctor told me."

Marlis sat down beside the bed and held his hand in hers. "I'm sorry I wasn't home when Sondra called, otherwise you know I would have been here sooner."

"Yeah, telling the doctors how to do the operation, no doubt."

"At the least," she agreed. "If not volunteering to do the surgery myself."

"Then I would have been finished," Bob complained with a grimace. "Where were you anyway?"

At Marlis's hesitation a smile curved his mouth. "Out with Mr. Macho?"

"His name is Kevin, and you know it. You also know I don't like nosy brothers getting involved in my love life—"

"Oh, you mean there *is* a love life, Sis?"

Marlis sighed. "Why can't I ever outsmart you?"

"Because I'm two years older than you and, therefore, have the wisdom of the world in here." He tapped his head and Marlis groaned.

She stood up. "The doctor says you need your rest so I'm going to leave and not argue that point, but I'll be back tomorrow."

"Promise?"

"You bet. Maybe since you're flat on your back, I can make your life miserable for a while and not worry about retaliation."

Her brother squinted at her in warning. "I'd be careful, little Marlis. The day will come when I'm out of here, and then you'll have to pay."

"Uh-oh, then I'd better behave myself."

"Except with Kevin King."

"You are terrible," Marlis whooped. "Throwing me to the wolves."

"Not wolves, just one wolf. You know, don't you, that wolves mate for life?"

Marlis shook her head and left Bob in good humor, but

on the way home she sank into a bad mood. If she'd been honest with her brother, she'd have told him that Kevin King was every bit the predatory wolf who had preyed on her. In fact, he had made a fool out of her, giving her romantic attention on the one hand, criticizing the way she ran the Sunrise Inn on the other, then telling Amanda Stuart she was the perfect woman for him.

There was no doubt it was easy for him to attract women, Marlis figured, for they would either like his sophistication, as she had, or his devastating masculinity, as she had, or his sense of humor, success, and complete control, all of which she also had. What a mess she was in.

If she had just married Steve Alexander, she wouldn't be feeling as wretched as she was right now. And angry. Mostly angry that there were other women in Kevin's life even though he had made her feel she was the only one.

Lights were on in nearly every room of the inn when Marlis arrived home—a cheery welcome to a weary soul. She climbed the porch steps and went in the front door instead of the side one. From the reception desk she heard sobbing. It was Amy, crying and dabbing at her eyes with a big white handkerchief.

"Amy!" Marlis rushed to her. "Whatever is wrong?"

"Mr. King just talked to me."

"About what?"

"The new instructions for my job the two of you worked out."

Marlis stared at the girl. "New instructions?"

"Yes," Amy sniffed. "That from now on I'm to work five days a week instead of four, that my hours are to start at ten instead of noon, that my lunch hour is cut to a half hour, and that I'm only allowed six sick days off a year with pay." She blew her nose loudly into her hanky.

"He said all that?"

"Not only said it, he wrote it down." Amy thrust a legal-size sheet of paper toward Marlis, who took it in amazement, recognizing the firm, authoritative hand of

Kevin King. "Oh, yes, and I'm going to be carrying out people's luggage."

"What?" Marlis gasped.

Amy stood up, a hurt look wrinkling her face. "I may be a big girl, Marlis, but I don't have muscles for carrying heavy things. Mike is going to be furious when he hears that."

"And I wouldn't blame him. Amy, you will not be carrying luggage."

Amy sniffed, not ready to totally forgive. "That's good, but what about all those other things?"

Marlis was as astonished as Amy over the list. Yes, she and Kevin had discussed each of those points, but no, there had been no firm decision to implement any of them, and certainly no suggestion that he be the one to inform her employee. The bad mood Marlis had been in when she'd gotten home deepened.

"Amy, you look tired. Go home. We'll talk about this tomorrow."

Amy raised her head high. "I may not be in tomorrow. I don't have to work, you know. In fact, Mike doesn't want me to. But if I do come back, will Mabel still give me lunch?"

"Yes, she will. About the rest of Mr. King's instructions, put them out of your mind. Just remember, Amy, that I need you."

"Yes, you do." With a decided swagger, she left the house.

Where is that man? Marlis raged, turning purple. *I'll tear his hair out when I find him.* She strode into the kitchen to see if he was there, but he wasn't. Mabel was, though, shuffling around the table, setting it lethargically with plates and silverware.

"What on earth are you doing, Mrs., at this hour?"

Mabel threw her such a hostile look that Marlis actually took a step backward.

"I'm getting ready for tomorrow."

"Why?"

"Because Mr. King says I'm wearing myself out doing everything in the morning. He says it will be more efficient to get some things ready the night before." Mabel burst into tears. "He doesn't think I'm organized, Marlis." She sobbed into the tea towel she was carrying.

"It isn't that," Marlis tried to comfort her. "Mr. King just thinks it would be less of a burden on you to be able to concentrate on your cooking in the morning instead of putting out dishes."

"I've never complained at how hard you work me."

Marlis's eyebrows shot up.

"Or that I don't like all the menus you plan."

Marlis's mouth slowly dropped open.

"I've given you good service for five years now, Marlis, and I'd like to continue working for you, but not if I have to share my kitchen."

"Share?"

"Yes. Mr. King said Kathleen will be helping me more, and even taking over some of my days."

Marlis sank down in the nearest chair, her anger with Kevin bubbling up like a caldron of sulfur.

"He said a well-run inn needs more than one cook who knows exactly what to do. He reminded me that the first time he came here I was out sick, and Kathleen was in Ireland. I couldn't help being sick, could I? He made it sound as though I stayed home deliberately to cause you trouble. And why shouldn't Kathleen take a vacation?"

"It was unfortunate, Mrs., that both you and Kathleen were unavailable at the same time."

"Which meant you had to fix breakfast." Mabel pursed her mouth together. "We both know you can't cook water, don't we, Marlis? I gave you the recipe, and you lost it."

"Yes, Mrs."

Mabel went back to setting the table. "Why does he want two full-time cooks?" she said with a loud sniff.

"He doesn't."

"Kathleen's coming in three days a week."

Marlis jumped to her feet. "I can't afford to pay Kathleen for that much time, not when you're here, too."

"I may not be here."

"Mabel."

The cook put down the knives and forks on the table with a clang. "I don't need help in the morning setting up, and I don't want to do at the end of a long day what I can do just as easily before breakfast. It doesn't require two women to cook a simple breakfast, and seven o'clock is too early."

"For what?"

"Mr. King says our serving breakfast at eight-thirty is too late. Most guests want to be on their way by that time, he said, and we should serve at seven o'clock."

"That's ridiculous. We've never had one complaint that our breakfasts are too late."

"Or, he said, we can serve two breakfasts. One at seven and a later one at eight-thirty."

"How would you feel about that?"

"I think it's a bother, especially when Mr. King thinks I could do one and Kathleen the other." She tossed her head to one side. "You know the old saying about too many cooks spoiling the broth. In my opinion," she placed her chubby hands on her chubby hips, "all this fancy thinking the two of you are doing is just complicating what used to be an efficient way of doing things. Therefore, I'm not sure I'm going to fit in anymore. Perhaps Kathleen will. Why don't you choose which one of us you want?"

Marlis let out an exasperated sigh. "Mabel, there has been a misunderstanding here. Mr. King was not supposed to—"

"Did I hear my name mentioned?" The devil himself appeared in the kitchen door and both women whirled around at the sound of his voice.

"You go home, Mabel, and finish that in the morning," Marlis instructed, "as Mr. King and I have some business to discuss. Breakfast will be at eight-thirty, and will remain at eight-thirty.''

"You'd better tell the guests, then," Mabel pouted. "Mr. King informed everyone breakfast would be at seven o'clock." She shuffled out of the room with a quick, sulky glance at the man who had been her hero only that morning.

Marlis folded her arms across her chest and stared with undisguised hostility at the obnoxious person who was turning her B&B upside down. "What in the name of common sense are you doing?" she asked him in barely controlled words.

Kevin frowned and moved toward her. "Helping."

"I have a housekeeper and a cook who are threatening to quit.''

"Don't give that a second thought." He reached out for her, but Marlis backed away.

"Don't give that a second thought? That I might not have anyone here tomorrow morning to cook breakfast for seventeen people, at eight-thirty and not at seven, or clean up the rooms after those seventeen people, for the full house I'm expecting tomorrow night?''

"All employees threaten from time to time," Kevin assured her with an unconcerned grin.

"Really? Do yours?"

"Of course. I'm always soothing their ruffled feathers."

"Why are they ruffled in the first place?"

"Through no fault of mine, I assure you. They're just temperamental.''

"Or disgusted with their employer." Marlis whirled around and stormed out of the kitchen, flipping the light off on her way.

Kevin followed her into the parlor, where every light in the room was on.

"You really should urge your guests to be more cost conscious," he said, turning off a floor lamp and a Tiffany lamp on one of the tables by the windows.

Marlis spun on her heels and faced him, again folding

148 / KATHLEEN YAPP

her arms across her chest, which meant she was almost to the boiling point, and if the man were smart, he'd run for his life instead of standing there with a smug look on his face that indicated he thought he had solved all her problems.

"That brings up a good point. Since this is my inn," she said through gritted teeth, "I should be the one to tell my guests of any changes in policy, and I should be the one to discuss job situations with my employees."

"I'm glad you're willing to do that because while you were gone I made a list of things that need correcting."

"You did what?"

"Don't take offense. We're both in the same business, and should help each other out, although I don't need it."

Marlis exploded. "I'm going to help you out the front door and out of my life, Mr. King. Thanks to you I may lose two valuable employees whom I've been training for years."

"Hire new people."

"I don't want new people. I want Amy and Mabel." Marlis's eyes were fiery balls of determination.

"You're upset," Kevin stated calmly.

"Upset? Upset? You think I'm uspet?" Marlis yelled at him, appalled that she was doing so. She had never yelled at full volume at any adult in her life, not even her pesky brothers. "I'll tell you what's upset—"

"Pardon me." A cool, high-pitched woman's voice came from the doorway. It was a guest who had been there several days. "Miss Kent, may I speak with you?"

"Of course." It was an effort to calm herself down. "Mr. King will excuse us, won't you?" She turned to him.

"Actually," the woman said, "I'd like Mr. King to hear what I have to say, since it is a complaint about him that has brought me here."

Oh no, Marlis groaned. *Now what has he done?*

TEN

"Please tell me what is troubling you, Mrs. Dunsmore."

The tall, elegantly dressed woman walked into the room and stood with perfect poise in front of Kevin and Marlis.

"Miss Kent, I have been a guest at the Sunrise Inn several times in the past few years."

Marlis smiled. "Yes, you have, and we're always delighted to see you."

"You may not be seeing me again, I'm afraid."

"Oh? And why is that?"

"For one thing, I have always chosen your inn because of its cozy, homelike atmosphere. I can relax here surrounded by lovely antiques and beautiful flowers. You and your staff have created a warm and friendly ambience, Miss Kent, and you are gracious and helpful without being intrusive in my privacy. Those are the reasons I have recommended your inn to so many of my friends." She sighed. "Frankly, a regimented schedule is the last thing I want while on a vacation."

"I couldn't agree with you more," Marlis assured her.

Mrs. Dunsmore gazed at Marlis with question. "Then why have you made these horrendous changes?"

"Changes?"

149

Mrs. Dunsmore held out a piece of paper and Marlis took it. "This was given to each guest this evening by Mr. King," she explained, looking over at Kevin with disdain, who returned the look with a respectful smile. "If I must follow all these rules to the letter, then I'm afraid the Sunrise Inn will not be the delightful haven it has been for me in the past."

Marlis studied the paper, and could not believe what she was reading. Every item was something she and Kevin had discussed, the pros and cons, but never, never, had there been a decision to implement them. She had wanted time to think and decide whether or not they could become a part of her inn's character.

"Why don't you read them out loud," Mrs. Dunsmore suggested, taking a seat, as Kevin and Marlis did also, sitting beside each other on one of the sofas.

" 'Item One,' " Marlis read. " 'Breakfast will now be served at seven o'clock rather than at eight-thirty.' " She threw a withering glance at Kevin.

" 'Item Two. Checkout time will be ten o'clock instead of twelve.' " Another glance.

" 'Item Three. Please turn out all lights not absolutely necessary for use.'

" 'Item Four. Shower water should not be run for more than five minutes.'

" 'Item Five. Luggage will be picked up outside your door at time of departure. Please notify management.' " This time Marlis stared a little longer at Kevin, who merely gave her a confident smile. The questions she had for him were mounting.

" 'Item Six. For safety, all doors will be locked by midnight. Please notify management if you *must* be later coming in.' "

Marlis laid the paper down on her lap with deceptive calm. "Mrs. Dunsmore," she addressed the woman kindly, "please disregard every item on this list."

"But Mr. King—"

"—made a mistake in thinking I wanted these regulations for my inn. I shall tell the other guests."

Mrs. Dunsmore rose with a beautiful smile on her face. "And breakfast will be at the usual time?"

Marlis stood. "Yes, at eight-thirty. I know that you prefer that time."

"I do. Back home I must be up early every day. While here, I want my time to be more relaxed."

"I understand. Good night, Mrs. Dunsmore."

"Good night, Miss Kent, and thank you for making the Sunrise Inn such a special place."

When the woman had left the room, Marlis turned to Kevin. "I want to talk with you about this," she rattled the paper of instructions, "after I slip a note under each guest's door telling them to forget this rubbish—"

"Rubbish?" Kevin queried.

"Rubbish. Then I shall return to this room and you and I will talk."

Kevin pushed his glasses further up his nose. "If that's what you want, but I don't see what the problem is."

"You will," Marlis promised with deathly sweetness. "You will."

A half hour later Marlis was back. Kevin was calmly reading the day's *Wall Street Journal*.

"Are you ready?" she asked, standing squarely in front of him.

"You sound like I'm about to face a firing squad."

"What a good idea, since you have interfered where you should not have. I won't stand for it!"

With that imperturbable spirit of his that now aggravated Marlis to no end, Kevin laid down the paper and gave her his full and dispassionate attention.

"To come into another person's business and usurp her authority is the epitome of gall." Marlis ground out the words.

"I didn't usurp anything," Kevin defended himself. "We talked about every one of those points this afternoon."

"Talked about, yes. Decided that you were now running the Sunrise Inn in place of me, *no*."

"You were gone somewhere, and it was my opinion that the sooner these new rules were implemented, the sooner your bed and breakfast would be raised to the degree where it could be included in my book."

Marlis leaned toward him. "Shall I tell you what you can do with your blankety-blank book?"

Very slowly Kevin stood up, and every inch of his body and face went rigid. "No one, but no one, criticizes my work."

"Really? Then I would appreciate the same courtesy."

His eyes narrowed. "You're not in a mood to talk about this rationally."

"Sit down," Marlis ordered.

He did not move.

"Please."

He folded his arms across his chest. There was no doubting he was angry. Marlis didn't care.

"Fine. If you want to stand up, I can give it to you standing up." Marlis snapped the paper in the air as she brought it up to be read, wishing she were taller, so she wouldn't feel so much like little David accosting the giant Goliath.

"Item One. Breakfast at seven instead of eight-thirty. My guests are not dashing out to be at an office by eight o'clock. They like to retire at leisure, rise at leisure, and eat a quiet-paced meal *at eight-thirty*."

"For most people that time is too late," Kevin parried, his jaw as rigid as Marlis's. "They have to be on the road to their next destination, or they're going off on some sightseeing junket. Then there are those guests, I've noticed, who hang around the table till nearly ten o'clock."

"What's wrong with that?"

"It wastes time. Mabel can't clean up."

"She cleans up at ten o'clock. Besides, it's not as though she has to hurry to have another meal out by noon."

"True, but she's still wasting time waiting for guests to leave."

"I wouldn't call it wasting time when she's chatting with them, or," and Marlis's eyes pierced his, "giving them seconds of something they've particularly liked."

"Ah, yes, the pear almondine."

"And the cinnamon chocolate chip coffee cake?"

"Well . . ."

"The words *rush* and *hurry* are not in the vocabulary of the benefits to staying at the Sunrise Inn. Breakfast will remain at eight-thirty."

Kevin shrugged.

"Item two. Checkout time at ten instead of twelve. Why?"

"Because Amy can start cleaning the rooms earlier, and if breakfast were at seven—"

"Breakfast is at eight-thirty, and there's no need for Amy to be cleaning earlier than noon. She's always—"

"Didn't she tell you?"

"Tell me what?"

"When her husband gets home from work, he wants her there, and his supper waiting."

Marlis glared at him, waiting for a smug expression to appear. Fortunately for his health, it did not.

"Amy has said nothing to me about this."

"She was going to, but I solved the problem by letting her come in early so she can go home earlier."

"You did not solve the problem. I will not upset the routine hundreds of guests have gotten used to over the years just because a chauvinistic husband wants his supper on time. Why doesn't he cook for Amy, since he gets home sooner?"

"You'll have to ask him that. I'd be willing, if it were I."

Marlis gave him a skeptical scowl. "You would, would you?"

"Anything for love."

"Baloney." She dragged her eyes away from his. So,

he'd be willing to share responsibility for household tasks if we got married? Good grief. Marlis almost had a stroke. *I'm losing my mind if I'm thinking what it would be like to be married to Kevin King. It would no doubt consist of a daily list of instructions on how I could better pick up his socks, do his laundry, and make love to him by candlelight.*

She cleared her throat. "Items Three and Four: lights and water. I cannot regulate things like that."

"You can, because you have bills to pay." He was looking at her in a way that threatened her train of thought. Those eyes caressed with the same scintillation as his hands. For a man whose anger had been white-hot when she had dared criticize his book, he certainly had cooled down. But she hadn't. Wouldn't.

"Yes, electricity and water cost money," Marlis continued, "but my guests are paying handsomely for the privilege of being a little careless."

"I hope they appreciate your generosity. Do they know that in California we have to conserve water?"

Marlis bristled. "Don't you dare insinuate I'm insensitive to that problem."

"How long are your showers?" he asked her, imagining her standing wet and soapy and naked in one of his showers, her hair piled on top of her head, damp tendrils of it surrounding her face and trailing down her neck, her body—

"I have no idea how long my showers are," Marlis declared. 'Would you like to time one?" She knew she'd said the wrong thing the minute Kevin grinned.

Marlis resumed reading before her mind conjured up a picture of him standing naked in a tub, water cascading over muscular shoulders and chest, his hair wet and curling . . . "Item Five: luggage. Amy said you were expecting her to take the luggage out?"

"Since she's here, why not?"

"It will be too heavy."

"Have you looked at the size of your housekeeper

lately? I have no doubts she could carry me out if she wanted to."

"What an intriguing thought," Marlis mused without humor. "The problem is that Amy does not want to carry luggage out, and, therefore, Amy will not carry luggage out."

"Aren't we coddling our staff, Miss Kent?"

Marlis's eyes spit fire. "No, Mr. Kent, *I* am not coddling *my* staff. I'm merely thinking of their health. And I cannot hire a man or boy to come in and just sit around waiting for guests to check out."

"I thought it would be a nice touch. Like a European hotel."

"This is not a European hotel. Do you offer that service at your inns?"

"Yes."

"Who does it?"

"My gardeners."

Marlis grunted. "I'm the gardener here, and I'm not injuring my back carrying luggage. Neither is Amy. Item Six. Now this one is really the silliest thing I've ever heard: giving my guests a midnight curfew. They're not teenagers, for heaven's sake."

"I've noticed you don't lock your doors at night."

"The only one open is the back door. Please remember that this is a small town."

"There's no crime in Sutter Creek?"

"Not compared to Sacramento, Santa Barbara, and Huntington Beach, obviously. Look, you may have to keep everything locked tight as a drum in those big cities, but here we live differently, and I'm glad."

"You could give guests a key to let themselves in if they're going to be back late."

"I don't need to do that. I want them to feel free to come and go, as if the house is their own. Besides, it's not as though I have a huge sign by the front door that says, 'Attention Burglars: Please walk right in and take anything you like.'"

Kevin's mouth tightened across his teeth and he reached down and grabbed up his *Wall Street Journal*. "It's your inn, Miss Kent. Do what you want."

"I will, thank you, because I know what people enjoy when they come here, and I'm determined to do everything I can to make the experience pleasant for them. Now," she tore the list into several pieces and dropped it in a nearby wastebasket, "that's the end of that. It's late, and time for bed."

Kevin rose. "I agree."

They walked without speaking out of the room, up the stairs, and right to Marlis's door on the third floor.

"Your bed is not here," Marlis said, pointing to her door, her back to Kevin.

"I know, but I've made you angry, and I'm sorry. I . . . probably shouldn't have interfered."

"Probably?" Slowly she turned around and gave him an incredulous look.

"I only meant to help."

"I didn't ask you to."

"I did it because I . . . care for . . . the inn."

"The inn?"

"And certain people in it." He shrugged and gave her an innocent grin. "But the way I did it was wrong. I guess."

Marlis shook her head from side to side. "Are you apologizing or not?"

Kevin nodded yes. "Apologizing," he said.

"Accepted, then." It took a strong man who was sure of himself to admit he'd made a mistake. Her brothers weren't good at it. If Kevin was, Marlis would admire him for that.

He leaned one shoulder against the wall and dropped the paper on the floor. "You see, I have this little fault," he stated softly. "Nothing major, mind you, just a minor flaw in my character."

Marlis eyed him skeptically. "What is this minor flaw?"

He gave her a crooked smile. "I think I know everything."

She giggled.

"Don't laugh," he said, pretending hurt.

"I'm not. I'm giggling."

"It isn't funny."

"No, it isn't." She began to snicker.

"There have been a few other times when I've stuck my nose into other people's business."

"What happened?"

"They bit it off, just as you did tonight."

"But you keep doing it."

"Like I said, it's a minor flaw. I'm working on it."

"Good."

"I don't like it when I upset people," he said, and Marlis suspected he was being facetious. When his lower lip began to quiver, she knew it.

"Stop that," she demanded, fascinated at how he was able to make it move so fast. Then she started to laugh. She couldn't help it; he looked so pitiful.

"Please remember there are guests sleeping just one floor below us," he reminded her with a pompous air which made her giggle all the more. "We don't want to be rowdy, do we, Miss Kent?" When Marlis bent over, holding her sides to keep from laughing more, he quipped, "Or do we want to be rowdy?"

Unexpectedly he captured her by the shoulders, and silenced her laughter with a kiss which only lasted for a moment because she broke the kiss with more laughter.

"I really get to you, don't I?"

Marlis tried to get serious, but just couldn't. Tears were running down her cheeks.

"If I have to, I'll keep this up all night to settle you down," he promised, giving her another kiss.

"I can't help it. You're so pathetic when you quiver your lip like that."

"Pathetic? You're destroying my ego. I've been called many things by women, but never pathetic." Then he started tickling her and she yelped for him to stop, and they both forgot the people downstairs.

In desperation, Marlis opened the door to her apartment and pulled him inside where they fell into each other's arms, both laughing until they could laugh no more. He feathered her lips with light kisses until she forgot about his interference with her guests and the two seductive women who had called him on the phone. With his arms around her, and his breath gentle on her cheeks, she couldn't think of anything but how much she wanted to be the woman to this man.

"So," Kevin said after what seemed a long time, "this is the private world of Miss Marlis Kent." He released her and wandered through the combination living room and library as Marlis turned on some lights. "There must be a thousand books here," he said in awe, pulling out this volume and that from beautiful mahogany bookshelves built into the wall.

"I lost count after seven hundred," Marlis admitted. "What can I say but that I love to read."

"Are those your books downstairs in the parlor, too?"

"Yes. I was always the easiest of the four kids to buy presents for. 'Just get Marlis a book and she'll be happy—and quiet,' my dad always used to say, and still does, now that I think of it. My particular fondness is for books of the seventeen and eighteen hundreds."

"I'll remember that," Kevin said, eyeing her over his shoulder from his position in front of one of the shelves where he was examining with care a signed copy of *Gone With The Wind*. He walked past a modern couch upholstered in blue-and-rose flowers, over a white alpaca rug, to a fireplace that had a half dozen framed pictures on the mantel. "Which one is your boyfriend?" he asked, peering at various members of her family posing at significant moments in their lives.

"I don't have anyone at the moment," Marlis admitted honestly, "which I'm sure Mabel told you."

"She did, but I find that hard to believe."

He moved to a sophisticated stereo system, picked out an instrumental tape from a glassed-in shelf of cassettes, and turned the machine on, slipping the tape into place. Soft violins drifted through the room. "Can we turn off some of these lights?" he asked, giving Marlis a long, smoldering look.

When she did not move to do so, he did it himself, then walked to her, took her hand, and put his arm around her waist, leading her into a slow dance.

"Do you always just make yourself at home in a woman's apartment?" Marlis questioned.

"Always."

Marlis remembered the sultry voices of Amanda Stuart and Susan Roberts. Since he knew she didn't have a man in her life, she felt it only fair to find out about those two women, and any others who might be panting for him from one end of California to the other. "Are there any particular women in those apartments where you make yourself at home?"

"No" came the straightforward answer that took Marlis by surprise. She had thought he would be coy with her, make her work to get him to confess that he was seeing at least two other women besides her.

"That's surprising," she said, "since two of your fan club have called here."

Now he was the surprised one, as he whirled her around in a circle. "Oh, you mean Amanda and Susan?"

"Are those their names? I'd forgotten," Marlis lied, to which lie he chuckled.

"No, you didn't forget their names," he said, moving her hair away from her face with his nose and nuzzling her earlobe. "You're jealous and want to know how serious the competition is."

Marlis was embarrassed but wouldn't let him know it. "I have no ties to you, Mr. King, nor interest in your women." The lovely strains of the music drifted over them as his arm tightened and their bodies moved as one.

"Is that right? Why did you ask about Amanda and Susan then?"

"Idle curiosity. Let's talk about something else."

"All right." Kevin leaned over and turned off another of the lamps. There was only one now that was casting a gossamer veil of light over the tasteful furnishings of Marlis's apartment. "Let's talk about falling in love."

They had danced the length of the living room and were now at the door of Marlis's bedroom which was wide and open. Kevin led her through it. It was a small room, taken up mostly by a double bed, two nightstands, and a blue upholstered chaise with a book lying on the end and a floor lamp beside it.

"Let's talk about the very, very private world of Marlis Kent," he whispered in her ear, scooping her effortlessly off the floor into his arms and dancing with her that way for a minute, his lips finding hers, her arms loosely clasped around his neck.

Their response to each other kindled familiar hungers in them both. Kevin gently lowered Marlis onto the bed where her hair fell away from her face and lay over the comforter like a shimmering blond crown. She could hardly breathe, and her lips slowly opened as she waited for Kevin's next kiss and the arousing feel of his body on hers. She had never slept with a man, and she wouldn't sleep with Kevin now, but she yearned for just another moment or two of the blissful intimacy he had created for them.

Kevin stood beside the bed looking down at her, wanting her, aching for her. She was so beautiful, so vulnerable, and he was a man, after all, with a man's desires. But he was also aware of feelings that told him this was not the right time, or place. He gazed down at her, soft and feminine, her eyes and body expectant of his touch. Why was he hesitating?

Marlis's heart beat faster in anticipation of his touch. He would bring her alive. He would start a flame that she longed for, but was afraid of. He, and only he, made her vibrantly aware of her womanhood. Was this how it felt when you found the man you could love forever? she wondered. Her eyes melted into his. *Touch me*, hers invited. But his touch never came.

With a slow shake of his head, Kevin whispered, "Now is not the time, my love," and he turned on his heels and strode from the room. Rising onto her elbows in surprise at her deprivation, Marlis heard the door of her apartment slam shut. Not just close, but slam. She was greatly disappointed—and relieved.

Marlis looked up into the sky and frowned. The white puffy clouds of the past few days had turned gray with moisture and threatened rain. "I'd better fix those leaks around the vent pipes on the roof," she announced to the nearby shrubbery.

After she changed into bright-red shorts and a pretty matching polo shirt, she lugged the sixteen-foot aluminum ladder out of the garage and was struggling to carry it across the side lawn when Kevin came along.

"Here, let me help," he offered.

"Gladly," Marlis agreed. "That thing is awkward."

Their eyes met, and questions danced silently between them. *Why did you leave so suddenly?* her jade-jeweled eyes asked. *Do you know why I left you?* his darkened blue eyes asked. There were guests about, so they could not speak then of the unfulfilled intimacy, and Marlis had to be content to admire his trim and muscled body in a red and black short-sleeved shirt and black slacks, sharply creased, that hung over slim hips and strong legs to his soft leather loafers.

They reached the back of the house, away from people. "Where do you want this thing," he asked, "and what are you doing with it?"

"Right here will be fine." Marlis pointed to where she wanted the ladder leaned against the house. "I have to caulk three vent pipes. We had some leaking the last time it rained."

"You're doing it yourself?"

"Sure, why not?"

"It just isn't your typical female way to spend a morning."

Marlis threw him a grin. "I thought you knew by now that I'm not your typical female." She extended the ladder until it reached two feet over the roofline and tested its position to be sure it was braced properly. When she turned around, Kevin was an inch behind her, leaning forward, extending his arms past her to grasp the ladder, which imprisoned her against the cold metal.

"If anyone knows you're not typical, it's me," he said in a low, rumbling voice. "Every day you surprise me with some new facet I haven't seen before."

"I hope that's good and not bad," Marlis remarked as his mouth descended to hers.

"Mmm." Kevin murmured. "Kissing you at the beginning of the day is almost as nice as kissing you at the end of it. Uh, about last night, Marlis—"

"You were playing the gentleman?" She laid her hand momentarily on his cheek.

"Or the fool? You were so tempting, so desirable, there on the bed. But I can't promise if there's another night of soft lights and romantic music that I'll walk away. Consider yourself warned."

"I'll be careful." *But it won't be easy,* she could have told him. She'd been sorely tempted herself to give in to feelings that were new to her, and almost overpowering. Of course, it was her own fault that she'd let things go as far as they had. She shouldn't have let him create such a mood in her apartment with the music and the lights, and she never should have let him into her bedroom. Easier said than done, though, for Kevin was not a man a woman wanted to say no to.

Now that her mind was clearer than it had been while in his arms the night before, she recalled that he never did explain to her what Amanda Stuart and Susan Roberts meant to him.

"I have work to do," she said, gently pushing him away, but not before he had taken a kiss that sent her blood throbbing.

"Let me do that for you. It doesn't seem right for you to be teetering on a roof, ready to fall off."

Marlis grunted. "I don't teeter, Kevin King, and I've never fallen off a roof yet." She pulled a putty knife from a slot on the tool belt she was wearing and used it to open the quart can of black caulking paste.

Kevin looked up to the darkening clouds. "That caulking needs twelve hours to dry. I hope you get it done in time."

"I will if a certain someone will go away and not keep me from my appointed task."

"Are you sure I can't do that for you? That roof is a long ways up there."

"Have you ever caulked before?"

"No."

"Then let me at it. I'm sure you have something more interesting to do." She started up the ladder.

"Well, I was thinking of talking with Mabel about the menus."

Marlis stopped and turned with a start, her alert system registering DANGER.

"While what she cooks is excellent," Kevin went on, "she needs to consider the people who are on low cholesterol diets."

"Kevin, please, don't talk to Mabel," Marlis pleaded. "Or to Amy. Or to anyone, for that matter." She climbed again.

"Speaking of Amy, did you call her last night to tell her she didn't need to come in at ten o'clock."

"No, I forgot."

"It's just as well if she gets here early. There are a few things I want to talk with her about."

"Kevin, no." Marlis turned again from her perch ten feet off the ground. "If there's anything you're questioning, talk with me about it."

"It's nothing earth-shattering, Marlis. I noticed Amy uses some cleanser that is too abrasive for most sinks and countertops. I can recommend some wonderful stuff my housekeepers use."

"No, not one word to Amy unless I'm in the room." She went higher.

"You don't trust me." He sounded wounded. "Don't worry, love, I won't make any major policy changes while you're incommunicado on the roof."

"Nor minor ones, either. No changes at all. Promise?"

"Will you watch what you're doing. You're wiggling all over that ladder."

"Don't talk to me then about changes."

"Okay. Oh, there's Amy now. I'll be back in a minute to keep you company."

Kevin strode toward the approaching housekeeper and Marlis whirled around on the ladder to face the other way so she could see them. "Kevin King, don't you dare . . ."

That's when her inattention caused her right foot to slip off the rung and her left one to get caught under it. Losing her balance, she grabbed frantically with her hands for a hold, but she missed.

"Kevinnn!" she screamed, as she plummeted to the ground.

ELEVEN

Kevin spun around just as Marlis hit the ground. Her head bounced against the side of the ladder and she collapsed like a rag doll tossed out a window.

"Marlis! Marlis!" he yelled, frantic, sprinting to her faster than he'd ever run before and skidding onto his knees.

There was blood on her forehead and her legs were twisted under her in a bizarre way that made him fear one or both of them was broken. She appeared to be unconscious, as her eyes were closed. He didn't move her.

"Marlis. My darling Marlis. Speak to me, sweetheart."

With agonizing slowness, Marlis's eyelids fluttered, then opened.

"Kevin," she whispered. Then her face contorted in a grimace of pain.

"Amy, call the paramedics, nine-one-one," he yelled. "Then bring me a blanket."

The astonished housekeeper ran to obey.

"You'll be okay, honey, you will," he said to Marlis as he took out his handkerchief and pressed it against the cut on her head to staunch the flow of blood. It was hard to resist the temptation to lay her out flat on the ground and cradle her head in his lap, but he knew that if there were any bones broken, to move her might mean they would puncture a vein, an artery, or a muscle. "Help is on the way, sweetheart. Soon. Soon."

Amy dashed up with the blanket and helped Kevin drape it around Marlis. "The paramedics are on the way," she said, in tears. She bent down to look at Marlis. "Is she hurt bad?"

"I don't know." Kevin lifted his handkerchief away from the wound and found it was still bleeding.

"Kevin." Marlis's calling of his name was barely audible, and she started to move.

"Lie still, darling. Please don't move."

Marlis obeyed, except for her hand, which found one of Kevin's and squeezed it so hard it almost hurt him.

Oh, dear God, he prayed, *please let her be all right*. To see her like this, defenseless, hurting, made him feel pain, too. There were times when he'd thought she was too strong and independent for her own good, wanting to do everything herself, not knowing when to lean on others, like him. Now he would have given anything to see her so again, scrapping with him over this principle or that, scrambling up and down the ladder, caulking the whole darned house if she wanted to.

The medics arrived in three minutes, examined Marlis carefully, and moved her onto a gurney for transporting to the hospital in Jackson, the county seat, four miles away.

"It doesn't appear that she has any broken bones," one of the men told Kevin and Amy, "but X-rays will tell us for sure. She'll need stitches for the cut on her head."

Kevin told Amy to stay at the inn to take care of things. "Call Marlis's family," he instructed, then followed the paramedics in his car.

In the waiting room, while Marlis was being examined, Kevin paced and drank coffee, drank coffee and paced. He was angry with himself for having distracted her and making her fall, angry at Marlis for doing the kind of work that would take her up on a high ladder, and most of all angry because there was nothing he could do at that moment to help her but pray. And that he did, in a small chapel down the hall.

The waiting drove him crazy. He was a man used to making things happen. Now, when someone important to him needed help, he was not the one who could give that help to her.

Marlis's brother, Willy, and her sister, Sondra, arrived and joined Kevin in pacing and drinking coffee. When they were informed that Marlis had been taken from Emergency to a regular room, Kevin hung back, letting her family see her first, then he went in.

At first glance he saw that both her ankles were bandaged and at her right temple there were three or four ugly-looking stitches. But she didn't look so deathly pale, which was a good sign, and she was smiling.

"How you doing?" he asked, wanting desperately to take her in his arms and hold her forever, never ever letting anything like this happen to her again, but afraid to until he knew she was all right.

"I'll live," Marlis said weakly, holding out her left hand to him, which he took as he sank down in a chair beside the bed.

"How's the head?"

"The doctor says I have a slight concussion, but it's not serious. The cut will heal nicely, he promised. I do have to stay here overnight, though, for observation."

Kevin's eyes traveled down her body to the gauze bandages.

"Two sprained ankles," she informed him, reading his thoughts.

"Two?"

"Yes, but fortunately no broken bones."

He sighed with relief. "You came out of that accident pretty darn good."

"I know. Lucky for me you were there to take care of me."

Kevin's jaw tightened. "Maybe not so lucky, Marlis. If it hadn't been for me, you wouldn't be lying here now."

"Kevin, don't blame yourself. It was my own carelessness. I've been climbing ladders since I was five, and this is the first time I've fallen. I was overdue, I'd say."

Kevin pressed her hand to his lips. "I'm so very, very sorry, Marlis. What can I do to help?"

At her sudden grin, he held up both hands, as if to back off. "Don't say a word. I know what you're thinking: the last thing you need right now is my help, when you're flat on your back and can't stop me from making trouble. I should get as far out of your life as possible." Swiftly he rose to his feet and was at the door of the room before Marlis was able to call out his name.

"Kevin, don't leave me."

He stopped, but didn't turn.

"I need you," she said.

He spun around and saw the tears in her eyes, and in a second he was across the room, burying his head in her shoulder, his face lost in the fullness of her tangled hair. "I'll stay as long as you want me to," he said, thankful that his prayer had been answered and that she would be all right. And then he kissed her so gently on the lips it was, to Marlis, like an evening breeze stirring slightly as it passed by.

"The doctor is going to release me tomorrow," she told him, "but I won't be able to get around by myself because my ankles are too weak to use crutches. I have to stay off them as much as possible for four or five days." She managed a little smile. "Could I interest you in a temporary job?"

"Doing what?"

"Carrying me around the house. I need your muscles."

Kevin grinned. "I always knew those workouts at the gym would come in handy some day. What does this job pay?"

"Room and board?"

"Mmm . . ." he contemplated. "Not enough."

"How about the everlasting gratitude of the patient?"

"You're getting closer." To Marlis's look of puzzlement he said, "It's a word that starts with L."

Love? Marlis knew exactly what he meant. He wanted her to say she loved him, and she did, for a whole lot of reasons. She also was afraid to say so, for a whole lot of other reasons, two of which were named Amanda and Susan.

"If you don't have the time, Kevin, to do this," she said, choosing not to tell him what he wanted to hear, "I mean, with your writing and your B&B's, I'll understand."

"To help you in a way you really want. I'll stop my world if necessary."

"Oh, Kevin, thank you." Then she winced.

"Are you in pain?" he asked with great concern, starting this way and that. "Should I call the doctor? Do you need water? Is it too hot in here? Too cold?"

Marlis was laughing. "Kevin, stop. It hurts to laugh."

He sank down in the chair beside the bed. "It does me good, though. You scared the heck out of me, lady, when you did your flying trapeze act off that ladder."

"I scared myself," Marlis admitted, yawning. "My ankles are throbbing, but the doctor's given me some pain medication which should take effect soon."

"I'd better leave then."

Marlis held out a hand. "Not until you answer my question: Will you stay?"

Kevin's face relaxed for the first time since he'd entered the room. "Do you think we can get along in this situation for four or five days?"

"Probably not, but I don't have much to choose from. My brother, Bob, is recovering from surgery. My other brother, Willy, is going out of town on business tomorrow. Neither Amy nor Mabel is strong enough . . ."

"I get the picture. What about Steve Alexander?"

Marlis shook her head back and forth. "He's more used to toting mushrooms and asparagus spears than crippled ladies, I'm afraid." Her eyes grew serious. "You're the one I need, big guy."

Kevin beamed. "Well, then, I guess you're stuck with Kevin King's Carting Service."

Marlis grasped his nearest hand. Her eyes were soft with feelings. "I truly will be grateful, Kevin. More than I can tell you."

"Good enough," he said, giving her hand a squeeze. "Tomorrow I'll take you home, and for as long as you need me I'll be your humble servant."

"Humble servant?" Marlis chortled. "That will be the day."

He leaned over and kissed her on the cheek. "You have a few days to boss me around, lady, but after that, it's a different ball game."

"Okay. And Kevin?"

"Yeah?"

"Just be sure my inn, my employees, and my guests are all still there when I get home tomorrow."

"Sure." He blew her a kiss from the door and was gone.

Kevin brought Marlis home from the hospital the next morning, and that's when the trouble began. "I'm going to take care of everything while you're off your feet," he insisted.

A warning bell clanged in her brain and Marlis struggled to sit up on her bed where Kevin had brought her.

"I'm not asking you to do my work for me," she said.

"I know, but I'm offering."

"But if you carry me downstairs later, I can sit at the desk—"

"The doctor gave me strict orders to make you rest today. No sitting at a desk for Marlis Kent. If you're a good girl, tomorrow I'll take you downstairs, if you really want to, but only to sit in the parlor and read one of those hundreds of books of yours. You're getting over a concussion, remember?"

Big, gentle hands eased her back onto the pillows he had fluffed for her. "And don't look up at me with those beseeching green eyes. I cannot be seduced into giving you special privileges. Of course, if you really want to try . . ."

"Oh, Kevin," Marlis giggled, "you're so good for me."

His eyes twinkled. "It certainly took you long enough to realize that." He leaned over and kissed her forehead. "Get some sleep, honey. I'll bring your lunch up later. Any special requests for Mabel?"

"Whatever she has will be fine."

"What about dinner? I'm cooking. Seems to me I owe you a meal I reneged on recently."

"So you do. Well, then, make it chateaubriand."

Kevin coughed. "Anything else?"

"Caesar salad with honey mustard dressing, warm oatmeal muffins, and homemade apple pie for dessert."

"I knew you'd be a bossy little thing."

"Too late to back out now. You hired on for the duration."

Kevin got serious. "Yes, I did, and don't you forget that."

They stared at each other for some time, each considering what that meant—the duration.

He got her a cup of water from the bathroom so she could take her pain pill, and also brought a damp cloth which he placed gently on her forehead and eyes. "Don't worry about the inn, Marlis, I'm going to take care of everything for you."

All the worry buttons in Marlis's system kicked into action at once. Having Kevin in charge of the Sunrise Inn was like a mother turning over her precious child to Godzilla. The man, no doubt, would come up with a four-page list, single spaced, by three o'clock, of things that needed correcting.

As if reading her thoughts, Kevin called out from the

door, "Stop worrying. I know how to run a bed and breakfast. There's nothing to it."

It was the pounding on a door later in the day that awoke Marlis from a lovely dream in which she was windsailing with Kevin in Hawaii. She couldn't determine exactly what door it was, but she did know it wasn't hers.

Oh, well, she told herself. *Not to worry. Kevin will see to it.* She fell asleep soon after.

Dinner that night was an unbelievable surprise: Kevin had fixed everything she'd requested, right down to the honey mustard dressing. "I was only kidding about the menu," she said, consumed with guilt at all the trouble he had gone to for her.

"Now you tell me," he replied. "As a loyal employee, I thought I was supposed to obey the boss to the letter."

"Did you cook the chateaubriand yourself?" she asked, still not able to believe the gourmet meal that sat on the tray on her lap and suspecting it came from Steve Alexander.

"Of course. One of my many talents is in the kitchen."

Marlis giggled. "I know. I've seen you eat."

"That's not nice," Kevin responded.

"No, it isn't, and I do apologize. But, honestly, Kevin, I was expecting peanut butter sandwiches, not . . ." she gestured toward her picturesque plates, "this masterpiece."

Marlis took a bite of the tender beef covered in a delectable béarnaise sauce and ran her tongue around her lips in appreciation of its delicious taste. Then she tried the salad, the muffin, and even a forkful of the apple pie.

"You should open your own restaurant," she told him with enthusiasm.

"I can't. I have too important a job carrying around the beautiful owner of a bed-and-breakfast inn in Sutter Creek."

Marlis snickered. "I see. Oh, by the way, I heard some

pounding this afternoon, or was it this morning? Anyway, what was it?"

"Have some more salad," Kevin offered, ignoring her question.

"Thank you. Kevin, what was that pounding?"

"Nothing to worry about. Mr. Germane broke his key off in the lock which, by the way, brings up an interesting contradiction. You say you're not concerned about leaving a door to the inn open at night, but you give your guests a key to lock their rooms."

"Most people are uncomfortable about leaving their personal belongings in a room they cannot lock."

"And you don't think it would bother them to know the house itself is unlocked?"

She gave him a look of resignation. "You think I'm foolish to leave it open, don't you?"

"Yes, I do. Times are changing, Marlis. In my opinion you're asking for trouble leaving the back door unlocked."

"You're probably right. I'll think seriously about what to do. Back, though, to Mr. Germane. Did you call the locksmith? If I'd been up, I would have handled it myself, but we have an excellent man here in town."

"I decided to save you some money by taking the lock off the door and delivering it to him. He'd have charged an arm and a leg to come to the house."

"That's true. So how did it go?"

"Fine."

Marlis eyed him with skepticism. "I don't like that word fine."

"What's wrong with it?"

"It sounds like something should come after it. Fine, but . . ."

"Well . . ."

"Oh, no. You had trouble getting the lock off."

"A little trouble, yes."

"How little?"

Kevin cleared his throat. "There are a few scratches . . ."

"Scratches?"

"The screwdriver slipped."

"Scratches in my two-thousand-dollar door? I purchased that from a house in Gettysburg where Abraham Lincoln once stayed, you know."

"It's unique all right, and not made like any door I've ever worked with. That's why I got a few gouges in it, too—"

"Gouges?"

"I had to pry the door open."

"But I heard pounding."

"Prying didn't do the whole job. I had to pound."

Marlis put down her fork. "I'm not hungry anymore."

The next day, the system worked pretty well: Amy, who'd magnanimously volunteered, helped Marlis get to the bathroom for her more intimate needs. Marlis leaned heavily on her, putting as little weight as possible on her two injured ankles, but Kevin did the other moving around, which consisted mostly of going from the bedroom to the living room of Marlis's apartment and back to the bedroom.

Marlis, who'd thought she'd be good as new after a long night's rest, found that not to be the case.

"I guess I'm not Superwoman," she told Kevin, as he scooped her off her bed after a midafternoon nap and carried her effortlessly into her living room where he had a bone-china cup filled with her favorite coffee and some of Mabel's famous chocolate brownie cookies waiting.

It felt wonderful being in his arms, Marlis admitted to herself, so she decided to be a willing patient and make full use of Kevin's athletic strength.

When they came to the couch, instead of setting Marlis on it, Kevin sat down and kept her on his lap. "Have I told you today how much I'm enjoying this job?" he asked her, lowering his mouth to hers.

"That's surprising since it doesn't pay much," Marlis answered.

"You're right, boss, the pay is lousy, but the benefits

are first class." He smiled warmly and with the back of one hand, caressed the curve of her cheek and the straight plane of her nose, ending with two fingers brushing across the fullness of first her upper lip and then the lower. "Yes," he breathed deeply, settling her more comfortably in the circle of his arms, "definitely first class." He kissed her again and wondered if he'd ever get tired of doing so.

Marlis laid one of her hands on the muscle of his arm that draped over the front of her, and then that hand traveled over his rough, hairy skin, from shoulder to wrist, which brought a sharp intake of his breath.

"Unless you want to be taken back to the bedroom, boss lady, you'd better keep your hands to yourself."

"Is that what you really want?" Marlis's voice was husky.

"No," Kevin murmured, "but now isn't the time to tell you what I do want and plan to get."

"Do I have a say in this?" She played with a lock of his hair above one of his ears.

"Sure, but I know you want the same thing."

"How do you know that?"

"Because of the way you respond when I do this," and he bent over her and kissed her mouth a half dozen times before taking it in earnest and tenderly exploring its interior with his searching tongue.

Marlis was intoxicated with him—his tenderness and his strength. His consideration of her was patient and intuitive, and she found herself more and more thinking of all the positive aspects of his dynamic personality and putting aside the negative.

"I feel guilty taking you away from your work," she said with the greatest sincerity, although she did not know what she would have done had he not been willing to stay.

"Don't worry, love, you'll receive a bill for services rendered." He playfully roughed up her hair.

"And will I be able to pay it?"

"Oh, yes," he assured her, "you'll find it very easy."

As he started to kiss her again, Marlis cleared her throat and said, "My coffee is getting cold."

"So it is," Kevin agreed, and went right on kissing her until the telephone rang and he had to get up to answer it. It was Marlis's sister, Sondra, and Kevin left the apartment so the two girls could talk.

Fortunately, for Marlis's mental healing, there were no crises at the inn that day for Kevin to handle in his own inimitable way. But on the second morning, as Kevin was carrying her downstairs so she could work in her office for an hour or so, he stepped on a skateboard in the foyer and nearly sent them both crashing into the grandfather clock. Only an incredible ballet of balance kept Kevin on his feet, with Marlis clinging to him in horrified fear.

"Where did that board come from?" Marlis gasped, once they were safely in her office and Kevin had deposited her in her chair.

"It belongs to that Jorgansen boy," Kevin fumed. "You really shouldn't allow children here, you know."

"I don't if they're younger than sixteen," she told him.

Kevin threw himself with a weary sigh on another chair nearby. "Then why did the Jorgensens bring that ten-year-old terror with them?"

"I have no idea."

"I let him stay because they had a reservation. I assumed from that, you knew he was coming."

"I didn't. Is he a problem?"

"Not unless you count riding his bicycle as fast as he can along the path around the house and almost knocking down people. I've had three complaints already."

"Oh, dear. Keep an eye on him, Kevin."

"I intend to." Then he smiled, not wanting Marlis to worry. "I'm bigger than he is, so there won't be any trouble."

After Marlis worked on bills for a while, Kevin moved her into the parlor. "I want you here on this sofa, with your legs stretched out, reading your favorite book."

"Yes, sir."

"And no arguments."

"No arguments."

"Dr. King knows best."

Marlis giggled. "I believe he does," and she poured herself a cup of herb tea he had thoughtfully brought and placed on a small table beside her, along with a bell to ring if she should need him.

"You're spoiling me," she told him with appreciation dancing from her vibrant eyes.

"You ain't seen nothin', boss," Kevin promised, and Marlis settled herself comfortably on the couch and thoroughly enjoyed her reading until Kevin brought her her lunch. He had a complaint.

"Mabel will have to be dealt with."

"Oh?"

"I tried to talk with her about using less salt in her recipes."

"I was going to do that, too."

"I should have let you. When I offered to send her some recipes a doctor friend of mine has made up, she almost threw waffle batter at me. Ordered me out of her kitchen saying you never interfered with a true chef at work, which I suppose she meant was herself."

"Mabel is very touchy about her cooking. I'm surprised she got upset with you, though. She's your biggest fan."

"Only as long as I'm praising her, I guess. The woman is definitely unable to take constructive criticism."

"Cooks are sensitive people. One has to handle them carefully."

"Oh? I never have trouble with the people who cook at my inns."

"You're very fortunate." Marlis made a vow to visit all three of Kevin King's bed-and-breakfast inns. She just had to see how "perfect" inns were run.

* * *

A man's voice shouting startled Marlis a half hour later. She heard Kevin's voice, too, but his wasn't angry. The disturbance kept on for some minutes.

"What was all that shouting about?" she asked him when he came to carry her back to her apartment and keep her company for a while.

"How do you like the name Rory Bruiser for a professional football player?"

"Fitting, I'd say. He's a linebacker with the Dallas Cowboys. Is he the one who was yelling?"

"Yes."

"Why?"

"Would you like to have your hair brushed?" Kevin asked, clumsily trying to change the focus of the conversation.

"I can do that myself later. Why was Rory Bruiser yelling?"

"But I'd like to do it," Kevin insisted, walking over to the dresser and bringing back a silver-handled brush. "Is this an antique?"

"Yes, from an antebellum mansion in Natchez. It's been brushing women's hair for over a hundred years. Now tell me about Rory Bruiser."

"Let's see how it works. He's not worth discussing."

With surprising gentleness, Kevin worked through the tangles in Marlis's hair. "I can't believe how soft your hair is," he said. "And it's the color of pure gold." He stopped brushing and just ran his fingers among the mass of waves. Then he turned Marlis's head toward him, kissed her, and finished his task.

After he put the brush away, Marlis asked him, "Weren't you going to tell me something about Rory Bruiser?"

Kevin pulled up a straight chair from a small desk close to the sofa and sat on it backward, leaning his arms over its back as he eyed her.

"Has he stayed here before?"

"No. He just got married, and the Sunrise Inn was

recommended by a teammate of his who comes here every spring.''

"So you've never seen his wife, Angel?''

"No. What's she like?''

Kevin whistled and looked up at the ceiling. "On a scale of one to ten I'd say about a twelve and a half.''

"That good, huh?'' She wasn't jealous, Marlis told herself as she remembered the only concession she had made to her beauty that day had been to apply a little mascara and lipstick.

"She's a model, for lingerie,'' Kevin said.

"I hope she's keeping dressed while she's here.''

"I hope so, too, because her husband is one jealous man.''

"Who told you that?''

"No one told me. I just about got my jaw broken for messing around with his wife.''

"Kevin.''

"She's a flake, that woman. This morning she called downstairs to the desk to ask if I could open her suitcase. The lock was stuck.''

"Where was Rory?''

"Out getting some aspirin for a headache Angel had. So, I went up to her room and got the bag open for her. Then, not long ago, she called to say she needed help getting her necklace on. Once again, Rory was off somewhere. So I went up, leaving the door open. I'm not stupid. She brought out this long gold chain with a tiny clasp, impossible for her to handle with those long claws she calls nails.''

Marlis smiled.

"On the end of the chain was this huge green emerald, and when I draped the necklace around her neck, it fell right between . . . uh . . . in the center of . . .'' He made gestures that Marlis understood.

"So you got the necklace in place and were ogling her when Rory came back.''

"I wasn't ogling her.''

"But Rory thought you were."

"He got the wrong idea and nearly slugged me."

"That's what the shouting was I heard?"

"Yes. Angel just stood there and let me defend myself against her two-hundred-forty-pound husband."

"But he believed you?"

"Finally, when I told him he had nothing to worry about. That I was going to marry you."

Marlis gulped. "What made you say a ridiculous thing like that?"

"Because, Marlis darling," Kevin leaned over and deposited a long, sensuous kiss on her mouth, "that is exactly what I am going to do."

_____ TWELVE _____

The next afternoon, Marlis was writing letters in the gazebo, enjoying the balmy spring air. Rather, she was *trying* to write letters. Kevin's declaration of his intention to marry her kept playing through her thoughts like a scratchy, broken record.

Marry him? Was he serious? Whereas yesterday she had thought only of his good qualities, today, for some reason, she was dwelling on the bad ones.

Marry him? With all his quirky faults? His compulsion to run everything *his way*? Oh, sure, he liked helping her, and he could be kind and considerate, and they kissed well together, and sparks flew when they touched, *but* they argued with just as much passion. Could she put up with that for fifty years?

The man of her thoughts materialized by her side. "Monster Boy is at it again," he declared with undisguised frustration.

"Oh, no."

"That ten-year-old tyrant plays his music on a cassette player and turns it up so loud it splits your eardrums."

If Marlis did not know that Kevin King never lost his cool, she would swear he was chilling rapidly over this

181

child. "I heard that awful music awhile ago and was going to ask you about it," she said, deciding not to remind him of his previous assertion that because he was bigger than the boy, there would be no trouble. "Is he doing anything else?" she asked.

"Only painting heat registers."

"What?"

"Actually, only one. I decided to paint another room for you on the first floor."

"Oh, you shouldn't have done that." Marlis was touched.

"Yes, I should have. The room needed it, and I don't want you anywhere near a ladder for the next hundred years."

How wonderfully protective he is, Marlis thought. *That makes up some for his also being stubborn. I wonder if now is a good time to ask him if he was joking when he said he was going to marry me?*

"I was only gone for five minutes," Kevin went on, "to accept a package downstairs from the postman that needed a signature. When I got back, the little monster had painted one of the heat registers in the hallway and still had brush in hand when I caught him. Believe me, I gave him a talking to, until his mother came along and chewed me out royally for being angry with her darling." Kevin leaned back and stretched his legs out, crossing his ankles. "I'm afraid I've lost you a customer."

Marlis cocked her head and studied him for a moment with sympathy. "Some are better off lost. You're having a rough time, aren't you?"

"I wouldn't say rough. Just a few minor inconveniences."

"But you're handling them?"

"Sure. Didn't I say I would?"

"Yes, you did."

*   *   *

It was the fourth day after her accident and Marlis was feeling much better. That afternoon she had an appointment with the doctor who would tell her whether or not she was ready for crutches. She hoped so, although she was a little concerned about climbing all those stairs to her room.

She had to admit she would miss being carried about by Kevin. When his arms were around her, she felt safe and secure—like she was exactly where she ought to be.

He was surprising her with his patient care, cheerfully doing what needed to be done, and even accepting with humor any problems that cropped up. The cases of Rory Bruiser and the boy painter had been exceptions.

Both Amy and Mabel were solicitous of her condition and Marlis appreciated their concern. It was funny, though, that whenever she brought up Kevin's name, both of them would not talk about him, but would, instead, stare down at the floor and not look her in the eye. Something was going on between the three of them, she began to suspect.

Marlis was sitting on a white wicker chair out on the grass, near a circular garden of delicate bearded iris which bobbed in lavender splendor in the playful breeze that was cooling the rather warm day. She felt wonderful; marvelous, actually. Amy had washed, blown dry, and curled her hair that morning and she was wearing a pale turquoise jumpsuit she'd bought a month before but hadn't had a chance to wear, until today.

Marlis's eyes drifted away from the magazine she had been enjoying, and up to the marshmallow-clouded sky. While she was anxious to get back on her own two feet, instead of being carried everywhere like a helpless lump of potatoes, she knew she would miss the companionship of one Kevin King. He'd spent a lot of time with her, away from his work, so she was sure he'd be anxious to be on the road again, even though he had made that unbelievable statement that he was going to marry her.

Had he meant it?

"Do you really want to marry me?" she imagined herself saying to him.

"Of course I do, darling. I adore you. I can't live without you."

"Then why haven't you pestered me for an answer? Wouldn't a man in love do that? But you haven't. Is it because you don't really want to marry me and you only said you did to Rory Bruiser so that he wouldn't wrap you around the nearest goalposts?"

"Well, yes, honey, you figured it out. I don't want to marry you. You're too stubborn and opinionated and independent for me."

Marlis slammed the magazine shut with a huff. *Fine,* she thought, *if he doesn't want to marry me, then I certainly don't want to marry him, either. He's too stubborn and opinionated for me.*

The sudden yelling coming from the open window of Rory and Angel Bruiser's room made Marlis sit straight up. There was quite a row going on here, but it wasn't between the football player and his model wife. Kevin's voice came through loud and clear.

Oh no, Marlis thought with dismay, *now what's happening?*

She found out fifteen minutes later when Rory Bruiser himself came to her.

"Who is this King fella? Is he part owner? Handyman? Your lover enjoying a free handout?"

"He is a famous writer," Marlis felt compelled to defend Kevin, "kindly helping me for a few days until I get back on my feet."

With a grunt that sounded like he had just been hit by an opposing player, Rory declared, "Then you'd better tell the guy to go write while he still has two hands to do it with, and stay away from my wife."

Marlis gulped. "Do you have a complaint, Mr. Bruiser?"

By the time Rory was finished, Marlis was barely able to keep from laughing out loud and could hardly wait to hear Kevin's version.

"Tell me about your shower with Angel Bruiser," she said to him with a straight face later, when he brought her some lunch on a pretty white wicker tray that matched the chair in which she was sitting.

Kevin gave her such a disgusted look she couldn't keep a wee grin from curving the corners of her mouth.

"Who told you about it?"

"The injured husband, Rory Bruiser himself. Just an hour ago. He was ready to use your head for a football. Only my reassurance that you were a new, overly enthusiastic employee without much experience, or common sense I had to add, made him promise not to squash your insides and check out immediately."

"That wife of his has a problem."

"Does she?"

Kevin gawked at her. "Well, you didn't believe him, did you?"

"Tell me your version. Then I'll decide."

Kevin began gesturing dramatically and pacing back and forth in front of her. His cool, unflappable nature was hot and flapping, and Marlis coudln't have been more amused or anxious to hear his accounting of what had transpired.

"Rory was on his way out to buy some cold pills for Angel when he saw me in the foyer by the desk and complained that the shower door in his bathroom was sticking."

Marlis gave Kevin a sweet, attentive smile. "And how were you to know when you went to fix it sometime later that Angel was taking a shower?"

"Exactly." Kevin's mouth twitched. Marlis had never seen it do that before. Maybe it only did when he was trying to defend himself. "I didn't even see her," he explained. "I just barged into the room, yanked open the shower door, which wasn't stuck all that much, and there she was."

"In all her glory."

Kevin swallowed and, incredibly, looked embarrassed. "She has a lot of glory."

"Does she? At which exact moment her husband walked in."

"Yes."

"And saw you gawking at his wife . . ."

"I wouldn't exactly call it gawking."

"What would you call it."

A pause. "Looking."

"Simply looking? Or was your tongue hanging out and your breathing ragged?"

Kevin stopped pacing and leaned over to glare at her. "You're enjoying this, aren't you?" he boomed.

"Enjoying what?" Marlis asked innocently.

"Putting me through the wringer because of this silly misunderstanding."

"It wasn't a silly misunderstanding to Rory Bruiser. He thought you were about to rape his wife—"

"Rape?" Kevin exploded.

"Or at best, an attempted seduction."

"The man's a loon."

"He's in love with his wife, and protective of her. What's wrong with that?"

Kevin flung himself into a chair beside Marlis and stared at her with a dangerous glint in those diamond-blue orbs. "Nothing's wrong with that. Love makes a man do crazy things. Finish your lunch, Marlis. We have to go."

"Go where?"

"To the doctor's for an examination. Remember?"

"You're right. How could I have forgotten? It must have been the excitement over the Angel Bruiser episode."

Kevin made a low, growling noise in his throat, accompanied by some words Marlis could not quite make out but fully understood.

"Just think," she said with enthusiasm, "in a few hours I might be walking again, by myself."

"Then you won't need me."

"That's right."

The doctor said Marlis could try the crutches, "but only for a few hours a day, to start."

"I'll have to stick around awhile then," Kevin told her on the way home.

"Do you mind?"

"No, ma'am. I'm hoping you'll give me a good recommendation, saying that I was hard-working and dependable." He wanted a lot more from her than that, but not yet.

"Dependable all right—to get into trouble," she joked with him.

"Now if you're talking about Amy's husband coming over to complain about the new hours I gave her . . ."

"When did he do that?"

"Last night. He's really a hothead."

"Why did you change Amy's hours?"

"She's going to help me on the desk while you recuperate—"

"But I can handle the desk myself. I haven't lost my mind as well as the use of my ankles," Marlis insisted.

"It's too soon for you to be full-time innkeeper."

"Kevin, you're treating me like a fragile china doll about to break."

"I like treating you that way."

"I don't."

Silence hung heavy in the car as they drove home until Kevin finally said, "Marlis, I can't help wanting to take care of you." He reached for her hand, and she did not pull hers away when he found it.

"I know, Kevin. I'm just not used to being incapacitated. I've never been the helpless female, and I never will be, so if that's what you want—"

"It isn't."

With a big sigh, Marlis gave in. The doctor had, after all, told her to get back to her routine gradually. "You can't rush the body's healing," he'd warned.

"One question, Kevin, before I agree to let Amy help on the desk: Did you discuss this with her first or just announce that she was going to be working longer hours?"

"The work has to be done. Amy knows that."

"You didn't answer my question."

"Trust my judgment."

"I'm afraid to," she snapped.

Kevin slowed the car for a stoplight and glanced over at her with a repentant smile. "Don't get upset, please. What do you want to do about Amy?"

"Let her keep her regular hours if it's going to bother her husband, and call Winifred Lutz. She helps out when I need her."

"Not anymore."

"What do you mean?"

"She's moving to Florida. Her husband's retiring, and so is she."

Marlis slumped down in the seat and felt bad that she had come down so hard on Kevin. She should have known he would think of an alternative to simply giving Amy longer hours, but experience had taught her he did not always handle a situation in the same way she would. What made it worse was that he hadn't gotten defensive with her, or angry. He'd defended his position, but then had given in to her wishes. It was refreshing to find a man who didn't always have to be right.

"Kevin . . ." she turned toward him, admiring his strong profile, the determined set of his jaw. He was a man who got things done, and that was good. What was bad was that they weren't always done the way she wanted. But then she was beginning to see lately that she wasn't always right, either.

As Kevin turned toward her, expecting another tirade, she figured, she said, "I'm afraid I'm not sounding appreciative for what you're doing for me. I wouldn't blame you if you packed up your computer and moved on."

Kevin winked at her. "I've told you before that it's my nature to just barge ahead and handle things. Sometimes that's good, and sometimes not." He gave her one of his most charming smiles. "Don't let me intimidate you. If you think you're right and I'm wrong, then fight me on it."

"You mean that, don't you?"

"I wouldn't say it if I didn't."

"But I thought most men wanted a woman who knew how to salute and say, 'Yes, sir.' "

A low chuckle rumbled through the front of the car. "It's obvious you don't know 'most men.' And you certainly don't know this man. I want you to be yourself, Marlis Kent, because if you don't respect who you are, and what you believe in, you can't expect other people to."

"I'll remember that." Marlis rested her head against the window, totally disarmed by his forthrightness.

"Are you tired?" he asked.

"A little. I don't have as much energy as I'd hoped I'd have."

"Don't rush yourself. Your body will heal in its own time. One last thing about Amy's husband, before you fall asleep on me: he really isn't a bad guy. When I explained the change would only be for a few days, till you were feeling better, he didn't mind. In fact, he offered to help by replacing the hinges on the front gate. Had you noticed that its sagging?"

Marlis was surprised. "No, I hadn't."

"And some of the pickets are warped. He's going to put in some new ones."

Marlis gazed at Kevin with new appreciation. "You really know how to motivate people, don't you, Mr. King?"

He gave her a devilish wink. "I'm more interested in motivating one woman."

"In what direction?"

"Mine."

They held hands all the way home.

It felt marvelous to be on her feet again, even though her arms ached from leaning on the aluminum crutches and her getting around was agonizingly slow. The stairs were a particular difficulty. She did not find it hard to abide by the doctor's suggestion to only be up for a few hours a day, and promised everyone to take his advice and use the crutches for at least a week.

Amy and Mabel welcomed Marlis back to the world of the walking with enthusiasm, and Kevin said, "I'm going to miss carrying you around, although you still need me until you're up and running."

"Yes, I do," Marlis admitted.

She wondered when Kevin would be leaving to pick up the thread of his life again now that she was more able to take care of herself. Every time he started a conversation with her, she was sure he was going to say good-bye. Well, wouldn't she be glad? she asked herself. Hadn't he caused more turmoil than she needed in her life? Wasn't he too hard to figure out?

Yes, yes, she answered to those soul-searching questions. But then the truth always came back to her: *But I love him, oh, I do love him, and I've gotten used to having him around.*

Their relationship had been on rocky ground from the beginning, but it had grown, despite numerous setbacks, into something special and real, at least for her, and she had to believe it had for Kevin, too. The way he held her, and set her body on fire, and cared about her welfare, all spelled love. Yet he had never come right out and said, "I love you." Oh, he had hinted at it several times, but had always stopped short of a firm declaration.

Marlis was in her tiny office paying bills when the shrill screech of a fire detector going off nearly bolted her off her chair. It droned on and on, high-pitched and grating, and even though it was coming from the second floor, it was still excruciatingly irritating.

Fire! There's a fire in my inn was all Marlis could think about. Grabbing for her crutches, she hobbled into the parlor and was on her way to the foyer when Kevin dashed in.

"Where's the fire?" she questioned anxiously, at the same time sniffing for smoke.

"There is no fire. Don't worry. Everything is under control."

"Kevin," Marlis yelled, "when the alarm goes off, everything is not under control."

"I repeat: there is no fire. The electric smoke detector on the second floor has shorted out. I've practically lost my hearing trying to disconnect its wires, but I can't, so where's your electrical panel?"

"In the basement, by the furnace."

As he dashed away she shouted, "Are you sure there's no fire?"

The firm answer came back: "No fire."

Marlis stood rigidly in place, waiting for word from Kevin, until she realized her ankles were aching. Hobbling to one of the chairs by the game table, she sank down and fiddled with the chess men lined up on the onyx board.

Finally the ear-piercing scream stopped. With a sigh of relief, she sniffed the air again, and when she still did not smell smoke, she assumed Kevin's evaluation of the situation had been correct. A few minutes later he came bounding into the room, a thin line of perspiration lying across his forehead in the grooves made by a deep scowl.

"That noise is enough to drive a man insane," he announced. There was a decided snap to his words. "Had your detector been battery-operated, like the ones I have in my bed-and-breakfast inns, instead of electrical, I could have stopped it easily and a lot quicker."

"I'll change them over, if you think they're better," Marlis offered, wanting to show she could be cooperative.

"I do."

The sound of a fire siren and engines rumbling along the street toward them stopped the conversation. "What now?" Kevin grunted, racing out the door without even waiting for Marlis. She managed to get into the foyer when Kevin returned with two volunteer fire fighters with him.

"A conscientious neighbor of ours turned in an alarm,"

he explained succinctly to Marlis, "but the men want to check the place out."

"Of course," she agreed, thinking how this was going to disturb her guests.

Dressed in regular work clothes—one was a plumber and the other a dentist—the efficient firemen did their job quickly and without dramatics.

"Looks like everything's fine," Joe Blake, who knew Marlis, told her and Kevin. "You should replace that faulty detector today."

"I will," Kevin promised.

After the men left, and their trucks drove away from the inn, Marlis ventured to say, "They were nice not to be annoyed by a false alarm."

"I wouldn't have been, I can tell you," Kevin growled.

"What's the matter with you?" Marlis asked.

He turned to face her, no longer a man of cool unflappability. He was angry. He was disgusted. "It's one thing after another at this place."

"Now, just one minute, no one can help a smoke detector going berserk."

"Just like no one can help a broken water pipe, a cook who doesn't leave extra food, a breakfast that burns, and a housekeeper who brings her elephant dog to romp on the lawn and knock people down?"

"Right."

"No, Marlis, wrong." He pointed a long index finger at her. "I told you once that a competent innkeeper must be able to handle all inevitabilities, or, better still, prevent them from happening in the first place."

"The way you prevented the boy from painting the heat register, or Mr. Germane from getting his key stuck in the lock, or Angel Bruiser from being in her shower?"

Kevin's eyes blazed. "You don't sound grateful for the fact that I was here to handle those problems."

"Or make them worse," Marlis grumbled.

"Since you feel that way, I guess you'd prefer that I wasn't around." Kevin waited for Marlis to beg him to stay, but she didn't. With her jaw thrust to one side, and looking around the room—anywhere but at him—she sent the clear message that she didn't give a hoot whether he stayed or left.

I know she loves me, he told himself, *but why hasn't she ever come right out and said so?* Two different emotions, love and frustration, warred for supremacy and Kevin wasn't sure for how much longer he could keep from throwing Marlis over his shoulder and taking her someplace where he could kiss some sense into her. As long as she was here, in her inn, she didn't think straight, or understand him at all.

"Since you don't have anything to say to me," Kevin said flatly, "I'll leave today. Then you and your crazy Sunrise Inn can go back to your own brand of insanity."

To her continued silence he added, "And don't ever, *ever,* expect to be listed in my book."

Now she whirled to face him. The crutches crashed to the floor as her small hands tightened into fists and landed squarely on her hips. "Who cares, Mr. Know-it-all."

Kevin was more angry with himself than with her. He never should have said that about his book. It sounded like a boyish tantrum and was, he knew, the lowest blow he could have delivered. So much for love conquering all. What a joke.

Kevin turned without another word and marched away. By noon he was gone. By two o'clock, under impatient orders from Marlis, Amy had cleaned his room, and by five o'clock it was occupied by a gentle retired couple from Spokane.

"So much for that episode," Marlis declared to the emptiness of her room as she sat and sulked that night. "Now maybe I can live my life the way I want to." The tears in her eyes didn't change her mind that she was glad he was gone, and gone for good.

Mabel had, unfortunately for her, chosen the minutes after Marlis's argument with Kevin to ask for a raise, "since I'm going to have to be figuring out and fixing low-calorie, low-cholesterol breakfasts as well as regular ones from now on." When her request was met by stony silence from Marlis who, obviously, had not heard a word she'd said, Mabel shuffled away, wondering what on earth had happened.

Six days passed. Marlis put away the crutches and was relieved to find herself able to walk without pain—pain in her feet, that is. There was infinite pain in her heart. She missed Kevin more than she would have believed possible and gradually came to regret their disagreement.

Her sister and brothers called to see how she was, and commiserated with her when she told them the fiasco of events that had led to Kevin's leaving.

"He'll be back," Bob assured her. "If he doesn't know what a great gal he's giving up, then he's too dumb for my sister."

"I don't want to talk any more about me," Marlis said. "How are you feeling? Are you missing your appendix?"

"Nope, and I'm feeling great."

"I'm glad to hear it."

"I'm even back to teaching my Sunday school class."

"How are the boys?"

"Rowdy, as usual. Say, did you know that Jason may be adopted?"

"No. How wonderful. By whom?"

"Some couple in Santa Barbara. He's with them now for a few days."

That piece of good news momentarily lifted the melancholy pall under which Marlis had spent the days since Kevin's departure. Jason was a darling little boy, and deserved to have a loving home.

The next morning the phone rang, and a voice Marlis had known she would never forget asked for Kevin King. It was Amanda Stuart.

"I'm sorry, Ms. Stuart—"

"Mrs. Stuart."

"I see. Mrs. Stuart, Kevin is no longer here. In fact, he's been gone about a week."

"Really? He was here a few days ago, but when he left I assumed he was going back to you. It's unusual for him not to keep me informed as to where he is."

I'll bet, Marlis felt like saying.

"I really do have a problem here that needs his attention," Amanda went on.

"Well, if I hear from him, which I don't expect to, I'll pass on the message."

"I'm afraid that won't do. I need to speak to him today, otherwise Pierre is going to quit."

"Pierre?"

"Our chef."

Good heavens! Marlis gasped. *Did Kevin and Amanda Stuart live together?*

"He's always been temperamental, but I've handled it in the past without having to tell Mr. King."

Why was she calling him Mr. King? Marlis wondered.

"Well, I'm sure Kevin will know what to do. He's thoroughly experienced in solving problems, isn't he?" Marlis hadn't intended the remark to sound snide, but that's the way it came out.

Amanda Stuart laughed attractively in a low, throaty way. "Perhaps at his other bed-and-breakfast inns he solves problems, but here at the Ocean Nook my husband and I take care of most of the difficulties and only bring in Mr. King when we absolutely have to. I'm afraid he thinks there are no dilemmas."

Marlis almost dropped the telephone in amazement. *Amanda Stuart has a husband? And together they run one of Kevin's inns? And run it so well he doesn't even know he has problems? Oh, that man,* Marlis growled inside, *coming here with all his criticisms of how I don't handle things well, making me think his inns are superior when they aren't any different at all.*

"Mrs. Stuart, I'm Marlis Kent, the owner of the Sunrise Inn."

"Yes, Miss Kent, I've heard of you and your inn."

"From Kevin?"

"No, from experienced travelers who say that the Sunrise Inn is a very special place."

"Why, thank you. That pleases me greatly to know my guests are satisfied."

"More than satisfied, I'd say. They're enthusiastic fans." There was a pause as Amanda stopped to talk to someone. "Miss Kent, there's someone here who'd like to speak with you."

"To me?"

"Yes, he heard me mention your name. It's Jason Winters."

"Jason? What is he doing there?"

"My husband and I are hoping to adopt him. Mr. King met him while he was staying with you and, knowing that we've wanted a child for years now, thought Jason would be perfect for us. And he is."

Marlis could hardly speak she was so overwhelmed with the news and the recollection of time she had overheard Kevin, on the phone, telling Amanda, "You are the perfect woman." Perfect to be Jason's mother, not Kevin's lover.

Marlis eagerly spoke to Jason, found out he loved it with the Stuarts, and that Kevin had taken him there and spent a few days with him before leaving.

No wonder Kevin had been so attentive to little Jason, Marlis thought. Imagine finding the boy a home. Amanda Stuart sounded like a truly lovely person. Marlis smiled. Funny how Amanda sounded motherly now, whereas before she had seemed a seductive temptress.

"So Mr. King isn't with you now, Jason?" she asked the boy.

"No. We had fun, but he wasn't as happy as he was when we were panning for gold."

Marlis knew why. She wasn't at all happy herself, but there was nothing to be done about it. She and Kevin King got along about as well as two wounded polecats in a very small gunnysack.

THIRTEEN

That evening, just after six, the doorbell rang, and when Marlis went to answer it she found Steve Alexander standing there, grinning.

"Hi," she greeted him warmly, realizing how much she'd missed him in the past weeks.

"Everything's under control," he said.

"What?"

"For your picnic dinner. If you'll follow me to the rose garden . . ."

Marlis gave him a funny look. "Steve, what are you babbling about?"

"Just come with me and you'll see."

Always ready for a surprise—and heaven knew she needed something to lift her out of the doldrums—Marlis hooked her arm through Steve's and they went outside and around the brick walk to the garden she had pampered for so many years. It was rich tonight with the scent of pink and white roses.

There she saw Kevin, in a white dinner jacket and tie, looking incredibly handsome and debonair, standing beside a huge white tablecloth spread over the lush grass Amy's husband had cut the day before.

"Thanks, Steve," were the first words he spoke, then he walked up to Marlis and took her hand, raising her fingers to his lips. His eyes were soft and liquid as they swept over her face. "I'm back," he said, "to claim what's mine."

Steve disappeared as Marlis gazed first at Kevin, then down at the cold supper lying on bone china plates, surrounded by sterling silver cutlery, pink flowers, and pink candles, reminiscent of another night Kevin had had a dinner catered for her.

"What exactly did you leave here, Mr. King?" she asked nonchalantly, not knowing why she was acting as though she hardly cared he was there. What was the matter with her, when she'd been longing to see him again?

Marlis wasn't ready for the explosion that followed. Kevin gripped her arms at the shoulders and nearly lifted her off the ground. "You know perfectly well what I'm talking about, Marlis. I'm back for you. I'm going to marry you."

Marlis's eyes flashed defiance. "Are you? And when did you decide this?"

"The first day I saw you."

"Well, thank you for *telling* me instead of asking." She gave a little laugh. "Although I can't imagine why you want to marry me when everything I do is wrong—"

"Not wrong."

"Stupid."

"Don't be ridiculous."

"Inept then—"

He kissed her, hard on the mouth, and crushed her in his arms, his hands molding her against him, then murmured, "You're intelligent and beautiful and compassionate and spunky and I love you, Marlis, just the way you are."

Marlis caught her breath but said nothing.

Kevin held her away from him and his dark eyebrows slid downward. "Don't you have something to say?"

"No."

"You're supposed to say Yes."

"I'm not sure I want to say 'Yes.' "

"Darn it, woman. Why is everything so complicated with you?"

Marlis removed his hands from her shoulders. "I am not at all complicated. A woman has a right to think a little before she promises her life to a man, doesn't she?"

"What is there to think about?" Kevin roared. "You love me and I love you." Some guests, reading nearby, looked up in surprise at the same time Marlis put two fingers to her mouth and said to Kevin, "Shh."

With a gigantic sigh, Kevin tilted her chin upward with one of his fingers. "I want to marry you, Marlis Kent, because I love you. You know that."

"I do not know that."

"Yes, you do, and you love me, I know you do."

"How do you know that?"

"Well . . . just because I do. It's obvious."

"Not to me."

He shook his head as though he had just gone through a revolving door a hundred times. "What is the matter with you today?"

"Nothing, absolutely nothing." She was irritated with his brash assumption that when he said jump, she would leap—right into marriage. "I just know my own mind," she insisted, "about how to run a bed-and-breakfast inn, and how to choose a husband."

Kevin slipped his arms around her waist and pulled her toward him. "Marlis, sweetheart, you know we're good for each other." He leaned down and kissed her cheek. "I can't stop thinking of you. I want you day and night."

Suddenly, Marlis was scared. She had always dreamed one day of being married and having a husband whom she adored. Now that it was possible, she wasn't sure she could blend her life successfully with a man. She'd been on her own, made her own decisions, had confidence in herself, until this oaf came along with his opinions and suggestions and . . . help.

Oh, but she did love him. He was strong and intelligent

and interesting and successful. She had new respect for him, because of Jason. He was caring. He could be tender.

He was insensitive and too often exasperating.

Kevin cupped her face between two large hands. "Marlis, just say yes. You know you want to."

"No, I don't." She met his gaze as unemotionally as she could.

Kevin groaned. "Since this is going to take time—"

"What is going to take time?"

"Convincing you to marry me. We might as well eat."

Marlis felt a little giddy. He was pursuing her. Her mood mellowed from serious to flattered. She liked being pursued.

She looked around the beautiful grounds. A new couple who had checked in an hour before were enjoying tea in the gazebo. Mr. Hankins was taking a nap in the hammock under the big oak tree. "All right," she agreed, gracefully lowering herself at the edge of the tablecloth and spreading the wide skirt of her emerald-green dress in a circle about her knees; "we'll eat, but you mustn't disturb my guests."

Kevin followed her glance and nodded as he settled down beside her. "We both know we love each other . . ." he began but stopped when Marlis shook her head no.

"Did I ever tell you I love you?" She challenged his statement, feeling the greatest of hypocrites, for she knew she loved him with a frenzy.

"Yes."

"When?"

"In a hundred ways: the way you looked at me, the trembling of your skin when I touched you—"

"Skin doesn't tremble."

"Something trembled when I touched you, because you responded."

Marlis picked up a piece of salmon and slid it onto her tongue. "Is it all right to begin, or are we waiting for the National Anthem to be sung?"

Kevin motioned toward the food. "By all means, go ahead."

"Thanks, I'm starving." She pulled six glistening red grapes from their stems.

"I know we have had our differences . . ." Kevin began.

And popped them into her mouth.

". . . but I'm sure we can work them out . . ."

She stabbed a piece of imported cheese with a long toothpick and pulled it off with her teeth.

". . . because when two people feel toward each other the way we do . . ."

Marlis dipped her fingers into a silver bowl filled with pistachio nuts and put exactly three on her tongue.

"Are you listening to me?" Kevin roared.

"Shh." Marlis held up a finger to her lips and glanced toward the people in the gazebo.

Kevin sat up straight. "I wanted this to be a special, romantic moment for us, but you're finding it more amusing than serious, aren't you? I can see I shouldn't have come back."

He started to get up, but Marlis laid a restraining hand on his arm. "Wait, I'll behave myself if you'll answer two questions for me."

Eyeing her with skepticism, Kevin slowly relaxed, spread his long legs out, leaned back on one elbow, and gave Marlis his attention. But he was frowning.

"Who is Susan Roberts?" she asked.

Kevin shrugged. "She manages my bed-and-breakfast inn in Sacramento. She's a widow with four children."

"How old a widow?"

"Fifty-one."

"Why were you so secretive about her?"

"I didn't know I was. It was a business call, Marlis." The frown eased. "Were you jealous of her?"

"Yes. Her, and Amanda Stuart. I thought you had women in every bed and breakfast in California."

Kevin chuckled. "Two months ago the idea would have appealed to me, but not anymore. There's only one woman I'm interested in." His gaze traveled the length and breadth of Marlis's body, and she felt the electric warmth of those blue eyes. "What's the second question?"

"Are the Stuarts really going to adopt Jason?"

"How did you know about that?" He was surprised.

"I had a long talk with Amanda today. In between courses you'd better give her a call. Pierre is about to quit."

"Quit? Why?"

"It seems he's temperamental. Did you know that?"

"No. We've never had a problem with him before that I can recall."

Marlis leaned toward him. "The reason you can't recall any trouble with him is that Amanda and her husband took care of it, as they do all the problems, just as I suppose Susan Roberts does in Sacramento and . . . and . . ."

"Jack and Joan Reesner in Huntington Beach." Kevin took a deep breath and let it out all at once. "I'm beginning to get a picture there. The things that went wrong here go wrong at every bed and breakfast."

"Something like that."

"Probably at mine, too."

"I'm sure of it."

"No wonder you thought I was a jerk when I criticized you and made it seem as though the Sunrise should run smoothly every hour, every day."

"That did occur to me."

He grinned at her. "I have a confession to make."

Marlis's eyebrows raised in anticipation.

"I never really thought you were an incompetent innkeeper or that you needed any help from me."

"Oh?"

"In fact, I've already written up the 'unique and be-sure-to-visit' Sunrise Inn for my next book."

Marlis's mouth moved into a pucker. She should have been thrilled, but something was not quite right here. "Go on."

"I just wanted your attention long enough to make you fall in love with me."

"What?" she screeched. "You put me down; you patronized me; you . . . you . . . hurt my feelings."

"I know, darling—"

"Don't darling me." She jumped to her feet. "This is what you call male logic? To point out all my faults so that I'd fall in love with you?"

A sheepish grin played across Kevin's handsome face. "It worked, didn't it?"

"No, it certainly did not."

Marlis reached down for the bowl of nuts and a dish of bright red cherry tomatoes and she dumped both bowls on Kevin's head. Turning on her heels, she walked right across the middle of the tablecloth, kicking the flowers and candles aside and marched, stiff-backed, toward the house.

"Don't walk away from me, Marlis Kent," Kevin's warning voice followed her. She kept walking.

"Come back here or you'll be sorry."

Marlis got only to the brick path before she was scooped up in a pair of powerful arms and carried into the house.

"Put me down," she ordered Kevin as he marched into the foyer, past an open-mouthed Amy.

"If you don't put me down, I'll have Amy call the police," she warned as he started up the first flight of stairs.

"Amy, call the police."

Kevin reached the second floor and started toward the third.

"Either you put me down this instant or I will scream and kick and—"

"Go ahead."

When they got to the door of her apartment, Kevin kicked it in. There was a shattering of wood that shocked Marlis into silence that turned to concern as he strode through the living room and into her bedroom where he threw her on the bed. Threw was the right word, for it was not a gentle laying down, a romantic sinking onto the covers. Kevin tossed her there as though she were a bag of oranges.

When she started to get off, he leaned down and grasped both her wrists, forcing them down beside her head into the pillow. Slowly he came toward her, and though she struggled as hard as she could, there was no breaking his iron grip. The bed sank beneath the weight of his body as he leaned over her.

"You eogtistical, self-centered, puffed-up—"

"Marlis, will you shut . . . up . . ."

Kevin kissed her with all the meticulous attention a man in love gives to the woman who has captivated and captured him. Every part of his body spoke of his love and passion as he shared this with her body. His lips persuaded, his fingertips caressed, his voice spoke her name as though it were an anthem in a great cathedral. He created a poetry of feeling for her and knew she read his every intent. He wanted to possess her and give himself in return.

She was beauty and gentleness and fire and mystery and he couldn't get enough of her. She was woman, and he needed her as he had never needed another.

He pulled back from her, gasping.

Pulling himself up into a sitting position, his legs on the floor, Kevin struggled to breathe as Marlis clambered to her knees and gripped his shoulders in alarm.

"What's wrong?" Merciful God in heaven, he wasn't having a heart attack, was he? Men didn't have heart attacks in their early thirties. Yes, they did. Even in their twenties. Oh no, he was going to die in her room! On her bed. "Kevin, speak to me. What's happening?"

He gave her a boyish grin as he continued trying to catch his breath. "I guess I'm not in as good shape as I thought. Why couldn't you have lived on the first floor?"

She frowned. "What are you talking about?"

"Did you happen to notice that I carried you from the path into the house, through the foyer, up two flights of stairs, and into this room? At top speed? How much do you weigh, anyway?''

Marlis let out a yelp. "How much do I weigh? You don't know that after all the times you carted me around when I first got hurt?" She fell back against the pillow and began to laugh.

"What's so funny?"

"You are." She continued to giggle until she was holding her sides because they ached.

"I'd like to be in on the joke."

"Sure. I thought you were having a heart attack," she told him, noticing that he was already breathing normally again.

"I guess I'm not, which means it should be safe to do this." Kevin kissed her for a very long time, without taking even one breath.

Then he said, "Since I have learned that there are problems at my three inns, could I hire you to do some management consulting?"

"It'll cost you." Marlis gazed into his love-softened eyes with loving eyes of her own.

"How about a marriage license and a wedding ring?"

She smiled and caressed his face with her hand. "Not enough," was her answer.

"What can I do to convince you?"

They had moved from the bed to the swing on the back porch, having decided it was a cooler place to be.

"I want you to admit it," Marlis said.

"Admit what?"

"That even though you told me one night that a competent inkeeper must anticipate every problem and prevent its happening, even you were not able to anticipate the things that went wrong while you were in charge of the inn."

"Uh, right," Kevin agreed reluctantly.

"And since you did not anticipate them, you did not prevent them from happening."

"Also true. Now can we get married?"

"Not yet."

Kevin looked puzzled. "What else can I do except to tell you I adore you, and love you with all my heart."

"That'll do it." Marlis was so in love at that moment she didn't think of a major problem that could come between them, but it did leap into her thoughts over dinner—that she cooked herself—after making Kevin sign a waiver relieving her of all fault if he died of food poisoning.

They were having coffee in the gazebo when Marlis brought up the problem: "Where are we going to live?"

"In Santa Barbara, of course. That's my home."

"Why do you say *'of course'*? It's not as though I live on the back of a motorcycle. I have a home, too, and not just a home, but a business."

"Do you want to keep the Sunrise?"

Marlis looked at him as if he were daft. "Yes, I definitely want to keep it. My family has had it for years."

"All right," Kevin said in that Don't-worry-I'll-take-care-of-everything voice, "keep it, then. Hire someone to run it."

Marlis's brows knit to a frown. "And give up doing something that has given me such pleasure for so many years?"

"You'll be my wife. You won't need to work."

There was stunned silence before she said, "But I want to work. I want more than just to be married to you."

Kevin put his coffee cup down more forcefully on the table in front of them than he needed to. "You make marrying me sound like a sentence rather than a deliverance."

"Deliverance? From what do I need deliverance?" Marlis scooted a little away from him. "In case you never noticed, I love the Sunrise Inn. I thoroughly enjoy running it and, frankly, don't want to give it up."

"Are you saying that I should move in here?"

Marlis's eyes brightened. "Couldn't you? Kevin, your main occupation is writing, which you can do here just as easily as you can in Santa Barbara."

His voice was low when he answered. "My home is in Santa Barbara."

Marlis sighed. "And my home has been Sutter Creek for twenty-eight years."

The crickets chirping in the approaching night air were the only sound for some minutes, then Kevin said, "We have a major problem, Marlis, and I'm not sure it can be settled to please us both."

Sadly, Marlis knew he was right.

Marlis knew now why most people got married when they were younger, before they were both established in careers that conflicted one with the other. Of course she wanted to marry Kevin, but to do so, under his terms, meant giving up a great deal. How could she abandon the Sunrise, even for him?

"Get married and work out the details later," her brother Bob advised.

"You'd better have a long talk and work out all the details now," her sister Sondra advised.

Marlis agreed with her sister, but having a long talk with Kevin was impossible right now because he was in New York, meeting with his publisher. The company wanted him to do a sophisticated travel book on the many special places in California to vacation.

"It might make a nice honeymoon," was the olive branch he'd offered before driving off.

"Researching your book—or me?" Marlis had joked.

As she'd watched his bright-red Porsche drive down Main Street out of town, she'd reflected sadly on the fact that in the books and movies love was supposed to be enough to conquer all, but in real life love was only the beginning. They had said good-bye locked in each other's arms, kissing heatedly, touching with fondness, but no definite plans had been made: no date for the wedding, no decision on where to live or what to do with the Sunrise Inn.

For the next week Marlis was moody, and both Amy

and Mabel complained about it, while also giving advice on what to do with Kevin's proposal.

"I'd marry him in a second and go live in Santa Barbara," Amy drooled. "You know the man has gobs of money, and you'd never have to work again."

"But I enjoy working, Amy."

"I think you're nuts."

Mabel's advice was a little harder to figure out. "I think you should marry him, but not give up the Sunrise Inn."

"But he doesn't want to live here."

"Then live with him in Santa Barbara."

"If I do that, I won't be able to run the inn."

"Take it with you."

For about thirty seconds Marlis thought of that crazy idea: dismantle the house and relocate it. Then she shook her head no and said, "The inn belongs here, in Sutter Creek, surrounded by its own memories. There has to be another way to work this out."

"I hope you find it," Mabel shrugged, "because a man like Kevin King doesn't come along every day." She had gotten over her hurt feelings about the diet menus, finally agreeing that Kevin had been right in suggesting the inn begin offering them and now was back to sighing over him.

"He's so intelligent and up-to-date and caring on what is best for people." She tugged her apron straighter as she and Marlis stood by the kitchen stove chatting. "I've talked with our guests for years, you know, and it's true that more and more people are changing the way they eat. But it's hard giving up my treasured recipes, even if they are rich in salt, sugar, white flour, calories, and cholesterol."

"Mabel," Marlis assured her, "as talented as you are, you'll be able to make healthy food taste as good as unhealthy."

"Do you think so?"

"Yes, I do, and so does Kevin."

"Did he say that?"

"Exactly that. He has great respect for your culinary talents."

That look appeared on Mabel's face—half adoration, half wonder—that this well-known man of the world would even deign to think of her. "If Pierre, his chef in Santa Barbara, quits," Mabel said with sudden excitement, "I could work for him."

Marlis exhaled. "No, you couldn't, Mabel, because you work for me, here."

"But you'd be there, too, so we'd still be together."

Marlis's confusion didn't get any better. She wanted to marry Kevin because she agreed completely with Mabel that a man like him didn't come along every day, but she wanted the life she had formed for herself, which she so thoroughly enjoyed, to go on, too. At times she felt guilty for her selfishness; at other times, justified.

Kevin called her every day from New York. Even over the phone she experienced the power of his being and felt light-headed. His rich voice soothed her troubled heart, its deep tones, so loving, so manly, washed over her anxieties and gave her assurance that things would somehow work out.

Marlis, though, was reminded by Amy one day that she hadn't ever said yes to him. "I'll bet there's not another woman alive who would hesitate the way you are," she added.

"You're right, Amy. If I lose him, I'll have no one to blame but myself."

Kevin called on a Monday morning. "I'm coming home Wednesday," he told her.

"Home?"

"I meant there, to you. Sweetheart, I have a terrific idea I think will solve our problems."

"Really?" Marlis's smile was broad for the first time since he'd left.

"I'll tell you about it when I have my arms around you."

"That can't be too soon for me."

Marlis didn't get much sleep that night, anticipating

seeing Kevin again. She needed to be in his arms. She prayed with all her heart that his plan would enable them to set a wedding date.

Tuesday afternoon a stunningly beautiful woman wearing a raspberry linen suit, fashionable gold jewelry, and her sleek black hair pulled back in an attractively large chignon, appeared at the desk of the Sunrise Inn.

"Are you Marlis?" she asked, pulling off a pair of expensive kid gloves. Upon receiving an affirmative reply, she held out her hand. "I'm Susan Roberts."

Marlis blinked. This couldn't be the Susan Roberts who worked for Kevin, whom he had described as a widow, mother of four children, and fifty-one years of age in a way that made her sound dowdy, tired, and thirty pounds overweight. None of these descriptions even remotely represented the striking, sophisticated woman standing there.

To Marlis's momentary silence she added, "I manage Kevin King's bed-and-breakfast inn in Sacramento."

"Y-yes," Marlis finally stammered, "we spoke once on the phone. It's nice to meet you in person."

"Thank you. The reason for my visit is that Kevin said he would be coming here tomorrow from New York. I have some legal papers for him to look over. Could you give them to him?"

"Of course. And then have him call you?"

"He'll rush to call me," Susan said with a smile, "as soon as he reads these. We're being sued."

Sued? Marlis wanted to ask why, but decided not to. It still was not her business yet. Poor Kevin. For a man who thought he had no problems with his bed-and-breakfast inns, this lawsuit was going to be a jolt.

After Susan left, Marlis stared at the door a long time. Lots of men preferred older women, she ruminated. Had Kevin ever been attracted to Susan? He couldn't be blamed if he had been, for Susan Roberts was intelligent, capable, and lovely to look at, as the old song said.

The fact that she had not acted as though she knew Kevin had proposed, or even that Kevin was romantically involved with Marlis, bothered Marlis more than she wanted to admit, as though she were a secret Kevin didn't want anyone to know about. You'd think Susan would suspect something was going on between them, Marlis mused, since he'd spent so much time at the Sunrise Inn. Oh, well, maybe she thought it was none of her business to mention it, just as Marlis had not felt it proper to ask about the lawsuit.

Marlis's down mood brightened the next morning when Steve Alexander came over with a freshly baked apple pie, her favorite.

"How did you know I needed cheering up?" She had confided her relationship with Kevin to Steven several days before.

"I got the vibes all the way down the street, around the corner, and two blocks away," he kidded her. "Still haven't made up your mind yet?"

"No, but Kevin is coming back tonight and hopefully we'll figure it out."

"Maybe your folks will have an idea," he offered.

"They probably would," Marlis agreed, feeling a real hunger to see her parents again. They always had been good at solving problems. "But they're still on their vacation."

"No, they aren't. I saw them driving down the street on my way here."

"You did?" Marlis shouted. "Maybe they're at Sondra's. I'll call right away. Oh, thank you, Steve, you're wonderful." She threw her arms around him and gave him an enthusiastic kiss on the cheek.

The sound of a suitcase being dropped to the floor was heard from the doorway. Marlis and Steve whirled around, still in each other's arms, to see Kevin standing there.

"It looks like I haven't been missed as much as I thought I would be," he said brusquely.

FOURTEEN

"Oh, darling." Marlis flew from Steve to Kevin. She leaned up and kissed him. "I wasn't expecting you till much later."

"So I see. I took an earlier flight. Didn't want to be away from you another minute."

Marlis stood back and surveyed with amusement the stern look on his face. "And now you think you've caught Steve and me at something."

Kevin continued to scowl. "Maybe you've decided to marry him. It would make more sense since he lives right here in your beloved Sutter Creek. Then you could run his and hers bed-and-breakfast inns."

Marlis made a face. "My, my, what a Grumpy Gus we are today." She was so happy to see Kevin again nothing could spoil his homecoming, not even his suspicions. "Come to think of it, though," and she turned with tongue in cheek to Steve, "we could make quite a success of such a union. I can see the advertising now: One free night at the Heritage Inn for two nights at the Sunrise."

"Wait a minute," Steve joined in the fun, "how about one free night at the Sunrise after two extraordinary nights at the Heritage?"

"We could get a discount by buying our sheets and towels in large quantities," Marlis added.

"And on groceries, buying by the gross."

"Think of the possibilities."

"They're endless."

"All right, you two," Kevin gave in with a grin. "I guess you're innocent."

"Not me," Steve denied. "I'll marry Marlis any time she wants to."

"Oh, goodie," Marlis exclaimed, clapping her hands together. "Shall we have the ceremony in your rose garden or mine?"

"Mine, because my Summer Sunshine roses are in full bloom."

"My Red Masterpieces are, too, Steve, and I much prefer their glorious deep red to the wan yellow of your Sunshines."

Kevin shook his head as if he were witnessing a squabble between two five-year-olds. "When you two decide where the ceremony will be, and when, let me know. In the meantime, I'm going to grab a nap."

He turned and started toward the door of the parlor, but Marlis stopped him. "Not until I give you this," she announced, throwing her arms around his neck and kissing him with such fervor that Steve blushed and tiptoed out the door, while Kevin groaned and hungrily pulled Marlis against his aching body that began to relax now that he had the woman he loved right where she belonged: in his arms. He wanted to tell her how much he'd missed her, but words would have to wait, there were more important things to do.

"Tell me what your special plan is for us," Marlis said, running her fingers along the soft hair of his mustache when they finally came up for air. "I'm anxious to know."

"Later, sweetheart. I've been on the go for thirty-six hours, and I want to be fresh when we talk." He pulled Marlis into an embrace and another long and sensuous kiss. "Why do I want to do that every time I see you?" he asked with a lopsided smile.

"Maybe because I want you to," Marlis said. Then she went to the desk in the foyer and came back with a key which she handed to Kevin.

"To your apartment?" he asked hopefully.

"To the Dog House. We're full tonight."

With a sigh, he remarked on his way out, "I always knew I would end up there."

"Oh, Kevin, I almost forgot," Marlis said as he turned to go. "A beautiful woman stopped by here today to see you."

"To see me?"

"Yes. I believe she's fifty-one, a widow, and has four children."

"Susan?"

When Marlis nodded her head Yes, he asked, "What was she doing here?"

Marlis got the envelope of legal papers from her desk and handed it to him. "Bad news, I'm afraid."

Kevin whipped the papers out and glanced through them. "So, the old man is finally going to try to get his land." He didn't seem too upset to Marlis.

"Were you expecting this?"

Kevin nodded. "Mr. Henderson has been threatening me for years to sue over a strip of land that adjoins both our properties. I've had a survey taken which proves beyond doubt that the land is mine."

"But he must have some basis upon which to make a claim. A law firm is representing him."

"It's nothing to worry about." Kevin closed the matter by dropping the papers into his briefcase.

"You're taking this casually," Marlis remarked, surprised that he hadn't displayed the temper she probably would have had she been served such a notice. It was just one more example of the positive way Kevin looked at life and handled problems with ease.

"I have more important things on my mind today than a lawsuit," he said, giving her a wickedly sensuous look.

"I'll be here," Marlis promised.

"You'd better be, or I'll call out the volunteer fire department of Sutter Creek and have them track you down."

"They handle fires, not missing women."

Kevin laid his hand over his chest. "I know where there's a fire. It's here in my heart, and you started it."

Marlis took advantage of Kevin's rest to contact her folks. They were still at Sondra's and promised to come right over to see her.

"I sure miss this place," her dad said when he walked in the front door and gazed around the hallway. "You've made a few changes, I see, but they're good ones. Don't you think so, Mother?"

"Marlis is very talented, yes."

"Let me get you some tea," the talented daughter said, "and then I really need some words of wisdom from you two."

An hour later, when Kevin came in and found Marlis at the desk, he took her hand. "Put up your Out To Lunch sign, woman. We have some serious talking to do."

"Okay. Amy's here to take over."

In the gazebo Kevin held her hand and said, "Where are all your guests? You said you were full."

"We are, but they're either eating lunch or sightseeing."

"Good for them, because I don't want any interruptions." He pulled a blue velvet box from his trouser pocket and opened it in front of Marlis. She gasped when she saw a wide gold ring with seven rows of diamonds. Never had she seen a band like it and all she could say for the moment was a long "Oooh."

"This is a wedding ring, not an engagement ring. I don't expect us to be engaged more than a week, at the most."

Marlis lifted her eyes from the ring and said, "Isn't

that a little optimistic, considering what we have to work out?"

"I'm a positive thinker."

Marlis could see the determination stamped on to every plane of his face.

"Before we leave this gazebo, there won't be any more problems to work out," he added.

"I think you're right, because I have something to say, too."

"Great. Who goes first?"

"I do." She pulled one leg underneath her, sitting on it, and bounced up and down in her excitement. "My parents are back from their trip and I saw them while you were resting. Kevin, they shocked me, I mean really shocked me, by saying they are tired of retirement. 'All fun and no work makes Ray a dull boy' is the quaint way my father put it. 'Your mother and I need some challenge in our lives,' he said. 'We're too young to sit around a retirement village in Arizona all day, playing shuffleboard and bridge.'"

"Does he want to go back to work?"

"Both of them do—here, at the Sunrise Inn."

Kevin stared at Marlis in happy surprise. "They want to buy it back from you?"

"No, they still want money for traveling, but they would like to manage it for me."

"Honey, how do you feel about that?"

"I love it." She clapped her hands together in joy, feeling like a teenager revealing to her very best friend the most wonderful thing that ever happened to her. "Now I can keep the Sunrise, knowing that it is being run by people of experience, whom I trust, and live with you in Santa Barbara." A radiant smile spread her lips wide. "Isn't that great?"

To her amazement, Kevin didn't share her enthusiasm. He was pondering something behind those dark-rimmed glasses that worried her.

"Half your problem is solved," he said, rising and pacing around the gazebo thoughtfully as he spoke, "but what about your working? That's important to you. If you let your parents take over the Sunrise you'll be without a job."

Marlis jumped up and went to him, putting her arms around his waist. "I'll be your wife. That's the most important job any woman could have."

Kevin drew her against him and held her for a minute, but then he stepped back and gazed at her seriously. "You are willing to sacrifice your own career and ambitions to marry me?"

"Yes, but that doesn't mean I'm retiring to a life of knitting afghans and raising stray kittens. Goodness, Santa Barbara is a thriving town. I can get involved in worthwhile community activities if there's too much time on my hands—after making you as happy as I can." She snuggled against him. "Lots of women are fulfilled in devoting themselves to their husbands and children."

He kissed her with great tenderness, then fastened his eyes on her and said, "Sorry, Marlis, I can't accept that." When she started to protest he said, "And that's the end of the subject."

Marlis pulled away from him. "Aren't you being a little dictatorial here? It is my life, after all. Don't I have the right to decide what to do with it?"

"Of course, you do, as long as you remember there are two people in this marriage: me and you. I want you to be happy just as much as you want me to be."

"I don't understand."

"Sweetheart, some of the things I love most about you are your energy, your creativity, and the way you come alive when you talk about the Sunrise Inn—what you've done with it in the past and what you're planning for the future. I don't want to take that away from you."

"You're not taking, I'm giving."

"Then I'll give it back."

"Aha," Marlis exclaimed. "I've just figured it out.

Your *want* me to go on working so you can *stop* working and just be a lazy bum on the beach. That's it, isn't it?''

Kevin roared with laughter. "You clever thing. Of course, I want you working, but not in Santa Barbara."

Marlis was confused. "Where then?"

"Catalina Island."

She frowned. "The island off the coast of southern California, near Los Angeles?"

"Yes. It's twenty-six miles out in the ocean."

Marlis crossed her arms and gave him a sassy look. "So, we're going to get married but then you're going to stash me away on some lonely island while you roam through California writing your travel book?"

"Santa Catalina is hardly a lonely island. Millions of tourists go there every year."

"I know that."

"It's a paradise, Marlis, with over two hundred sixty days a year of sunshine and a balmy summer temperature in the high seventies."

"I know how nice it is because I've been there."

"Oh? Who was the fellow?"

"No one for you to be jealous of. We rode on those darling glass-bottomed boats through which you can see the fish swimming by."

"Yes."

"And went horseback riding and bicycling and played tennis and danced in the casino."

"And he's not someone from your past who is going to drop in on you someday and steal you away from me?"

"I think he's too busy politicking in the state Senate."

"He sounds like serious competition," Kevin said.

"No, not serious at all. He was one of the most boring men I've ever been with."

"Should we invite him to the wedding?"

"Kevin, why am I going to be on Catalina Island? Forget my former love life."

Kevin smiled, as broadly as Marlis had a moment before. "You're going to work there."

Her eyes widened. "I am? Doing what?"

"Running the Sunset Inn."

Marlis thought about that a moment before saying, "And what is the Sunset Inn?"

"Let me tell you." Kevin pulled her back down on the cushions and the words tumbled out of his mouth with the greatest of enthusiasm.

"There's an old, old house for sale. It belonged to one of the first families to live on the island."

"Cabrillo's? He discovered it, didn't he, in the early 1500s?"

"Yes, he did, bright girl, but the house isn't quite that old. It's more like a hundred years old."

A light dawned in Marlis's head. She got excited, too. "You want to turn that house into a bed-and-breakfast inn, don't you?"

"Yes."

"Filled with old Spanish things, since the island was given to its original American owners by a Spanish land grant."

"Yes."

Her eyes glowed with anticipation. "Wouldn't that be challenging—to create a unique inn incorporating the history of that beautiful island?"

"Yes."

"Kevin," Marlis groaned. "Will you say more than 'yes', please. I want to know all the details."

"The Sunset Inn will be a sister to the Sunrise Inn."

"I like that idea, but honey, taking an old house and turning it into a first-class bed-and-breakfast inn is going to take a lot of time. Years."

"I know."

"Won't you mind me being away from you so much?"

Kevin pulled her possessively into his arms. "You won't be. I'll be right there with you."

"You will?"

"Sure. Do you think I'm going to let you out of my sight once I put that ring on your finger?"

"Oh . . ."

"The diamonds are worth a fortune, and I don't want someone stealing it."

"Oh!" She hit him playfully on his chest.

"We'll start a brand-new life together, Marlis, in a place where neither of us has ties. I'll still keep my inns, and you'll have the Sunrise, but we'll live together on the island of Catalina and work together there."

"Kevin," Marlis breathed his name with all the love she felt for him at that moment. "What a perfect idea. An absolutely perfect idea."

"You're too talented with people to give it all up just to marry me."

"Don't put it that way. Marrying you is the best thing that will ever happen to me."

"Do you think so?" He pulled her close.

"Let me prove it to you," she whispered, curling her arms around his neck and leaning against him as she pressed her lips against his.

"On second thought," Kevin said softly, "I think we'd better get married tomorrow. I'm not a patient man." His ardent kiss proved the fact.

At the registration desk a new guest rang the bell, but no one heard it because Marlis was concentrating on Kevin, Amy was cleaning the only room with a television in it and was listening to her favorite soap opera, and Mabel was in the kitchen, sitting at the table and planning when to ask Marlis again for a raise.

On the second floor of the inn a faucet began slowly to drip in the Prospector Room, a light bulb burned out in the hallway, and a young father, driving the family car along Highway 49 toward Sutter Creek said to his pregnant wife, "I'm sure the Sunrise Inn won't mind having three children under six and a cocker spaniel puppy for four nights."

SHARE THE FUN . . .
SHARE YOUR NEW-FOUND TREASURE!!

You don't want to let your new books out of your sight? That's okay. Your friends can get their own. Order below.

No. 80 CRITIC'S CHOICE by Kathleen Yapp
Marlis can't do one thing right in front of her handsome houseguest.

No. 57 BACK IN HIS ARMS by Becky Barker
Fate takes over when Tara shows up on Rand's doorstep again.

No. 58 SWEET SEDUCTION by Allie Jordan
Libby wages war on Will—she'll win his love yet!

No. 59 13 DAYS OF LUCK by Lacey Dancer
Author Pippa Weldon finds her real-life hero in Joshua Luck.

No. 60 SARA'S ANGEL by Sharon Sala
Sara *must* get to Hawk. He's the only one who can help.

No. 61 HOME FIELD ADVANTAGE by Janice Bartlett
Marian shows John there is more to life than just professional sports.

No. 62 FOR SERVICES RENDERED by Ann Patrick
Nick's life is in perfect order until he meets Claire!

No. 63 WHERE THERE'S A WILL by Leanne Banks
Chelsea goes toe-to-toe with her new, unhappy business partner.

No. 64 YESTERDAY'S FANTASY by Pamela Macaluso
Melissa always had a crush on Morgan. Maybe dreams do come true!

No. 65 TO CATCH A LORELEI by Phyllis Houseman
Lorelei sets a trap for Daniel but gets caught in it herself.

No. 66 BACK OF BEYOND by Shirley Faye
Dani and Jesse are forced to face their true feelings for each other.

No. 67 CRYSTAL CLEAR by Cay David
Max could be the end of all Crystal's dreams . . . or just the beginning!

No. 68 PROMISE OF PARADISE by Karen Lawton Barrett
Gabriel is surprised to find that Eden's beauty is not just skin deep.

No. 69 OCEAN OF DREAMS by Patricia Hagan
Is Jenny just another shipboard romance to Officer Kirk Moen?

No. 70 SUNDAY KIND OF LOVE by Lois Faye Dyer
Trace literally sweeps beautiful, ebony-haired Lily off her feet.

No. 71 ISLAND SECRETS by Darcy Rice
Chad has the power to take away Tucker's hard-earned independence.

No. 72 COMING HOME by Janis Reams Hudson
Clint always loved Lacey. Now Fate has given them another chance.

No. 73 KING'S RANSOM by Sharon Sala
Jesse was always like King's little sister. When did it all change?

No. 74 A MAN WORTH LOVING by Karen Rose Smith
Nate's middle name is 'freedom' . . . that is, until Shara comes along.

No. 75 RAINBOWS & LOVE SONGS by Catherine Sellers
Dan has more than one problem. One of them is named Kacy!

No. 76 ALWAYS ANNIE by Patty Copeland
Annie is down-to-earth, real . . . and Ted's never met anyone like her.

No. 77 FLIGHT OF THE SWAN by Lacey Dancer
Rich had decided to swear off romance for good until Christiana.

No. 78 TO LOVE A COWBOY by Laura Phillips
Dee is the dark-haired beauty that sends Nick reeling back to the past.

No. 79 SASSY LADY by Becky Barker
No matter how hard he tries, Curt can't seem to get away from Maggie.

Meteor Publishing Corporation
Dept. 292, P. O. Box 41820, Philadelphia, PA 19101-9828

Please send the books I've indicated below. Check or money order only—no cash, stamps or C.O.D.s (PA residents, add 6% sales tax). I am enclosing $2.95 plus 75¢ handling fee for *each* book ordered.

Total Amount Enclosed: $_____.

____ No. 80	____ No. 62	____ No. 68	____ No. 74
____ No. 57	____ No. 63	____ No. 69	____ No. 75
____ No. 58	____ No. 64	____ No. 70	____ No. 76
____ No. 59	____ No. 65	____ No. 71	____ No. 77
____ No. 60	____ No. 66	____ No. 72	____ No. 78
____ No. 61	____ No. 67	____ No. 73	____ No. 79

Please Print:
Name _____
Address _____ Apt. No. _____
City/State _____ Zip _____

Allow four to six weeks for delivery. Quantities limited.